confessions

of

a bigamist

confessions

of

a bigamist

A Novel

Kate Lehrer

Shaye Areheart Books
NEW YORK

Published by Shaye Areheart Books, New York, New York.
Member of the Crown Publishing Group, a division of Random House, Inc.
www.crownpublishing.com

SHAYE AREHEART BOOKS and colophon are trademarks of
Random House, Inc.

Printed in the United States of America

Design by Lynne Amft

Library of Congress Cataloging-in-Publication Data
Lehrer, Kate
Confessions of a bigamist : a novel / Kate Lehrer.—1st ed.
1. Triangles (Interpersonal relations)—Fiction. 2. Voluntary simplicity
movement—Fiction. 3. Traffic accident victims—Fiction. 4. Identity
(Psychology)—Fiction. 5. Environmentalists—Fiction. 6. New York
(N.Y.)—Fiction. 7. Businesswomen—Fiction. 8. Deception—
Fiction. 9. Texas—Fiction. I. Title.
PS3562.E442C66   2004
813'.54—dc22   2003017686

ISBN 1-4000-5025-1

10 9 8 7 6 5 4 3 2 1

First Edition

For Shaye

and

For Malcolm, James, and Olivia

acknowledgments

I'D LIKE FIRST to thank all my friends who took the time to read and comment on this book. Special thanks, once again, goes to John Ferrone, who, along with encouraging words, looked at multiple drafts with his wise and skilled eye, and also to Erik Tarloff, who edits with a fine-tooth comb and leaves wry comments along the way. I owe a debt of gratitude to Gordon Rainey and David Busby for helping me with plausible scenarios on international lawyering, to William Laurance for critiquing my Amazon section, and to Tom Lovejoy for getting me there in the first place. Also, I am indebted to Jay Crum for his help with all kinds of Texas lore, as well as to the Heard Natural Science Museum and Wildlife Sanctuary in McKinney, Texas. Kris Gali contributed her typing services on one impossible draft and Amy McWethy not only typed but made suggestions and assisted in all possible ways from this book's inception. My gratitude goes to Deborah Artman, whose edits and insights were invaluable. Not nearly enough can be said about the importance of my editor, Shaye Areheart, for her belief in this book and me from the beginning and her nurturing of both in her always astute way. My daughters, Jamie, Lucy, and Amanda, deserve special recognition for their readings and suggestions, their support and their nudgings. My husband, Jim, gets a special medal because his enthusiasm for and help with this book never wavered. He tried his best to keep me on course.

The heart, like the stomach, wants a varied diet.

—GUSTAVE FLAUBERT

• • •

What is the victory of a cat on a hot tin roof?
I wish I knew. . . . Just staying on it, I guess, as
long as she can.

—TENNESSEE WILLIAMS

part 1

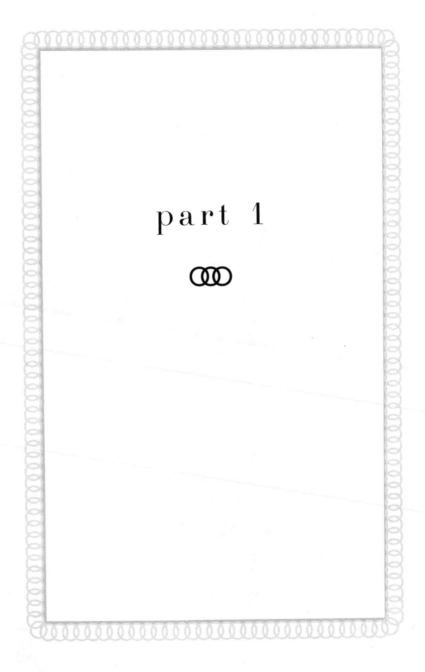

chapter 1

"DID I WAKE YOU?"

A male voice. I struggled to open my eyes. "Wake me?"

"I did." A guilty male voice.

I tucked my cell phone next to my ear. "I was dreaming . . . something about vines . . . ," I mumbled. "I was at a podium . . . and these vines . . . everywhere . . ."

A laugh. "Go back to sleep. I miss you."

"Me, too," I answered.

"That's all I wanted to hear." He hung up.

I willed myself into consciousness. Someone was missing? No, missing me. But whose voice? A husband's, that's whose.

Suddenly alert, I groped for a bedside lamp and tried to orient myself. Soft light suffused the room's surfaces, which were dense with cream and white and ivory. I saw bare walls and built-in cabinets, a down duvet, the mound of feather pillows that encircled me. A row of mirrored doors reflected the myriad lights that served the city as stars in this last decade of the twentieth century. New York, definitely: Fifth Avenue, upper Nineties, overlooking Central Park. This was the home I shared with my husband Steve—Steve Banyon—for twenty-eight years my only husband, and a fine one. When we married, I was happy to take his name. We were Mr. and Mrs. Banyon. Our friends knew me as Michelle.

Serenity usually reigned within these walls, but now,

crumpled pages of my notepad were scattered over the floor, on the bed, on my night table; my pencils, in equal disarray. A half-peeled orange, a soiled white towel, my white silk panties, and two lace gowns lay about in various states of abandon.

I sank back down into the bed and shut my eyes. Who was that on the phone? A husband. Someone was missing me. Me, too, I'd said, for I was missing me. Not so long ago, I had rowed merrily along in the shallows of my life. Innocent. Oblivious. Now I was groping wildly in rough waters, and the boat was definitely in danger of tipping. If only I'd been good at reading signs.

THE FIRST SIGN might have been eight months earlier, when I was running late. I liked to think I was a punctual person and I did hate being late, but Steve hated my lateness even more. He never was. He usually erred on the side of early. This night I was meeting him for dinner with friends. I was even looking forward to it, but I got sidelined by an unexpected call at the office.

Professionally, I was called Daisy Strait, a name I'd invented. Until I did it, I never thought I'd take a pseudonym, professionally or otherwise, though it immediately felt right. As Daisy, I wrote a monthly column for a dusty but sincere women's magazine and hopscotched around the country, lecturing the frazzled and hopeful about how to take the clutter out of life. Sometimes my fans called the office directly for advice, and most days I enjoyed the one-on-one.

"How late am I?" I asked Beth, my executive assistant, who held out my black mink-lined raincoat.

"Well—" she began softly, and I didn't even give her time to finish, just tossed a good-bye over my shoulder, chose the two flights of steps over the notoriously slow elevator, and rushed out of my Soho office building into the already-dark evening.

"Taxi!"

At least I was lucky there.

While people hunched their shoulders against the chill outside and stepped over and around piles of smudged snow, I hung on as my cabdriver lurched through traffic, jockeying for position. I took off my black-framed glasses and tucked them away in a case. I undid the clasp that kept my hair pulled back neatly at work, brushed out my chin-length, almost natural blond bob, and pulled down my long bangs. I was proud of my smooth mane. It took an hour every morning to achieve it. I opened my compact, grabbed a tissue, and rubbed away what was left of the dark red lipstick I wore at the office, then applied a more subdued mocha. I pressed my lips together. Voilà! Michelle Banyon—forty-seven years old, the fairly reserved, fairly chic wife of a fifty-year-old international lawyer, en route to dinner at Jean-Georges, where the waiting list for reservations was three weeks long. Everyone would be finishing their drinks by now and restless to order. I took one last look, snapped the compact shut, and, as the cab pulled in front of the restaurant, burrowed deep into the fur of my coat to prepare for the cold blast of February air when I opened the door.

"WE'RE GLAD YOU decided to come," Steve said, his drollness trumping my apology as he jumped up to pull my chair out for me. More a pouncer than a pacer, my husband was always alert, anticipatory, focused—qualities that made him an excellent and well-rewarded lawyer.

"I made the mistake of taking one last call," I explained quickly, sliding in between Matt Rogers and Buzzy Simpson, "and this woman was in hysterics. I couldn't cut her off. I'm sorry." I nodded toward the others, who murmured sympathetically.

Steve said nothing. He was leaving the next day for an eight-week stint in Hong Kong, and this was supposed to be his celebratory bon voyage.

"I'm sorry," I repeated.

"Steve, order Michelle a drink," Merin Gamble said, diplomatically. "While you, sweetie, catch your breath." She leaned across Matt Rogers to pat my hand. Merin was used to getting her way. Her swan neck and dark hair gathered in a French twist gave her an exotic air of distinction. Noisy conversation and swift waiters in their black suits swirled around us. I quieted my heart and took in the warmth of the room.

Buzzy Simpson turned to me. "Bad day?" he asked.

"Just a little dicey at the last minute," I answered, then asked about Roberta, his wife. I had hoped she would be here.

"She's in Florida—sweet-talking a new client who has too much money to be ignored," he complained. "But the kids and I are going down tomorrow to see her over Presidents' Day weekend."

"Mmm, sunshine and sailing—sounds heavenly," I said, knowing he'd take his boat out as soon as possible. We all teased him about his perpetual tan. I was going away for the long weekend, too, and like Steve's, my trip was work-related. I wondered if it would be warm in Texas and whether I'd even have time between seminars to see the sky.

Across the table, Merin said something to my husband, causing him to smile. His thin lips parted wide and the corners of his blue eyes crinkled. He looked to be enjoying himself. I hoped so. He was excited about the trip to Asia and I would miss him. I should have left work earlier.

"Steve Banyon, you are amazing," Merin said, raising her glass. "You gallop around the world and still manage to look like a young stud." She winked at me. "You're an inspiration to us all."

"Maybe it's all that gadding about that keeps him trim," said Merin's husband, Jack. "Maybe I should travel more," he added, patting his own round belly.

"Don't you dare," said Merin. "I need you right here." Which was true, since Jack, who was creative director at one of the hottest advertising companies in town, had helped to put Merin's new line of handbags at the epicenter of the fashion map.

"It can be grim sometimes," Steve said, not looking as if he thought his global lifestyle grim at all. With his lean, patrician looks and his seemingly attentive demeanor, Steve was often an inspiration to men and women, in one way or another. It was easy to become addicted to his practiced attentions. I was once, until I understood how Steve's mind worked: Behind those deep blue eyes, he was keeping another part of his brain clear for the dozens of balls he had in the air at any given moment. Over time this ability became disconcerting. There's something about sharing attention with a law brief even if you can't prove you've been shortchanged.

I scanned the menu quickly. Since everyone had been waiting for me, they all knew what they wanted to order, and a slim-hipped waiter stood by expectantly. "I'm having the duck," Merin announced.

"It's between the Rolled Filets of Sole à la Nage and the Veal Tajine," I said, stalling.

"Decide," Steve said firmly. He hated indecisiveness more than tardiness. Even shades of gray were categorized by him as either black or white. For Steve, happiness was a world of absolutes, a sentiment that appealed to me in the beginning. I, too, hated life's ambiguities and believed for a long time that he might stave them off.

I looked at the waiter. One of his nostrils seemed to move of its own accord. "What do you suggest?" I asked.

"The sole, the veal, both are excellent," the waiter responded with polite indifference.

"Go for the sole," said Merin, encouragingly.

"The sole, then," I said, nodding, then turned to listen to the others talk. Over the years, I had come to view my role as the provider of punctuation marks in our friends' conversations. Not the periods or exclamation points, mind you; more the commas, hyphens, and ellipses, maybe a semicolon, and frequently a question mark. As an organizing consultant, I facilitated daily living; as Michelle, I facilitated conversations. Even as a girl, I liked the idea of keeping parts of myself to myself, revealing a little here to one friend, a little there to another, and not too much to anyone.

Mostly, I tended to follow other people's scripts, another habit I developed growing up. Right now, for instance, Matt Rogers, on my left, was telling me about fishing and skiing in Utah. He spoke enthusiastically about what an excellent manager of houses his wife, Cissy, was and how I might pick up a few tips from her. At the moment, she was in Provo, overseeing the redecoration of their lodge. For one brief ego-driven moment, I wanted to remind him that I was the management expert and that his wife had picked up some tips from me, but I tended to play down my professional life, so who could blame him?

"Do you know, she keeps a database with all kinds of information?" Matt said proudly. "Take dinner parties. When we get home she records the evening's seating chart, the guest list, the cost of the food and wine . . ."

"Have you ever noticed," I heard Steve say, "how everyone who's gone to Harvard Law manages to work it in to the very first line they say about themselves?" I heard Jack's appreciative roar and Merin's bell-like twitter join the music from the speakers not far above our heads. Buzzy, who was applying to middle schools for his son, was weighing the merits of Dalton over Collegiate, while Matt, his beefy round face flushed from the wine, went on about Cissy's party planning, how she determined how much to spend and who to invite, and I nodded and added my "Oh"s and "Really?"s and meanwhile recognized the notes of Haydn's String Quartet in E-flat Major—op. 33, no. 2—threading its way through the conversation. *My center won't hold,*" the woman on the phone had said to me.

"Matt," I managed to interject, "do you feel you have a center?"

"Well, I am the center," he said, surprised, thinking I was referring to his investment banking company. "Others run the day-to-day stuff. I'm not much for details."

"I am," I asserted.

He shrugged. "We all do what we have to."

I thought about my center, whether it was like a room to walk into and how one could possibly hold it, and then I lost myself in the hum of voices, the glowing candles, and pale yellow wine, while the music, like a trick birthday candle you think you've blown out, ended and ended again until the final unresolved chord.

. . .

ON AN EARLY PLANE the next day to Fort Worth, Texas, I began anticipating with pleasure my lecture to a convention of alumnae delegates from Phi Delta Kappa. I thrived on my work. As Daisy Strait, I was quite the ham. By late morning, I was standing in full Daisy makeup—bronze foundation, darkly drawn eyebrows, red lipstick—before my audience of 150 women. They noted my slicked-back, utilitarian hair, my wrinkle-proof khaki suit, my honest face and warm expression, and the black-framed glasses that lent me substance. Receptive, the sorority sisters settled in.

Engaged and enthusiastic, my voice began its kneading: "Today we focus on your life as it can be with proper care and feeding. You say you have no extra time for one more thing in your life? Even if that one more thing is you? In that case, rule number one is this: Stop letting people, chores, or events wreak havoc with your destiny."

The women nodded, and I was pleased. They wanted to be cared for; they wanted to be fed. And they looked to Daisy Strait for the wherewithal, which was always, without fail, my favorite moment. Flaring to command the stage, I paused before offering deliverance through planning.

"Are you burdened by paper clutter? The piles of mail that never seem to disappear? Rule number two: Don't open *anything* that doesn't look relevant—and dispose of the rest promptly. The same with people clutter," I said sternly.

A groan went up. I nodded sympathetically.

"Rule number three: Think of people in the same way you do your papers." I could feel the women recoil slightly. "Are my methods ruthless? A little," I said, and then I whispered, "but act nice and you'll get away with it."

confessions of a bigamist

I winked. The women laughed, not because it was funny, but because they liked me, they liked being told what to do. I urged them to banish guilt as a waste of energy. "If you don't feel right without it, save it for when you fail yourself." Looking out at the sea of well-turned-out faces, I saw the weariness and struggle that wavered underneath their public masks. I reiterated: "Get ruthless, act nice, and stamp out guilt." In this last part I clowned around—a hand-chop to my throat, a broad smile, and a stamp of my foot at all the obvious places.

As Michelle, I could never perform in front of strangers, charming them with a willingness to make a fool of myself. In my home life, I was much too prissy, too self-conscious, and too private for any of this. As Daisy, though, I was confident. Reinventing myself was like an insurance policy, a fallback position to count on. If I failed at being Michelle, then maybe I could succeed as Daisy. People cared about Daisy.

"Don't forget—there are crimes against the spirit," I exhorted. "*Your* spirit. Those are the crimes you have to watch out for, or else you will end up with no spirit left at all, no *self* left"—I paused—"only the ghostly reminder of one." I let this image hang in the air and then bowed my head demurely. The pocket of silence was followed by appreciative applause.

The women were grateful to be told that it was all right to look after themselves. They flocked around me and I lingered with each a fleeting moment. My staff always admonished me to save my energy for the larger canvas, but I genuinely wanted to serve the people who attended my lectures. I enjoyed the individual contact, the small groups. I felt most effective this way, really, and would have stayed all day if time allowed, which it never did. Rule number six: Spontaneity must remain a luxury saved for rare occasions.

The next activity planned for me was an afternoon barbecue with the ladies of Phi Delta Kappa, but I had balked when my scheduler, Gloria, told me about it, back in New York.

"In the middle of winter?" I'd asked. "A barbecue?"

"Remember," she chided, "this is a regional meeting of women prominent in their hometowns. They belong to other clubs looking for speakers," she added emphatically.

"I'm already giving lectures in the next few weeks to half the state of Texas."

"*Regional* is the operative word," said Gloria, crossing her brown arms. "Think Arkansas, Oklahoma, Louisiana, New Mexico. Isn't that why we're opening an office down there?"

Gloria was right, of course. I was trying to expand my reach into the West and Southwest. I needed the exposure. Neither my talks nor my magazine column had yet brought me the kind of glory of, say, Martha Stewart. For the most part, I spoke to small, appreciative groups in small, appreciative towns. Although much of what I said was no longer very different from any other organizing advice or system in the current market, I came up with the idea of simplifying long before it became a fad. Unfortunately, the mother of an idea is not always rewarded as she should be.

Back in my hotel room, I changed clothes, replacing the khaki suit with jeans, a brown corduroy vest, and a moss green turtleneck that showed off my hazel eyes. I placed Daisy's Easy Spirit shoes in the closet and put on Merrells instead. My adrenaline rush was over. What I really wanted was to begin a quiet weekend working in the cocoon of the hotel. But this wouldn't take long, I promised myself, as I closed the door to my room.

chapter 2

THE BARBECUE WAS AT AN ELEGANT CONTEMPO-
rary house, nestled at the end of a driveway bordered with
azaleas. My hostess, Sonia Sartin, all graciousness in a white
wool caftan, her gray hair in a careless coil, apologized for
missing my lecture. She'd had a meeting with the director of
a wildlife sanctuary, she explained, "an interesting man who is
here somewhere, probably hiding." She laughed and looked
around. I marveled at the treasures that filled the foyer. A
luminous Rembrandt hung alongside the clean geometry of a
Stella; a playful David Smith sculpture complemented a dark
Caravaggio painting. I wished Steve could have seen these; he
would have loved them, too.

When I complimented Sonia on her collection, she gave
me permission to wander where I wanted. "The far hall
gallery is practically deserted," she said conspiratorially. "And
you'll enjoy the upstairs, too. You've worked hard enough
today. When you've gotten your fill of art and food, just sneak
out through the kitchen door." She smiled and added, "In this
crowd, we could both disappear and no one would ever
notice."

I thanked her and made my way to the hall gallery, where
only a docent, ostensibly positioned to answer art questions,
stood by quietly. From there, I wandered into a small sitting
room, where a Brancusi bird, a gleaming bronze blade, took

my breath away. It was a soaring wing, golden and defiant and lyrical. I stepped back to admire it from afar, to encounter it all over again, how the wing sliced the air. Did I ever define the space around me the way Brancusi did with his work? The bird embodied simplification, the radical reduction of an idea to its essence. An artist after my own heart, that's for sure. I couldn't resist and ran my finger lightly along the long curve of the sculpture.

"That guard is watching you." A low whisper over my shoulder.

I jerked my hand back and turned in the direction of the voice. He was a large-boned man with graying blond hair curling around his ears. His full lips formed an agreeable smile. He chuckled when he saw my startled face.

"I don't mean any impertinence, but the way you touched that sculpture, you looked like a kid asking for trouble." His slate-gray eyes were as friendly as his smile. "Do you know the story behind Brancusi's *Birds in Space*?" he asked.

The man had an imposing physique, not slender and tight like Steve's, but broad-chested and bear-cuddly. He wore a blue work shirt, khakis, a tan patch-pocket corduroy sport coat, and loafers like a familiar uniform.

"No," I said. "It's an incredible piece, though."

"He made twenty-seven in all," the man said. "The first was inspired by a Romanian folktale"—the drawl slow, emphatic—"about a magic bird with fantastic plumage and an extraordinary song—"

"How nice," I replied, slightly annoyed, cutting him off. I didn't really have time for this.

"—who was a messenger of love," he finished, undaunted.

While I was deciding if this was a come-on, he said, "Enjoy

the art, outlaw." Giving a little bow, he walked away and into the library. I watched, not without interest. Though I certainly didn't see myself as any kind of rebel, I felt a sudden surprising flick of desire to court a little danger in my life. Then I pulled myself together and turned to three severe Giacommetis that I had no desire to touch.

IN THE UPSTAIRS STUDY hung a series of Picasso's reclining nudes sketched in India ink. A small Picasso sculpture of a woman's head sat on the antique cherry desk. In the master bedroom I found a Matisse harem woman, a celebration of color and form. I tried to imagine the pleasure of waking to that every morning, which made me think of my own comfortable hotel room, and I began to feel weary.

As I brushed out my hair and bangs in Sonia Sartin's well-appointed marble bathroom, a harried woman stared back from the huge, spotless mirror. Only the art had saved me from fading long ago. The day had been long, and I had stayed up too late the night before packing and talking to Steve.

He had changed into his gray raw-silk pajamas, the ones I'd given him two birthdays ago, and was rummaging in his study for the books and papers he planned to take on his trip. Sitting in our white tufted bedroom chair, I peeled off my control-top panty hose.

"Imagine, ranking people's virtues by their wines!" I called to him. I was talking about Matt Rogers and his wife, Cissy.

"I always told you Cissy was a role model for you," Steve quipped, walking back into the room with papers and books under each arm. He suddenly looked very much as he had in law school—eager and cocky, a shock of hair falling over one eye. He'd been muscular in a low-key way then, too—wiry. Sometimes he still wore an old jacket and a pair of khakis that he'd had as an undergraduate.

"Maybe we should give up on them, Steve," I said, watching him arrange his books in a sturdy hard-case suitcase, his back to me. "We no longer have anything in common with them. Don't you agree?"

"You know Matt and his unedited mouth," he answered, continuing to pack. "He doesn't mean half of what he says." Matt Rogers had introduced Steve to many of the "right" people at a crucial juncture in his career, and to my husband's credit, he never forgot a favor.

"I still think we should reevaluate our lives, simplify them," I ventured. "Spend time with people we enjoy." A sprawl of indigestible conversations rose before me like the ghosts of dinner parties future. The Rogerses were not the only offenders.

"Why don't you call Daisy Strait? I understand she can help anybody—even the worst offender," Steve tossed back as he headed toward the bathroom.

The mention of Daisy made me think of the distraught woman on the phone just before I left work.

I followed Steve into the bathroom in my champagne-lace bra and panties as he brushed his teeth. "You know, I really did get hung up at work with some poor woman."

"Are we back on her again?"

"She wanted to know if the ends justified the means. She said she was etherized upon a table." I shook my head and sat down on the toilet seat. "I wasn't any help."

"You can't make everyone happy," he replied through a mouthful of toothpaste.

"Aren't we supposed to help one another through this vale of tears that we call a life?" I said, standing, then stalked off to pull my large suitcase and my carry-on out from under the bed. It was a little dramatic, I admit, but I wanted him to care about my cares.

Steve walked over and kissed me on the forehead, his breath minty. "And when was your last vale of tears?" he asked in that amused voice, half peace offering, half condescension, that drove me nuts.

"My point is that we're racing through our lives, too busy to live them," I said, quickly arranging my clothes just so in my two bags.

Steve clowned—held his head with both hands and rolled his eyes. "Michelle Banyon, you are one mass of contradiction," he said. "You get upset because Matt Rogers didn't see you as a management guru, yet you insist on playing yourself down. Tonight you want us to simplify, when the truth is you'd go batty even before I would."

I put another suit in my bag. "There are certain things we could trim, like our Christmas card list. Think about it."

"I'd rather not," Steve said, and placed his bedroom slippers by the bed.

Over the holidays we realized we'd been exchanging cards with one couple for sixteen years and neither of us could even remember who they were. We turned it into a joke at the time, but now it just seemed sad.

"Why do we send all those cards? Christmas isn't a big deal to us. We don't even spend it together."

"That is by mutual agreement, I'll remind you," he answered, holding out two suits to choose between. I inclined my head toward the pin-striped navy.

"I didn't say it wasn't!" For years now, Steve, the guilt-ridden, responsible son, had traveled to northern Vermont alone to visit his mother, who owned twenty cats and ignored me altogether. I'm not sure whether the cats or the deadly silence bothered me more, but we finally decided, after a few tear-filled years, to forget about holiday togetherness. Steve considered it some great sacrifice on my part, but I much preferred yoga retreats and spas. He enjoyed himself, too, for he could ski to his heart's content, and for a long time, he did so with his mother.

"And we do celebrate," he said, "just not on the day."

"We celebrate with a split of champagne for breakfast and an exchange of books, for goodness sake." I threw a sheaf of papers into my carry-on.

"That's all we could afford." He sat down on the bed with a sigh.

"Twenty-five years ago!" I stood before him, my hands on my hips.

"I thought you liked the sentiment of it."

"I do. The point is, why do we send all those Christmas cards?"

"Oh, for Pete's sake, it's good for business," he answered, and crawled into the middle of our bed.

I slipped into my sea-blue silk gown, the one he especially liked, and studied Steve in the mirror. He was lying on his side, and I could glimpse the bald spot on the back of his head. He hated that spot intensely. I found this small vanity much more endearing than the pleasure he took in his trim body. Poor Steve, always so conscientious, the good soldier.

He turned and smiled, held out his hand to me. "It's our last night for quite a while."

"Maybe the month will go fast," I said, sliding in beside him and giving him an Eskimo kiss. Eight weeks was a long time, even for Steve, to be gone, but I'd slotted three weeks in the middle to join him. I'd never been to Asia. He kissed me on the cheek. "Can you keep a secret?" he whispered.

I nodded yes.

"The Rogerses are hard to take."

I threw my arm over his waist. "And Matt has been a loyal friend to you."

A little later, after the Eskimo kiss had turned into something more substantial, I murmured, "Steve? Wouldn't it be nice to spend more time together, to—"

"Go to sleep," he ordered, putting his lips on mine to shush me before he turned away on his side. I snuggled up next to him and kissed his shoulder. Whatever else, Steve made me feel safe.

FOR STEVE AND ME, this wrangle was the closest we got to a real blowup. He always said his whole career was a fight and he didn't care to extend the battle into his personal life. I hated confrontation, too. I was a woman of moderation. A militant moderate, I used to call myself before realizing that part of me did long for a more extreme, more intense experience.

"At least you are tired and not etherized," I told the woman in the mirror in Sonia Sartin's bathroom. I felt grateful for my full life—my marriage, happy compared to most; a career that I loved; and a bountiful number of creature comforts that I wasn't too spoiled to appreciate. Besides, I could now return to my hotel room for a deliciously undisturbed weekend. I snuck out the back door as Sonia suggested, though I skipped the food.

As I walked down the handsome curving drive, blinking in the strong late-afternoon sunlight, I heard heavy and fast footsteps behind me. I walked faster, afraid I'd get trapped in a conversation about efficiency, but to my relief it was only my art comrade, who nodded when he caught up with me as if we were old friends. His smile was so unself-conscious that I found myself smiling back.

"You changed your hair," he commented.

"You noticed?"

"Well, I was looking for you. I saw a woman walking down the drive, and I suddenly realized it was you."

I gave him a puzzled look.

"I recognized your figure." He blushed. "I guess you were more fun to look at than the Henry Moore."

I looked away, trying not to smile, and didn't reply.

"Do you need a lift?" he persisted. "Could I buy you a drink?"

"I have a car and I'm awfully tired, but thanks," I answered firmly.

"I could lead you back to your hotel. It's tricky around here, the streets."

"I got here without a single problem. I'm sure I'll get back."

He held open my car door as I got in. "I hope I haven't offended you. My name is Wilson Collins. I had a meeting with our hostess earlier and she roped me into hanging around with the promise of good food and access to her collection. Believe me, I don't make a habit of coming on to strangers, even nice-looking ones. I can understand if you're suspicious, but I'm really just a normal guy who would like to buy you a cup of coffee."

He was so earnest, he could have been confessing to a robbery. "You don't look threatening," I answered, my tone less crisp, "but I really can't."

For the second time that afternoon, he bowed and walked away and again I was sorry to see his back, a good back, too—a chunky, muscular rectangle. It suited him. *Spontaneity is a luxury*, I reminded myself as I turned the key in the ignition and pressed down on the gas. The car lurched into reverse.

And then I heard a sickening thump. Afraid I'd hit an animal, I slammed on the brakes and jumped out. Crawling away from the back of my car was Wilson Collins—a bloody gash across his forehead, one leg trailing behind him.

"I've killed you!"

"Not yet," he tried to reassure me. He sat on the hot tarmac.

I began dabbing his forehead with a tissue from my vest pocket. "I'm so sorry," I said. "It's a rental and I haven't driven this model before." The gash didn't look too deep, though I couldn't tell about his leg. "Are you all right? Please be all right."

"I'm all right," he said stoically. We pulled up his pant leg. Already his knee had begun to swell and change to an ugly color, but he nixed returning to the house. "Too much commotion," he said, and tried to stand.

"You need help." I was only five foot seven, one hundred twenty pounds, but I did my best to support him. Somehow we got him on his feet.

"I just need to get home. Helen will help me once I'm at home." He tested the bad leg gingerly and winced.

"What about an ambulance?"

"Thank you," he said, "but the last thing I want is five hours on a gurney in an overheated and understaffed emergency room. Listen, there's no reason you should trouble yourself further." Pain and embarrassment had introduced an element of formality into his speech that I found touching.

"Don't be ridiculous. I've run over you. I'm driving you to the hospital."

"I'll be fine," he said firmly.

"What if you have a concussion?"

"I don't."

"People don't always know."

He suddenly buckled and clutched my arm, and that's how I found myself driving Wilson Collins home in his red pickup truck. His truck, he said, was reliable, implying that my car was not.

"What were you doing behind my car, anyway?" I asked him as we pulled onto the road. I turned the wheel of the pickup carefully—I'd never driven something that big before.

"I came back to get your phone number," Wilson Collins said. "I thought if I could at least talk to you again, you might be willing to see me. I didn't mean like this," he added, his smile more like a grimace as he shifted uncomfortably in his seat.

"But why were you standing behind my car?"

"I was just walking up and your car shot back."

"Well, it wasn't on purpose," I said, shifting into second.

TWENTY-FIVE MINUTES later we were still on a small highway in the middle of nowhere, hemmed in by gas stations and fast-food franchises. Wilson Collins's pale face had begun to turn shades of yellow. Worried that he might pass out, I asked for precise directions. "I will not faint," he replied. The suggestion that we call to alert Helen received an even more terse "Absolutely not."

To keep him focused, I asked questions about his life. He ran a bird and wildlife sanctuary; he lived on a farm; he had one son, who exasperated him; and Helen's only concern would be keeping his dinner hot. His one embellishment regarded his son: "A hippie," he declared.

I laughed. "That's what we were in the seventies."

"I was never a hippie." His voice had all the scorn my father's had when using the word. I glanced over at Wilson Collins's sun-etched face. I guessed that he was in his mid-fifties, seven or eight years older than I was. I also noticed that he was turning the color of skim milk. "Are we getting close?" I asked.

"It's no more than half an hour," he volunteered, slouching against the passenger door.

"A half hour!" I yelled, pressing harder on the accelerator. "Don't faint on me," I pleaded quietly.

"I promise," he answered, "but tell you what, a large coffee with four sugars and two creams would be helpful. There's a McDonald's coming up."

When we stopped, I asked him to call Helen. Again he declined. I decided the best course was to get him to his local hospital as soon as possible. This time I insisted, and I guess Wilson Collins heard my New York City resolve, because he gave me the directions. We pulled back onto the highway.

"Where are you from?" he asked after a few sips of coffee.

I looked over at him. This was the first conversation he'd initiated since his accident. "Oh, all around," I replied, and began the story of how my father, a career army man, a master sergeant, had instilled in me the love of travel, but Wilson Collins leaned back in his seat, closed his eyes, and told me his head hurt too much to talk.

SO I DROVE in silence, swept along by the last gleam of the day's sun, the bold black line of the straight highway leading me farther into the countryside. It felt different to ride so high. I passed rich dark fields with clusters of gray trees like stark winter sculptures. Now and then I passed new houses—Colonials, Plantations—somehow uniform in their boxy sprawl.

As we rode through the gentle swells of North Texas farmland, my spirits lifted. This unexpected—dare I say spontaneous?—turn of events had a sense of adventure about it, despite the shape of my poor companion. I felt excited just to be doing anything that had not been scheduled ahead of time. My whole life was scheduled ahead of time.

Daisy Strait kept me on the road throughout the year, which suited me fine. I loved it—the rushing to make planes, the lines at ticket counters, the hours-long wait on runways, the quick ins and outs of cities only to return to the sky once more. The world of bustle and harassed travelers was mother's milk to me. Much as I moaned like a disgruntled traveler, I thrived in the convoluted maze of airborne life. More than a room of one's own, I had a comforting, cozy citadel. But what a difference to be *in* the landscape rather than a couple of miles above it.

"I'm not very good company, Ms. Strait," Wilson Collins apologized. "That is your name, isn't it? Sonia told me a little about you."

"That's the name I use professionally. Michelle Banyon is my real name."

"You don't look like a Michelle," he said, studying me. "You look more like a Mickey—a plucky, kind Mickey," he announced, pleased with himself.

I laughed out loud. Plucky! I tried to remember the last time I'd heard anyone use that word. Not everyone got to be plucky.

"And do you enjoy giving talks, Mickey Banyon?"

"Very much." When I glanced at him, Wilson Collins seemed to be mulling this over, but he didn't ask me anything else. Why not be plucky Mickey for a change? "Who is Helen?" I asked.

"My housekeeper."

"Not your wife?"

"My wife left me."

"I'm sorry."

"Don't be."

Neither of us said much after that until Wilson spoke. "Are you married?"

I stared at my empty ring finger. As Daisy Strait, I had simplified my life by dropping my husband.

"Are you," Wilson said again, "married?"

I looked at him for a quick moment, then whispered, "No."

chapter 3

HIS DOCTOR, APPARENTLY AN OLD FRIEND, MET US
in the emergency room of the Rollins, Texas, hospital, located
just off the interstate and in Wilson's hometown. An orderly
pointed me toward a small waiting area painted the exact
pink of the Sweet'N Low packets that lay on a beige plastic
table holding two coffeepots and a stack of Styrofoam cups.
Breaking my rule of no caffeine after four, I poured a cup of
the real stuff, which was surprisingly good, and sat down on
one of the vinyl chairs.

The pink walls were oddly soothing and the silence had as
close to a calming effect as I was capable of receiving at the
moment. The emergency waiting room reminded me of Griffith, Georgia, my father's and grandfather's hometown. On
one visit to my grandfather, I fell from a tree and broke my
arm, and my father took me to the hospital there. Neither he
nor Grandpa talked a lot but both were comforting presences.
I loved the short pilgrimages my father and I made to Griffith
every summer, perhaps especially because my mother and sister seldom joined us. My mother hated it there. It must have
reminded her too much of her own beginnings, which she'd
managed to forget, with her parents dead. For me, though, as
an army brat, the small run-down house in that small run-
down town gave me the only solid sense of place I ever had

until I met Steve and moved to New York. I took another sip of coffee and willed the memories away.

Years had come and gone since I had sat so completely still. No laptop. No CD player. No idea what was going to happen next. I had a dread of stillness; I always had. It was just too dangerous. I always told my Daisy audiences that sitting in quiet reflection was a worthy goal, a part of the simplifying process, a way of finding your essential self. But like a doctor who smokes, I never practiced what I preached. What if my essential self was composed of nothingness? What then?

When the doctor returned, he predicted a quick recovery. "He's bruised up and has a nasty ankle sprain, but it's nothing too serious. I put a stitch in his forehead, a balloon cast on his foot, and an Ace bandage on his knee to hold down the swelling. Ice would be better, though. And he's got to stay off it for at least three days. You'll have to watch that he takes his pain medication and doesn't pull his stiff-upper-lip routine. Lucky thing he latched on to you."

"Didn't he tell you I backed into him?" I asked, incredulous.

"No," the doctor said. "He didn't mention that."

WE FINALLY PULLED UP to a white Victorian farmhouse, warm and appealing with a wraparound porch and well-tended flower beds. We were a good quarter mile from the highway, and no Helen, breathless with worry, appeared at the door. Not a single light greeted us. And what if Wilson Collins wasn't as hurt as he appeared to be? For the first time the foolhardiness of my adventure struck me. I no longer felt daring; numbskull was a better fit.

"So where is Helen?" I asked.

He shrugged. "I guess she must have left early. If you'll help me in, I can point out the liquor cabinet. I think we've both earned a drink."

"What do you mean, 'left early'?" I demanded, going around to his side of the truck and opening the door. As he eased himself out of the cab and negotiated his crutches, I noticed he had turned pale again.

The house was Daisy Strait's worst nightmare. The chaos was overwhelming. Wilson lurched sideways into me, and I poked my cheek on an old oak coatrack and then tripped on a pair of cowboy boots. As I reached for a hall table to steady myself and him, catalogs and mail cascaded to the floor.

"Damn it!" I yelled, exasperation overriding anxiety.

He managed to mutter, "Sorry," as he made his way in a staggered crutch-hop to an easy chair in what could only be described as a Victorian parlor, replete with knickknacks, pipes, papers of all kinds—magazines, books, and bills—covering every conceivable surface and fanning out over the carpet. It was almost eight o'clock. Wilson looked ready to pass out.

"Just sit right there," I said in a high-pitched voice that didn't hide my panic. "I'll get you some whiskey." Whiskey, that's what they gave in old Westerns, I was pretty sure.

He pointed to the hall. "The liquor cabinet is—"

"I'll find it," I interrupted, but instead I found the kitchen. Just as well, I decided. He needed food. And I was hungry, too.

THE ELUSIVE HELEN had left Wilson a note and eight meals with heating instructions. Apparently she had gone to her sister's for the week because her sister, who lived alone, had hurt her back. "Helen would think I'd want her to go. It's her kind of reasoning," Wilson called from the other room when I yelled to him what I'd found.

"Seems to be my kind of reasoning, too," I muttered as I put Helen's lasagna in the microwave. "But nobody has any idea where I am." I pressed the buttons and then looked up, surprised to see Wilson in the doorway. Had he heard me?

Woozy from the painkillers, Wilson insisted on pouring each of us a glass of wine—not the best idea for Wilson, maybe, but it could render him harmless, I reasoned, and he was a strapping man. But I didn't need to worry—he was barely able to make polite conversation. At the big pine table, I enjoyed the lasagna while Wilson went on about a dog of his that was nowhere to be found, his regret over my being inconvenienced, and a few other subjects that were just too rambling to make much sense. Somewhere in there I slipped in that I was divorced—amicably, I added, out of guilt. And somewhere in there it was decided I would stay the night in the guest bedroom, which Wilson assured me had clean sheets on the bed. What other choice did I have, really?

After he led me to the guest room, I wished Wilson good night, closed the door, and sat on the bed, exhausted. I heard him hobble down the hall with his crutches, but before I could kick off my shoes, I heard him return again to my door. His knock caused me enough anxiety that I considered not answering, then I realized I was being absurd, that I was more than a match for the wounded Wilson Collins. When I answered the door, I found him holding out an airline travel kit.

"Compliments of my former wife," he said. "There's a

toothbrush in here"—he paused—"and things. I brought you a T-shirt we give to people who donate twenty dollars or more to the wildlife refuge. I thought you could use it as a nightshirt."

"This is a very nice shirt," I said, fingering the heavy cotton. "How do you give this away to twenty-dollar donors and make a profit?"

Wilson looked confused. It could have been the painkillers.

"And thanks, but I keep a toothbrush with me. Some people wash their hands a lot; I brush my teeth."

"Tomorrow I'll drive you back. I'll be all right tomorrow," he said in parting.

He seemed to have forgotten he couldn't put weight on that leg. "Take the sleeping pill your doctor gave you. You need your rest," I called after him, not believing the nanny coming out in my voice.

I DIDN'T SLEEP because Wilson Collins didn't sleep. Sounds of his bumping around the house carried up to my room, and eventually, exhausted but concerned, I dressed and went downstairs. I found him in the Victorian parlor looking ravaged and helpless. For the first time I noticed the faded wallpaper, a gray background with small yellow flowers. It had lost its perkiness long ago.

"When did you take your last pain pill?"

"Well, I took the one the doctor made me swallow when we were leaving the hospital."

"You haven't taken *any* since then?"

Still fully clothed, he shook his head mutely.

"No wonder you look like hell," I said, and offered to fetch one.

"I don't like being doped up," he replied, a stubborn edge in his voice.

"And I don't like seeing someone in pain. Where are they? In your coat?"

Without waiting for an answer, I rummaged through the pockets of his jacket, which was tossed on the chair, and found the plastic container, then left the room and came back with a glass of water and a pill. "Take this, then, so we can both get some sleep." After making sure he swallowed, I led Wilson Collins to his bedroom. He followed with the reluctance of a four-year-old being put to bed before dark. And to think, only hours earlier, I'd been wondering if he was flirting with me. Now somehow I had ended up his nursemaid. So much for my life of danger.

I closed Wilson's door, then, feeling a bit wired, I crept back downstairs for a glass of milk. His house had the feel of an archaeological dig, one era after another just waiting to be unearthed. I padded through the rooms quietly, looking for clues about the man and his family. Curiously, there were no photographs. The walls displayed a few gilt-framed paintings whose subject matter varied from murky rivers and dark skies to green-black forests and dark skies—a depressing lot. They were probably inherited along with the rest of the Victoriana that crowded a fine early-American secretary and two chests as well as elaborately carved mahogany dining-room chairs and a becoming nineteenth-century French oak cupboard. Almost no sign of contemporary life intruded, unless a radio from the 1940s and a Barcalounger straight out of the fifties counted.

I hated to think what lurked behind the closet doors and inside the myriad of drawers. It had been years since I'd been in a house with so much clutter, although I could see the place had real possibility. The rooms were well-proportioned and stately without being formal in design, and the wide, lovely moldings had to be the originals. My guess was the house had been built in the early 1900s. With some effort and a lot of fun, I could turn it into a dream.

In my own apartment, there was not much left to minimize, except for Steve's and my erratic schedules. I spent so much of my professional time either writing about decluttering or giving speeches and seminars on it that I seldom had an opportunity for a real hands-on major sweeping-out of other people's homes anymore, and I really did love ordering disorder. This reductionist urge—almost a compulsion—to discard and simplify had turned into a rewarding career. I could think of few other actions that matched this delight, the sensation of virtue it instilled. I could feel myself being pulled in. What better place than this to practice my calling—for I thought of it as a calling, my small contribution to our times.

I shook my head to clear it. There was only one problem: I had no intention of sticking around. Yet tiptoeing up the stairs, I smiled as I thought about the day, Mickey's day. I wondered if my father had ever been called Mickey. I'd been named Michelle after my father, Michael Harmon. He named me himself. The second of two daughters, I would be his last child. He did not intend to try for a son. Maybe that's how my mother learned their marriage would be no sure thing. Maybe that's how she saw me: a reminder of a marriage gone awry. Maybe she had to keep me at bay.

But tonight I was Mickey. A spunky Mickey. Back in bed, I

heard the whistle of a train in the far distance and smiled again. Then I read a four-year-old *Newsweek* magazine until, with the first hint of morning light, I fell asleep.

I WOKE with my heart pounding and a man standing in the doorway staring at me. I was so stunned I couldn't react, and then I remembered who he was, where I was. "You startled me," I told Wilson Collins, my fright giving way to irritation.

"I'm sorry," he began, "but I wanted you to know that I'm ready to drive you back to your hotel."

"You can't drive. I heard the doctor say so."

"It's better. See?" He raised his leg about twelve inches off the floor before he grimaced. "Brian said I didn't have to keep it up all the time."

I pulled the covers around my neck. "I was there, remember? You can't drive. You still look like you might faint. You've got to call Helen and tell her to come home. She can drive me back and take care of you." Someone had to look after him, but, for a change, I didn't feel that it had to be me.

"I can't ask her to interrupt her trip."

"Let's figure out what to do over breakfast," I suggested, the bedroom becoming too intimate. "I'm starving and you shouldn't take your medicine on an empty stomach."

"No more drugs; they knock me out. But the diner in town is good." He turned to go but had to steady himself with his hand on a wall.

"Helen not only left an awful lot of prepared food for you, she left tons of groceries," I said. "No sense in letting it go to waste." I already knew better than to press the point with this Wilson Collins that he was in no shape to leave the house. He had a prideful streak. Fortunately, he did not argue and left me to freshen up, which I hurriedly did, more than a little ready for a cup of coffee.

WHEN I CAME DOWN showered and dressed, I found him shuffling around in the kitchen, a chair in front of him he was using as a kind of walker, frying pans all over the floor. At that moment he was peering under the sink, the chair precarious as it tilted under his weight.

"I'm looking for an omelette pan," he explained without my asking. "We used to have one around here somewhere. Helen must have borrowed it. I was going to make you an omelette in return for all you've done." He beamed at me and I smiled back gamely, the best I could manage that morning.

I started checking other cabinets. "I had no idea you cooked."

"I don't really, but I watched Connie, my ex-wife, make omelettes often enough that I think I can figure it out. Takes no time at all, you know."

I didn't know, but perhaps it would be just as well if we didn't find the pan. "Here, let me take over," I said briskly.

After making the coffee, I found a loaf of bread and the toaster. At home, Steve did the little cooking and cleaning up we required. He enjoyed whistling and swooping around with pots and pans as he concocted some favorite dish, and I enjoyed his kitchen noises. He considered the process therapeutic; I considered myself lucky. But where was Steve now when I needed him?

•   •   •

confessions of a bigamist

I SERVED WILSON Cheerios with milk and set a platter of buttered toast on the table, made him take a pill, then asked him about his birds. "What exactly do you do at your sanctuary?" is how I put it.

"As the director, I spend a lot of time trying to raise money for it and the Raptor Center," he said after a spoonful of cereal. "We try to educate people about birds and wildlife—the environment in general. Schools in this part of the country use it as a teaching resource."

"Are there interesting birds in Texas?"

"Oh, an amazing number of birds like this part of Texas. It's my job to convince people around here that birds in particular and wildlife in general need protection. Outside of the environmental and conservancy groups, it's still hard as hell to get over how important—" With a quick grin he stopped himself. "I'm sorry," he said, and laughed. "You don't need my lecture on the vulnerability of the bird population. There's a limit to what a good Samaritan must tolerate."

"Oh, no, please go on," I protested, for he clearly took pleasure in the telling, and I was curious. "But what exactly is a center for rapture?"

Wilson Collins's laugh was a deep gurgle that spread outward and upward, as expansive and unself-conscious as a child's. "Well," he said, catching his breath, "rapture, too, for some of us. But r-a-p-t-o-r is its official spelling, as in birds of prey. A bird hospital for birds of prey. You know, hawks and owls—birds that hunt live meat."

"That sounds, um, intriguing," I said, and he looked relieved.

"I'll take you to see it; it's the least I can do. You are the most wonderful person, Mickey. You are as special as they come." His look of admiration surprised me.

"But you don't know me."

"I know you better than you think." This time his eyes held mine a moment too long.

"So . . . you were telling me about your center?" I prompted.

He explained how it was strapped for cash. How a lot of Texas companies that could give money confused his setup with something involving the animal-rights activists. "Hunting is a big sport down here—" He stopped, considered. "They're good people, but . . . "

Now his gaze did not stray from my face until I broke the spell. "The activists or the companies?" I asked, and bit into a piece of toast.

He grinned. "Both." His enthusiasm made me realize how long it had been since I'd been with anyone who was so passionate about what he did.

With only a little prodding, Wilson told me how his mother had started the bird sanctuary thirty years ago. Having grown up on this large, beautiful farm, she dreamed of celebrating the land's primitive past by creating a protected environment and had gone on to do just that with the full support of Wilson's father, a banker. By then, Wilson was living in Houston with a young wife and working as a geologist in the oil business. He resisted his mother's enthusiasms until both she and his father fell ill. After that, he returned frequently to look after them and the property for what turned out, sadly, to be the last year of both his parents' lives.

He was thirty-three then, bored with his job. Still, Wilson loved the science of geology and, in turn, the farm where he was raised, and he soon became enamored of the many offerings found here, especially the birds, most especially the owls and hawks. The Raptor Center followed five years later. His wife and son, who was born on the farm, had not shared in this last passion. In fact, they came to resent the whole project because it was so time-consuming.

While I was interested in Wilson's story, I mostly enjoyed the play of his face, and my pleasure in watching made me notice the increasing discomfort that stilled his expressions, how he paused more often and closed his eyes.

"Pain's picking up, huh?" I asked.

"A little," he admitted.

Suddenly, the absurdity of the situation struck me. I dropped my toast and leaned toward him in frustration. "Look, you shouldn't be alone, and I can't stay here forever." I softened my tone but continued to lecture: "You've got to call your son. I'm sure he would want you to."

"My son has his own life," he said, rubbing a hand wearily across his forehead.

"Where is he? Couldn't he come for a few days?"

"He's on the West Coast, but it wouldn't matter if he lived next door."

"Well, I can't stay," I said gently. "I have to work. I have a schedule."

He agreed to call a friend who could drive me back and then look in on him after I left. Before any such call was made, however, his head began to nod as he sat upright in his chair. The medication. First it wound him up, then it knocked him out. Getting Wilson back to bed was a hopeless proposition, so I half-dragged him to the reclining easy chair and found a blanket to cover him and a pillow for his head. I silently cursed his stubbornness and the medication and our chance encounter the day before.

. . .

NO MATTER WHAT Wilson Collins had just agreed to, I knew he had no intention of asking anyone to see after him, although he seemed like a man who'd always been tended to. The location of an omelette pan wasn't the only domestic mystery for him. He looked surprised when I told him half the lightbulbs in his house were out. As for newspapers, socks, shoes, reading glasses—they remained wherever he'd discarded them. I wondered how many women, including Helen, had tried to step in after his wife left. As an attractive bachelor—more attractive than I had originally acknowledged—he must have had more than a few knocks on his door.

Other than his seeming ineptness around the house, Wilson appeared to be the model of independence, maybe even a loner. I wondered what really happened to his marriage and his relationship with his son. When he wasn't being completely direct, he could be downright opaque. I couldn't help feeling a little sorry for him, though I had spent a good deal of my life eschewing pity of any kind. I didn't give it and didn't want to receive it. Either way led to manipulation. For years I felt sorry for my mother, tried to please her, make her happier, only to discover that she depended on self-pity to get what she wanted, and was too preoccupied with her own issues to notice mine.

Abruptly, I started picking up the magazines and books scattered over the living-room floor. It looked as if Wilson single-handedly was trying to keep the magazine business going. I stacked copies of *Civilization, Preservation, National Geographic, Smithsonian, Harper's, Sports Illustrated,* and three newsweeklies. Then I began raising blinds and pulling back curtains. Before long I was rearranging anything light enough to lift. I created little still lifes, continuing my designs throughout the downstairs. It had been a long time since anyone had bothered about aesthetics around here, maybe never.

I lost myself to the task of making order. There was so much to do. I supposed I could stay another night. I called the rental company and asked them to pick up my car from Sonia Sartin's street. Steve was away. Who was there to miss me? I laughed at the idea of disappearing into the house of a stranger in Rollins, Texas. Talk about redefining your life! I ventured outside to collect branches for a kitchen table centerpiece. Our evening meal might as well be a little festive.

WORKING WITH LATE February's offerings, I put green twigs in two old fruit jars and sprinkled some pecans from a bowl around them. Under the kitchen sink I found some white candles, and by holding the flame of one to the bottom of the others, I used the wax for glue, pressing the slender tapers on an assortment of unpretentious saucers. I took out Helen's meal-planning instructions and decided to combine a homemade meat sauce in the freezer with a nice-looking dried linguine. That inspired me to search for some kind of cookbook, but all I found on the shelves were a multitude of cleaning solutions and storage containers. For the first time ever, I wished that I had learned a few rudiments of cooking. After arranging the centerpiece, preparing the pasta and a salad, and setting the pine table, I had to admit to a feeling of satisfaction. I sat down in the kitchen in an old black rocking chair and waited for Wilson to wake up. For the second time in two days, I allowed myself stillness, this one surprisingly resplendent with anticipation.

chapter 4

AFTER A LONG REST, WILSON'S RUDDY COLOR AND his vitality had reappeared. "You're still here!" he said on first seeing me. "I thought I dreamed you."

When he discovered I'd made us dinner and planned to stay another night, a big smile wiped out all the residue of pain left on his face. He kept thanking me for staying, for decorating, for cooking. He opened a bottle of wine, and when I protested his mixing the alcohol with his medication, he insisted, "It's a special occasion." To hear him tell it, my pasta beat out all the other pastas he had ever eaten. As for the salad, well, the salad must have come from an angel. Of course, the meal was mostly the product of Helen's culinary skill, but I was pleased anyway, and I allowed myself to bask in his praise. It wasn't so bad sitting opposite Wilson Collins at a table.

"What happened with your wife?" I asked him suddenly.

His face flushed red. "Nothing much to tell." He tipped back his head and drained his glass of wine. "One day she was living here with me and the next she left me for another woman." He poured himself a refill. I held out my glass, too, while trying my best to come up with an adequate response.

"At least her leaving didn't have anything to do with you," I said, taking a healthy gulp. "It isn't as if you were rejected for a better model . . . or a newer . . . What I mean is, she obviously needed something you couldn't give her, so your ego was not on the line . . . right?" We both swilled our wine and paid an inordinate amount of attention to the centerpiece.

"I thought I satisfied her," Wilson finally answered, his voice barely audible.

"Maybe you did, but she could no longer deny her other desires. . . ." I was definitely floundering and hoped he didn't notice. "I'm sure you were . . ." Finally I just held out the pasta bowl and he took another generous helping.

"I never satisfied her. She told me so herself," he said evenly. But possibly mindful of a tinge of pathos, he added, "I was clueless. That leaves enough self-doubt to last us macho men several lifetimes." He rose stiffly and hopped with one crutch to fetch another bottle of wine from a large cupboard. "We do have Connie to thank for the *vino*," he muttered, working the corkscrew.

"She chose well," I responded truthfully.

"Before she left she ordered several cases of both red and white," he said, sitting back down. "I tried to give them to her, but she said that I'd need them to seduce some worthier woman. She knows damn well I prefer beer, but this is really pretty good."

Leaning across the table, Wilson said in his earnest voice: "I hope you don't think I'm implying that I'm trying to seduce you." He touched my hand; his own was large. "At that party . . . I don't know. There was something about you. I felt like I knew you somehow, that I'd always . . . Crazy, but I couldn't just let you walk away and disappear. And look, here you are, by the oddest of circumstances, Mickey." He raised his glass to me.

I tried to figure out how to respond to this charming

frankness without getting in over my head. I took another sip of wine.

"I never talk this much. The medicine and wine... ," he said, and then abruptly passed out, his head just missing the plate of linguine.

"Wilson, Wilson . . ." I shook his shoulder gently and called his name until he stirred, then I managed to help him up the stairs and into bed. I took off his shoe—a Hush Puppy, comfortable and sensible, the kind Daisy Strait would recommend and I would never wear—and placed the foot in the cast on the bed as carefully as I could in what I hoped was a comfortable position.

"Would you stay with me until I go to sleep?" he whispered plaintively. So I eased down on the other side of the bed and lay on my back listening to his labored breathing. Another rare moment of stillness for me. Then I fell asleep, too.

THE PHONE. The phone? I rushed into wakefulness and bumped into a solid body next to me—Wilson. I don't know who was more startled. We had spent the night together. When Wilson turned to pick up the receiver, he let out a low grunt, then lied to his doctor: "Much better, yeah. Don't need a thing, Brian. Sure, yes, I'll keep you posted."

Even from a distance, I could hear Brian's strong voice at the other end of the phone. "Don't push yourself," he warned. "We're not in our twenties anymore."

While Wilson received the doctor's lecture, I slipped out of the room and headed straight for the bathroom. Sleeping in my jeans and shirt had left marks all over my body. I hadn't rinsed out my underpants or socks the night before, and I couldn't stand the idea of wearing days-old clothes. My mother's influence on me, I knew. Wilson must have had the same kind of mother, for by the time I finished showering, he had laid out a boy's shirt, socks, a pair of khakis, and Jockey shorts on the bed in the guest room. The briefs and khakis were so small, they probably were his son's from junior high. Only a little on the tight side, they reminded me of my tomboy days, and in turn made me feel reckless, frisky. Too bad it was time to get back to work. With Wilson out of commission, I had to figure out a way to get to the hotel.

"Do you have Enterprise around here?" I asked him when I came down to the kitchen.

"Haven't you noticed?" Wilson said. "I'm very enterprising."

I smiled at him. "Ha-ha. I mean the car rental company. I need to get back to Fort Worth."

"Oh," he said, disappointed. "But hey, I promised you a tour of the Raptor Center, Mickey. Do you have time before you leave?"

I hesitated—I didn't want to hurt his feelings.

"We can go the scenic route," Wilson said excitedly, "through the preserve."

I didn't have the heart to tell him a bird sanctuary wasn't high on my list of places to see. "Okay," I gave in. "That sounds like fun."

THE DRIVE did turn out to be fun. While I steered us along the paths, Wilson pointed out his favorite treasures. "Just over there is the creek where two regal alligators have taken up residence," he said. "Who knows? They might end up television stars."

"How so?" I asked.

"Green Earth, a TV production company from L.A., might do an adventure series set in the Amazon rain forest. If they do, they are thinking of using all this land as a backdrop. That's money, publicity—everything we need!"

I laughed out loud. "You can replicate a rain forest here in Texas?" I asked, more than skeptical.

"Sure," he said a little defensively, but confessed it would take some doing.

Looking out at the parched brush and stunted trees, I certainly agreed with the "doing."

"We've got hundreds of acres of wetlands and marshes right here," he said, waving his hand expansively. "And a wetland is a wetland is a swamp. Ours look like every swamp you ever saw in the world. I mean, we'd have to plant more trees and add some high grasses, but that's doable—with money." He pointed to the creek. "That could pass for a terrific muddy river. We've already got a variety of cedars and big oaks, too, and they can be shot in different ways. Speaking of which, drive over there, across that field." He pointed toward a patch of land holding mostly stones and stubble.

"But why Texas? Why couldn't they shoot the show in Florida, or even the Amazon itself?" I asked as the pickup bounced across the field. Wilson could use some new shock absorbers, I thought. Even he winced as he came down hard on his tender side.

"Doesn't cost as much here and the weather's real predictable—hot and no rain," he said. "The Dallas/Fort Worth airport is only about an hour away, and there are great studios right near there for postproduction stuff like editing. The crew could work up an authentic sweat here all day, and before they dried out, they'd be back in Dallas eating world-class food and sleeping in a swanky hotel. Lots of films are shot around here. TV shows, too."

"I never knew that."

"It's okay," he said, as if to console me on my ignorance. When we came to two small white rock hills, Wilson told me to stop, and he explained that, if framed right, they could look like mountains or a cliff.

"Really?"

"Hell, as kids, those two mounds took us around the world and back, and we didn't have cameras to reconfigure them. Hey, see that tree? I used to swing from that tree and drop into the creek below—still do sometimes." He looked at me and grinned. I had the feeling that, if not for his leg, he'd do it right then. His inability to play the host earlier had made him determined to entertain me now.

Our next stop was a low-slung modern building, circa 1960, with a simple brown sign in block letters that announced: COLLINS BIRD CENTER. Wilson's enthusiasm swelled—and for good reason: He had a much more elaborate setup than I'd ever imagined. There was a pleasant information volunteer, in her twenties, and a bookstore well-stocked with books on the natural sciences and a gift section selling bird and wildlife T-shirts, animal carvings, stones, and environmental postcards, among other items. Wilson seemed to have mastered his crutches, and he led me down a hallway with plate-glass window dioramas of local birds and wildlife—everything from sparrows and larks to wolves and rattlesnakes—stretching along the walls. Down another corridor, a colorful exhibit of regional seeds and grasses stood on display along with a selection of local wildlife photographs, some of professional quality, mounted by the county's photography club. Before I had a chance to take it all in, Wilson ushered me back into the car and directed me over to the Raptor Center.

Inside we were met by the Raptor Center's on-site supervisor. "He lives right here on the premises because some of these animal-rights people don't believe any animal should be in captivity, even if they can't survive outside," Wilson told me. He also told me that I was getting a rare, privileged look at the raptors; state regulations forbid their being on exhibit to the general public. As a result, each bird had a room of its own with a large darkened window that visitors couldn't see through unless a special light was turned on.

His pain almost forgotten, Wilson gave me the royal tour, every bird seeming more special to him than the last. "Now look at this hawk. Isn't she a sweet thing?" he asked, almost purring. "Some guy brought her in with a broken wing." I had never seen hands as gentle as his as the hawk perched on Wilson's fingers and he lightly stroked its forehead. "After two weeks here, she had created a nest and laid two eggs," he said proudly. "Only one hatched, though. She was so nurturing to that chick. It was great to see, I can tell you. Since then, we've given her baby orphans, and she's as good with them as with her own. We released her last foster babe into the wild just last week."

I felt a ridiculous pang of jealously, and Wilson placed the bird back carefully on a perch, then guided me down the hall. How could a hawk make me feel somehow inferior? I needed to get a grip.

"Now this screech owl will be released, too, as soon as he can catch live prey, but an old eye injury makes it hard for him to pounce on what he's supposed to," Wilson said as we looked through the glass at the serious-looking bird. The staff, he explained, had to keep any raptor to be released isolated from human contact as much as possible; otherwise the birds become too dependent on humans for food and goodwill to survive on the outside. "And this sharp-shinned hawk goes into the flight room after the great horned owl gets out. But you haven't seen the flight room yet," Wilson said excitedly. "You have to see this!"

We headed outside to a cage larger than my living room in New York. A flight room. I liked the idea of it—flying practice. Maybe I needed a flight room. If I had one, would I be able to leave my life? I honestly didn't know the answer. Wilson had pointed out that even raptors found it hard to resist taming when given the opportunity.

Wilson liked my company—and I was certainly beginning to like his. I decided to postpone my return to the hotel one more day.

WILSON SPEEDILY ACCEPTED my decision. He even obliged when I suggested he take a nap. Once he went to sleep, I took out my cell phone for the first time since driving to Rollins and put in a call to Steve. What time was it in Hong Kong? I looked at my watch and did the math. Five o'clock in the morning—he'd just be rising.

When either of us was away on business trips, we seldom communicated directly. We had learned years ago through trial and error that while Steve might write sweet e-mails, he tended to think three brisk, unsentimental sentences over the phone were adequate to convey any information. This created enough misunderstanding—the staccato exchanges didn't make up for my hurt feelings no matter how adult and rational I tried to be—that we basically decided to keep our exchanges to a bare minimum.

"Steve?"

"Something wrong?"

"No. Just wondering how you are."

"Busy. Very, very busy. But you know that." A pause. "So. And you?"

"Fine. I've been in Texas all weekend working on a column idea. This week, of course, I have to set up my new office in Dallas."

"Good, good."

He sounded so distracted that I wanted to scream.

"Michelle?"

"Yes?"

"Did I forget your birthday or something?"

"I wanted to talk to you, that's all. It already feels like you've been gone a long time."

"Oh? Well, I haven't, but the pace here is eating me alive. There's not enough hours in the day."

"I know, I know, darling. I'll e-mail soon," I said, cutting him off. This was why we never talked. I knew better than to call, but I wanted to give him a chance to pull me back from the edge of . . . of what exactly, I had no idea.

I thought about my drive with Wilson. He had asked me questions about my life, and I told him about growing up with no roots, how my parents were both dead and that I had a sister I wasn't close to. I also told him my former husband and I were friends.

"We grew apart, but we get along well now," I said. It seemed the least I could do for my marriage. I hated myself for lying in the first place. Wilson must have seen how uncomfortable that last subject made me, because for the rest of the ride we talked off and on only about my work, a subject we returned to over dinner that evening.

"I stay really busy," I told him as we ate a beef stew Helen had left. "But I'm ready to expand my reach. I think I've got something worth saying, and I'd like for more people to hear it."

"I would like to hear you," he said with utter sincerity, and for the first time I realized that Steve had never heard me speak, nor expressed any interest in doing so. I smiled at Wilson Collins. "From what I've seen of your life so far, you practice what I preach," I told him. "Maybe not your house," I laughed, "but your life seems focused ... uncluttered ..." In Wilson's case, house clutter didn't count, I decided.

"So with an office in Dallas, you'll be coming here a lot?" he asked, his fork halted midway to his mouth.

"I guess," I mumbled, suddenly quite interested in the carrots and potatoes on my plate. "But I have a lot of different exciting projects ... well, off and on I do. Actually, it's been a little slower than I would like recently. That's why I'm trying my wings. ..." Visions of flight rooms leapt into my mind. "Why I'm expanding my base," I corrected. "I honestly think what I do is important. It matters."

"Of course it does. Next time you speak, I'm coming," Wilson declared.

The thought of him sitting in the middle of a group of

earnest efficiency seekers was too much. "Maybe sometime," I said vaguely. "You know, I turn into a real ham," I confessed. "I get a real kick out of performing."

"No more than I get out of listening to you talk," he responded.

I, too, enjoyed our talking. He was so attentive. In Wilson's eyes, I was glamorous, maybe even a little mysterious.

Later, after he shook my hand good night at my bedroom door, I found I regretted the loss of his company. He seemed so interested in everything I had to say, and he did have such presence. All the more reason to get myself away from Wilson Collins. After all, I loved Steve. I loved my job. I loved my life.

chapter 5

PLEASE UNDERSTAND. MY LONG-STANDING MAR-
riage to Steve was important to me. It had held together better
than most unions of whatever duration. Though our travels separated us a great deal, Steve and I had a lot in common. We went
to hear any chamber music group, no matter how obscure. We
shared a passionate love of twentieth-century art, especially the
Abstract Expressionists—something about the aggressive colors and bold streaks appealed to us. We were both readers, and
years ago, we began reading the same book when we were apart.
It made us feel closer and gave us something more rewarding
than upcoming dental checkups and electricity bills to discuss
in our e-mails. At Steve's insistence, the book we had chosen for
this separation was *Lonesome Dove,* and I laughed now at how
its title fit my predicament so perfectly. Even Steve would have
appreciated the irony. We were a perfectly normal couple well-
suited to each other, and though our beginning was less than
spectacular, it also fell into the perfectly normal category.

"I'M PREGNANT," I had burst out exactly fifteen days after
missing my period and six months after we'd begun dating. I
was nineteen, an undergrad still undecided about my major.
Steve was twenty-two, a first-year law student.

"Fancy that!" he responded. Even then, Steve pictured

himself as someone more exotic and sophisticated than his middle-class and law-school status made him, and he experimented with odd bits of aristocratic dialogue. This affectation tickled more than annoyed me. For the moment, however, what mattered most was how he was taking the news. He recovered almost immediately. At four o'clock the following morning, he slipped a note under my door. I knew exactly when the envelope rustled against the wall-to-wall carpeting because I had been up worrying all night. I lay in bed another thirty minutes gathering the courage to get up and retrieve it. Then I returned to bed to read:

> *Dearest Michelle,*
>
> *We are not perfect but we are perfect for each other, and that fact alone should make us perfect to be parents of a baby who has no chance of being anything but imperfect in the same ways we are, therefore making the child perfect for us. Does next Saturday afternoon suit you for a wedding ceremony? The pumpkin will arrive and when you step in, it will turn into six white horses and a chariot, to be yours forevermore along with me.*
>
> *Steve*

I vowed there and then to love this man forever. He was good. He was kind. He was a class act. And he loved me. When his parents refused to give us any extra financial help, he didn't blink. My father was dead, killed in a car accident a year earlier, but my mother couched her rejection of us in moral terms, thereby contributing a tidy sum of anger to the desperation I already felt. Steve took my mother's anger in stride and helped me get over my own. I understood my good fortune in finding him.

Once ensconced in Steve's apartment at the university, I dropped out of my sophomore class to begin a frantic search for some kind of job that would give us needed extra income. In that Michigan university town abounding with overqualified, struggling young women looking to support their husbands and themselves, office jobs were hard to come by. But I was determined to show everyone that I could pull my own weight, and the baby's, too, and I came up with all sorts of schemes.

The housing complex we lived in was inhabited by other graduate couples, too, all mostly friendly and neighborly, but neighborliness had its price. Lacking children or a job, I became the one asked to let in the plumber or take the dog out, or to pick up a toddler from play-school when an emergency arose. Compensation usually took the form of tuna casseroles, but Steve and I didn't complain. If the young mothers had to hire a baby-sitter, they usually asked me. On those occasions, they actually paid cash.

My luck changed when a pregnant neighbor named Rose, a teacher of third grade at a private school, found herself showing a month or two sooner than expected and, to keep her job in that era, had to hide her condition until school was out in June. Inviting me to tea, she asked my advice on how to camouflage the small bulge in her belly. I had given the matter of "covering up" more than a little thought, as she knew from our casual conversations, because I was ever hopeful that a real job would open up and I, too, might need camouflage. In fact, I had gone so far as to imagine maximizing my bare-bones wardrobe by sketching out mix-and-match outfits, the kind so popular now in women's magazines and catalogs showing combinations for travel or the office or dining out. Since Rose could sew, I modified the sketches of my own ideal wardrobe to suit her taller figure.

More grateful and enthusiastic than I expected, Rose told everyone about my designing talent and how I was able to find new uses for seemingly old dresses and skirts, and my services became quite sought after. The ante for my input got upped to homemade fried chicken or hamburgers out and occasionally a case of beer or a couple of bottles of decent wine. If I'd known how to sew, maybe I would have pursued clothing design. I might have made some real money.

As it was, I didn't make us much, but my ability to re-imagine a woman's wardrobe sure reduced the grocery bill, which was no small thing, and I enjoyed myself immensely. I liked being helpful and I liked the casual friendships I made. They reminded me of the girls I'd known in the various high schools I had attended—fun and satisfying friends, even if there was never enough time to develop real intimacy.

Soon the women professors hired me also, and they paid in cash. Now, that was satisfying. For them the sorting of clothes turned into the sorting of filing cabinets and, many times, the sorting of research. In some instances, this last turned into my helping with their important papers. I loved that, the poking around, making order from multitudinous facts, but, in truth, no more than I loved poking around in people's clothes and junk, the artifacts of a life. I never imagined such bounty pouring forth from that first sketch of "camouflage." I hoped Rose would volunteer to make an outfit for me when the time came. Except the time never came.

The baby died in utero. One of those mysterious ends that no one could explain and which left me totally grief-stricken. As if that wasn't bad enough, a botched procedure to remove the baby's little body ended with an unexpected hysterectomy. Until then, I had not realized how much I was counting on this baby to give me a sense of family, an experience I'd never really had.

A strange and complicated period followed for Steve and me. We assumed we would pull through. We were young, after all. We had not counted on such anguish—or our even greater sum of sorrow.

When a severe staph infection occurred right after I was released from the hospital, Steve nursed me through it. Despite his workload at school, he rose in the middle of the night to give me medicine. When my fever soared, he gave me sponge baths. He learned to fix milk shakes that I could keep down and found foods I liked. Even after I began to regain my health, I'd wake in the night to find his hand on my forehead, checking. If his studies preoccupied him, he certainly never showed it. I accepted his ministrations with gratitude and all the love at my disposal.

We remained together, the best and most either of us could do, neither of us dreaming too far into the future. We had felt the force of randomness and discovered its treachery. Out of fear, we held on to each other and mourned the loss of our child, our suffering unstated.

Really, we were wiser than we knew, for we had as yet no clue that even early losses don't heal completely, and that a loss of such magnitude, not just our little child, but all possible future children, would have flattened couples less well matched than ourselves. I persuaded myself that being Michelle Banyon satisfied me. I had planned on it satisfying me for life.

chapter 6

I NEVER CONTEMPLATED ADULTERY. I STAYED ON
the straight and narrow, not giving my virtue a thought, blinders in place. After three nights on Wilson's farm, it was time
for me to get back to the Worth Hotel in Fort Worth for
another Daisy seminar. Wilson, meanwhile, was counting the
minutes until he could rid himself of his cast. As it turned out,
he had a meeting the next day in that city with an assistant
producer of the Amazon TV project—"Gotta show my face,"
Wilson said, "keep the sanctuary on their radar"—so we drove
back to the hotel together and he booked a room for the night.
Apparently, he planned to free his foot and drive himself
home after his meeting, and I decided it wasn't my place to
suggest his ankle might still be sore.

"But listen, Mickey," he said as I shook his hand good-bye
at the check-in counter, "let me at least buy you lunch for all
you've done for me." He gave my hand an extra squeeze, his
palm warm. "Don't say no." He looked at me searchingly and
flashed that winning smile.

Usually on these junkets, I slipped from lecture to meeting
to hotel room in a private bubble—a solitary traveler—and I
liked it that way, refusing overtures and social invitations by
well-meaning sponsors. Maybe I'd gotten used to Wilson's
company, I don't know, or maybe because we'd already punctured the balloon of my routine, but despite the deep grain of

my habit, I heard myself say, "Give me two hours. I need to clean up."

Upstairs in my room, twelve new e-mails stacked in a column on my computer screen allowed me to continue pretending nothing extraordinary was going on. Steve's, written before our call, had a cartoon with squiggles of a man defiantly tearing up a Christmas card. His drawing, a concession of sorts, made me smile. Merin Gamble had sent an invitation for dinner next weekend. There were numerous notes from readers, more than usual, and then I remembered it was Presidents' Day weekend and I always heard more from fans when they had a little extra time.

To think only three days had passed since . . . since . . . *Since what?* Since I'd been in New York, I concluded firmly. The brevity and substance of updates from my staff confirmed how short a time had really passed.

But one problem had not gone away over the weekend, as was evident from the pointed negative remarks from both Beth and Gloria, my two right hands. These women were godsends, really. Beth had been with me for nearly twenty years and Gloria for almost as long. Needless to say, in their own ways, they were both very protective of me. For whatever reason, they considered a new young assistant I'd hired both arrogant and ignorant of what Daisy Strait Enterprises was all about, and they were on a campaign to get "the newbie," as Gloria called her, out of there. Her name was Pam, and I tended to give her the benefit of the doubt and remained hopeful that she or they would come round.

Despite the gospel of Daisy, which promoted quick decisions and clean breaks, I hated letting anyone go and understood why entire industries were filled with liars who would say anything, promise anything, just so they wouldn't have to deliver bad news. I didn't like to confront difficult emotional situations either and had spent a great deal of effort protecting myself from just such unpleasantness in both my professional and private lives. For now, I tried to calm the troubled waters without taking any definite action.

I returned quick messages to everyone and then attempted to figure out what to wear for lunch with Wilson. Since I was giving an afternoon lecture to the Business and Professional Women's Club of Fort Worth, my outfit had to work for both activities. This was a challenge. Daisy's clothes weren't picked for attractiveness but to save a woman time and cleaning bills. In the end, I chose a black skirt and a soft pink ruffled blouse, purchased on a whim to soften a suit that was too severe even for Michelle. The blouse had been a rare misguided acquisition, too fussy for my Michelle life and not practical enough for Daisy. Still, I sometimes packed it on my travels—a small note of whimsy—and decided to wear it now. I could add the jacket for the lecture. Maybe Wilson was a sucker for ruffles, and the pink did make my complexion glow.

I TREATED MYSELF to a glass of wine, which should have been a warning all by itself. Wine with lunch was an indulgence I saved for long, lazy weekends—never for when I was on Daisy time. Today, though, a soothing glass of the house Chardonnay felt right. I asked Wilson to help me keep track of the time.

As I reached for my wine, my ruffled sleeve dipped dangerously close to the carrot soup. Without missing a beat,

Wilson slipped his hand under my arm briefly, catching and protecting my blouse. I concentrated on our conversation. The wine was obviously kicking in, and he was keeping up a steady stream of talk. Maybe he was anxious about his meeting with the TV rep the next day, because mostly he talked about the nature reserve and his frustration that it was underappreciated and misunderstood.

Sitting in the quiet dining room of the hotel with its Western decor, Wilson spoke with the zeal of a missionary to a possible convert as he expounded on how few people fully grasped the fundamental connection of everything on this planet. "Including," he said, his fork waving, "ourselves and ants. Even mosquitoes! Things might look disparate, but they're part of a whole. Everything is necessary!" His fork hit the wood table with a twang.

I nodded in vigorous agreement. I thought I was getting a glimmer of my disparate natures.

"Whenever I talk about this stuff, too often people's eyes glaze over," Wilson lamented.

"The whole is greater than the sum of its parts," I said.

Wilson paused. Since I had no idea what I meant, I was sure he didn't either. Then he nodded with enthusiasm. "You're a good listener, you know that, Mickey?" he asked, his slate-gray eyes flattening whatever meager barriers I had erected. Every time he said my new name in that Texas drawl of his, I felt a thrill.

"I like listening to you," I replied. It was true, but listening was also my best social talent.

"You're too generous. Now it's your turn," he said, wagging his knife at me. "Tell me about your lecture this afternoon. Can I come?"

"Oh, no," I said, alarmed. Daisy was for me and for total strangers. I didn't want him there.

"Don't be so modest," he said.

"It's a women's group," I said lamely. "Maybe another—" I stopped myself.

When he saw that I wasn't going to change my mind, he tried another tack. "So what do you do with your free time?"

"I read and . . . well, I read. I've always liked stories." It didn't feel right to mix Michelle's life up with Mickey's. Better to be vague. "I should probably make more time for some kind of physical activity."

"I bet you were a tomboy once," Wilson said, appraising me.

"It's true." I laughed. How could he tell that? "I was always getting scratched up and bruised. That's why it's easy for me to sympathize with you and your predicament," I added, tilting my head toward his knee.

"You still are a little reckless."

"Clumsy is what I was," I answered. I didn't want to confess that I was probably the most cautious tomboy ever. I liked climbing trees, playing ball, and riding bikes better than playing house, but I approached my activities with care. "Anyway, my sister, Andrea, cornered the market on the more feminine pursuits—she was like my mother that way—and I was the odd girl out." I paused. I hoped I didn't sound whiny. "I guess the outdoors was more fun—plus it gave me a way to snub my nose at them."

"A rebel you are," Wilson said, tapping my hand lightly for emphasis. "But stubborn as old barbed wire," he said, expanding his theory. When he saw the questionable look on my face, he added, "I admire that."

I was becoming attached to this idea of me as a gritty maverick, a daredevil, someone quite different from the me I knew. Someone who rescued strangers from disaster. Reckless. Impulsive. I reached for my wineglass.

Again Wilson rescued the sleeve of my blouse from an encounter with my plate, the more remarkable because while he was doing it, his eyes never strayed from my face. I was unaccountably flattered. His gesture seemed to have a kind of "looking after" quality to it.

Then Wilson lifted my wrist and did something I never imagined any man would do to me. He examined the inside of my wrist, lifted it to his face, and touched it lightly with his tongue. "You have to be more careful," he said in a whisper, "or no more wine."

My wrist, his tongue.

My pulse hammered furiously.

I took his hand. "All right," I said to his unasked question. It seemed like hours before the check came. We didn't speak.

AS THE DOOR to his room shut behind us, he placed me against the wall, his own readiness pressing through his trousers and against my skirt. We stood there kissing for a long while, and his tentativeness only excited me more. The slower his tongue in my mouth, the lighter his hands on my body, the more aroused I became. Unable to stand the tension any longer, I unbuttoned my blouse, unzipped my skirt.

In bed he continued to caress me, his eyes expressing wonderment. He was more muscular than I'd realized, his legs as solid as his upper body. "I'm glad you're fond of curves," he joked as I ran my fingers across his small paunch.

"I think I've found an angle that I like, too," I whispered when he turned me onto my belly. I loved the care he took, the slow, tantalizing motion of his hips against my ass, the playful nibbles on my shoulders. When I thought for sure I'd explode, I turned over and climbed on top of him. Wilson moaned with delight—or pain—and the sound shocked me into awareness. I jumped off him and the bed.

"Come back here," he pleaded.

I began scrambling for my clothes. "My talk . . . I'm late!"

Wilson watched, a look of confusion and frustration on his face. "What about dinner?" he said. "Will you meet me for dinner?"

"I— Okay," I said, running out the door, promising to return later.

IN MY HOTEL ROOM, my heart pounding, I pulled back my hair tightly, set Daisy's glasses on my nose, slipped on my suit jacket, and found my sensible shoes. I felt a sliver of shame. I had told Wilson I'd return. I could no longer pretend innocence to myself. Ten minutes later I was walking into the hotel ballroom as Daisy Strait. I didn't have my notes, but onstage I never referred to them anyway. Notes didn't lend the right air of artlessness, the handmaiden of simplicity. Running late didn't exactly fit the picture either. As I approached the stage, I composed myself, willing myself to become untroubled, clutter-free.

"ALWAYS BE CLEAR about your destinations," I heard myself say in my perky Daisy Strait voice to the well-dressed audience of Business and Professional Women. "But allow yourself a few minutes every now and again to give up control and stop reckoning with yourself." An arduous task that reckoning, I thought as I tried to remember how on earth I had planned to open this talk. What I was saying bore no resemblance to my usual sessions.

"Too often, we are mired in daily clutter, oblivious to the small indulgences that could ease our way, the small pleasures that could make life worth living," I declared, remembering Wilson's soft kisses on the curve of my ear. Oh, I was lost. Recklessly, hopelessly lost.

"You must focus on your life and make the most of every moment, every lesson learned. . . ." I resolved to do so, too. And then, as though someone had flipped a switch, I was back into my Daisy groove and the right words started coming, admittedly by rote. Throughout the lecture and the question-and-answer period, Wilson's tongue played against my wrist, my neck, my nipple until I became a lyrical instrument, an instrument that had never been properly played before. I could barely concentrate on the questions; my answers were short and vague. I had never experienced physical attraction like this; it had taken me over the moment he licked my wrist.

TO BE HONEST, inexperienced as I was with infidelity, I was surprised by how little my qualms interfered with my desire. I was not without discipline, however. After I cut short my Q&A and left my audience still applauding, I quickly returned to the hotel and stopped by my room to brush out my hair and remove my jacket. I was now free to bathe once more in Wilson's voice—or maybe his tub.

This last thought gave me a moment's pause as I stood in

front of the mirror, tucking in my butt and pulling in my stomach. I felt satisfied enough until I realized the impossibility of making love or even taking a bath with a sucked-in belly. Not that I was overweight—adrenaline, a good metabolism, and an ever-so-sensible diet kept me skinny. But toned I wasn't. I had stopped paying much attention to the condition of my body, mainly because Steve had, too. Neither of us really saw me anymore. Sit-ups tomorrow, I promised the mirror, and started toward the door.

This time shyness overtook me. What if I didn't live up to Wilson's expectations? Or I bored him afterward? Or my body bored him as soon as he'd conquered it, which I certainly full well counted on his doing? Heartsick, I sat down on the bed, resisting the urge to cry. What would become of me? For that matter, what was already becoming of me?

I couldn't remember when I was last overwhelmed by a lack of confidence. It was not my style. I dialed his room.

"You're back?" Wilson asked.

"Yes."

"Good." The relief in his voice told me all I needed to know. I felt steeped in his husky tones.

"Just checking my voice mail, things like that," I replied in as sexy a manner as possible—and made a note to do so.

"Should I join you?"

"Oh, no! I'll be right up." I answered a little too quickly, too shrilly. I did not want him on my territory.

As a last-minute stall, I checked my home voice mail as well. Dottie, my sister Andrea's only child and my only niece, had called on Friday morning after I'd left for Texas, wanting to know if I'd like to hang out with her over the holiday weekend.

She had ended with an uncertain, "If it's convenient." The call caused a surprising amount of anguish. I would have liked to have been with her and was sorry to have missed the opportunity.

I hadn't seen much of Dottie until seven years ago when she turned thirteen and my sister began letting her spend two weeks of the summer with Steve and me in New York. This winter, Dottie had decided to drop out of her small local college in Indiana and take lessons with a modern-dance company in Manhattan. My sister and I had almost nothing in common and talked only on Christmas or birthdays. When she called to tell me of Dottie's imminent arrival, she made a point of telling me that Dottie had always thought of me as special. My sister had choked on *special,* I don't know whether because of her own emotional state or because her daughter felt that way about me. This was as close as Andrea could come to asking me to be available. The truth was I would have done anything my sister asked, because she had never asked or wanted anything of me before. Those previous summertime visits had been at my request.

The truth was also that I was flattered to think my niece thought of me as someone special. I would have done anything for Dottie, too; she had always charmed me. I seldom heard from her between visits, though. And there was a difference between having her for two weeks—as if she were a precious object on loan that I mustn't grow too fond of—and having her actually reside in my city. So far we had only succeeded in having a couple of dinners with her. Every other time I'd called she'd been busy.

Maybe Dottie's message was a signal to toe the line. I could not go through with this. I would go to Wilson and confess my marital state, apologize—all in a dignified, calm manner. After all, I had come to my senses. This last, all too true.

IN HIS ROOM, I began in a rush, "There's something I have to tell you—"

He interrupted with, "I'm sorry."

"Sorry?" I echoed, puzzled that he knew what I was about to say.

"I was taking things too fast. If you'll stay and have dinner with me, I promise to behave myself. Please." He stood there awkwardly.

"No, no, it isn't that. I mean it's that but not just that. I can't . . ." I hesitated before deciding once and for all against a risky dinner. I held out my hand. "I am sorry. I've enjoyed your company and I apologize for my own behavior this afternoon. I turned out to be a tease and that's not nice. . . ." I took a deep breath. Don't talk, I thought. Leave. Right now.

But he had taken my hand in both of his. "You are very nice. It's all my fault. I shouldn't have . . . please. Let's just have dinner and forget the whole thing—not the whole thing, the part . . ."

I pulled my hand away. "I can't. Really."

Wilson looked crushed. Instantly, my urge to console turned into something more. I pushed him lightly into a chair. Standing in front of him, my hands enclosed his face, my lips found his eyes, nose, his ears, his tongue, his neck. I began unbuttoning his shirt. When I got to his belt and pants, he tried to help, but without thinking, I slapped away his hands. This had become my show.

I never behaved like this. Nobody would have put me in the *Guinness Book of World Records* for aggressive sexual conduct. But could I help it if his ex-wife was a fool and he needed reassurance? What else could I do? The man was about to be treated to the best my body could offer. And when I put my mind to something, my best can be pretty good.

chapter 7

THE NEXT MORNING, KNOWING WILSON HAD LEFT for his meeting, I called Dottie and made a date for dinner that night in New York City. This I did at considerable cost and effort. It was no more like me than going to bed with a man not my husband. Then I met with Amy Ward, the woman I had hired to run my Texas office in Dallas. By the end of the hour, Amy appeared overwhelmed even before I explained that we would be in touch primarily by e-mail for the next few days.

Long before Wilson, I had decided that Daisy Strait and Texas were perfect for each other. The plan called for setting up an office in Dallas and training some nice, young local women to be on-site advisers to the frantic and cluttered, in between special consultations from Daisy. Poor Amy Ward looked perplexed about my lack of time for her, but I concluded that she might as well get used to my preferred mode of communication sooner rather than later. I had numerous lectures in the coming days. And Wilson. He had asked me to stay with him while I continued my Texas lecture schedule and supervised my new office arrangements, and I had said yes.

ALL RIGHT, REASON wasn't my strong suit at the moment. This last crossed my mind as I watched my niece, so young and untested, her cheeks flushed from the cold, enter Balthazar, the trendy little restaurant I'd chosen in Soho. Fortunately I came often enough that I could wrangle a last-minute reservation. She seemed agitated but pleased to see me. I felt I'd had something to do with her move to New York, and I was thankful she wanted to spend time with me.

Someone in the family needed me—albeit a grown child and one who hadn't yet said so. Perhaps she saw me as someone who could provide . . . what? Inspiration? A role model? Another way of life? Whatever it was, I vowed to help her discover that nebulous something in any way I could—unless, of course, I was projecting onto her some nebulous something of my own.

"Auntie M, am I late?" Dottie asked, looking apologetic as she sat down. "I left rehearsal early so you wouldn't have to wait."

When I assured her that she wasn't late, that I'd wanted to be there first to welcome her, Dottie visibly relaxed. "I'm glad on both counts," she said, smiling, her eyes approving her surroundings.

"The food is good, too," I said. "Of course, you've probably hit all the cool spots by now." I wanted to elicit any information about her life that I could.

Dottie laughed. "Are you kidding? My folks think my dancing is a whim and they don't believe in indulging whims. They've given me enough to live on, but not enough to taste anything of the wicked high life."

"Nobody works as hard as you do without being serious," I said.

Blinking back surprising tears, Dottie could only nod her agreement. What had upset her so? I wondered, but thought better of asking. Whatever the cause, I wished I had the power to assure her a happy ending; instead, I asked how the dancing was going. When Steve and I had dinner with her, Steve tended to dominate the conversation with his knowledge of dance and his enthusiastic approval of her decision to study in New York. Tonight, though, I hoped to draw her out.

I knew about the tap classes my sister had enrolled her in at the tender age of three. At the time, Dottie had been much more enthralled with watching her arms move than her feet. Later in ballet, she told me now as she picked at a spinach salad, she toppled on pointe; but in high school, she attended a modern-dance recital by a visiting local company and later found she could duplicate the exact dance steps she'd seen executed. Thus began her love affair with modern dance, she said. "Since nobody else in our class took it very seriously, my teacher loved me, which helped. I might not have been the best, but I was the most earnest." Dottie laughed. "I got pretty obsessed." She pulled her wavy blond hair out of its loose knot and let it fall around her shoulders. "My dad believes football and basketball are the only proper objects for obsession. I like to play those games, too, but he isn't interested in girls' athletics."

"What about your mother?"

"She's not into sports—or obsession." This time Dottie gave me a knowing smile, which I resisted returning.

"It's easy for us who are older to get caught up in our daily refrains and not catch what's important," I offered. Did that sound too much like Daisy? I tried another tack: "When I was young, I became a tennis whiz because my father was interested in the game. By the time I was good enough to really show my stuff, he was off to some new war and I gave it up." As soon as I finished, I wished I hadn't told her that. Story for story wasn't what she needed. "I'm sure your parents must be proud of you, though. Your mother always brags about you." A lie. Andrea and I weren't in touch enough for bragging or complaining.

"Oh, they spend a lot of time hovering, but that's not the same as tuning in. They're a little out of it where I'm concerned," Dottie said, as if this were some big joke, but it was clear she was the one who felt out of it.

Until that moment I'd assumed, without realizing it, that my invisibility in my family meant something was wrong with me. My actions—so long as they didn't reflect badly on the family, and they didn't—always seemed of no consequence to anyone else. No questions asked; little notice taken. I guess I wasn't the only one who felt alienated from our clan.

"Anyway," Dottie continued, "I decided I might as well do what I want, whatever that is." Again, she laughed. I noticed all the stories she told about herself had a self-deprecatory quality to them.

At one point over our grilled salmon, Dottie confessed that her boyfriend since high school, Mike, had tried to talk her into staying in Indiana. He, too, didn't see anything special in what she did. "Maybe they all are right," she sighed. "This town doesn't exactly instill confidence." We both stared around us at the expensively maned young women in their Galliano pants and Blahnik stilts, drinking and bantering with young men who flaunted their own high-priced haircuts and Gucci loafers.

"It can be hard here," I agreed. "Most cities and institutions are blind, but your family, your boyfriend . . . they should be able to see you and what *you* want," I said fiercely. Fearing Andrea's wrath, I didn't want to get in the middle, but I recognized a piece of myself in this vulnerable child, a too-ready acceptance of being someone on the margins of family, of city, of self. Filled so with other people's needs, Dottie was on the verge of becoming peripheral to her own life. The self-absorption of the young usually is an inadequate ally against such odds. For better or worse, she now had me as a protector.

My last words of the evening to her were innocuous enough: "What's important, Dottie, is that you understand your possibilities and that you take a chance on them." And that, I thought, summed me up pretty well at the moment, too.

THAT NEXT AFTERNOON I made a beeline to Wilson's farm in a rental car straight from the airport. I was off on a lark. Everyone deserves a lark once, I told myself, and wondered if Wilson had ever rescued any larks.

As soon as we closed his front door, he began satisfying desires I didn't know I had, this time with the deftness of a messenger boy in traffic, despite his recent injuries. He lingered on my earlobe, my buttocks. I couldn't get enough of his touch and smell, couldn't get over the *newness*, the *strangeness* of him. Twenty-seven years with one man had not prepared me for lust of this magnitude—lust made even more acute by virtue of difference. We climaxed together and I laughed happily. He looked at me, surprised.

"It's so much fun," I told him.

"Just wait, lady. I've been storing up for you," he answered. We decided to christen his bed upstairs. In bed I once again became the aggressor, already fond of that new role.

By that night, sitting at Wilson's kitchen table, I could easily have been mistaken for a completely different woman. All flirty and soft, I hardly recognized myself. I was so besotted that over dinner (compliments of Helen's frozen meals), I belly-laughed at even his silliest jokes. I discovered that, when not in pain, Wilson was something of a raconteur, with stories about everything from riding cows as a boy on the farm to the time he came face-to-face with a rabid wolf to a lifetime of misadventures with Brian, like when they went down to Mexico once and got arrested for speeding. "The only Spanish I could remember was *'Atare los cordones de mis zatatos,'* which means 'I will tie my shoelaces,'" said Wilson, "which I kept repeating, Mickey, and I couldn't figure out why the police were not moved to let us go."

Inevitably he found his way back to his favorite subject, and I heard about a committee he had formed to help lobby the television bigwigs to do their series at his bird sanctuary. "I'm trying to get the town to see why this would be as good for Rollins as for the center. Filming here would generate tourists for us both," he explained. "But everything has to be spiffed up, including the storefronts and the look of downtown. If we could only raise the money that's needed!"

"You'll do it," I replied, with complete faith in his prowess on any front, so to speak.

Covering my hands with one of his, he smiled and said, "Mickey, you're the best thing that's happened to me in a long, long time."

FINGERS LACED, sex-sated, wine-drowsy, we lay in bed as I stroked his stomach and nuzzled my face against his neck. Perhaps because he was happy to have an audience and self-professed supporter, Wilson's idea of pillow talk was to tell me about an animal-rights group that kept protesting in front of the center. "They don't believe in breeding mice to feed birds. You'd think people would have better things to do with their time."

"Yes, you would." Certainly Daisy's people would, I thought. But like the selfish lover I was quickly becoming, I wanted him to talk about me, to elaborate more on his delight with me. I wanted to be the center of his universe, not those damned birds.

By the time he drifted into a deep slumber, my need for the same had disappeared. What if I snored? I knew for a fact that sometimes I slept with my mouth open, evidenced by a tell-tale trail of saliva, which wasn't exactly romantic. I couldn't handle exposing myself that way. No, I definitely did not plan to risk sleep. In the hotel I had left Wilson by making up an excuse about pulling an all-nighter to catch up on my work. But if this sex business required such constant vigilance, how long did I think I could last?

Finally, I decided to slip into the guest-room bed and tell Wilson in the morning that *he* snored, but when I shifted to leave, he pulled me closer and put my hand between his legs. "I can't promise, but ... ," he murmured.

"I like challenges," I answered, already on my knees.

THE REAL CHALLENGES began the next morning with the arrival of Wilson's dog, Luck, a large black mongrel—a scary dog color to me, but Wilson had adopted the dog a couple years earlier to ease the pain after his wife left and named him in hopes of a better life. Now Luck was back after days chasing some bitch in heat all around town. The way he kept sniffing up my skirt, he surely knew I was one, too. Wilson had the mistaken notion that I would adore his pet, but only my desire not to look like a complete wimp persuaded me to touch the massive brute. At one point, I swear, he snapped at me. Dogs and I had no affinity for one another.

A few days later, Wilson's housekeeper, Helen Carson, arrived, sniffed around a little, and also appeared ready to snap at me. To be fair, I already knew of her existence whereas she had no clue about mine. A dyed yellow-blonde, a color that suited her pale skin prematurely wrinkled by sun and cigarettes, she had the determined jawline that came with willing life to work for you. From her ample figure, I had to assume she enjoyed her own cooking. She resented my clumsy attempts to help in the kitchen and made it clear that I was an intrusion, unnecessary and unwelcome. With my trips to other Texas cities and Oklahoma coming up, as well as an overnight conference with the Timber Association of Arkansas, not to mention my plan to meet Steve in Hong Kong, Helen didn't have to worry about my bothering her too much.

This last commitment loomed on the horizon like a faint bruised sky that you worry might mean rain. I had no idea what it would be like to see him again. I'd never before even kissed another man, let alone made love to one. How could I look Steve in the eye?

As it turned out, a few days before I was scheduled to leave, Steve sent a contrite e-mail suggesting that I cancel the trip to Asia: *Miss you, love you, but no see you. Sorry, light of my life, but I'm in Hong Kong hell. It doesn't make any sense for you to come. I'll explain all when I see you again. Meantime, when you think of me, please be kind. Your beau, Steve.*

My heart was a tangle. I loved his notes, as he well knew. This was the softer side of Steve, the man who could tell me he cared. I craved knowing this, no matter how breezily expressed. I felt a familiar letdown, followed quickly by a complicated pang of remorse as I realized I did not regret the turn of events. In the past, I would have fought off my disappointment and tried not to feel rejected. Those reactions seemed foolish to me now, for I truly did understand his predicament. I always understood, really. It was just that sometimes I felt that Steve took advantage of all that understanding.

Years ago, after our hurried marriage and my debilitating illness, I constantly looked for ways to pay Steve back for his attentions and kindness. Since we'd had no semblance of a honeymoon and romance hadn't figured much in our courtship either, I decided on a romantic retreat during his next spring break. For weeks, I studied travel brochures and took on extra jobs running errands as well as organizing clutter. Then I surprised Steve one cold morning with a fully financed plan to head for a relatively inexpensive place in Nassau. He smiled and rumpled my hair.

"You like the idea?" I asked.

"Sure. A weekend away with you sounds great." For emphasis he hugged me, and added, "I can hardly wait." I still remember how happy and secure I felt to think that he truly loved me.

The day before our vacation, I left work at five o'clock to run errands and pack. Around eight, just as I was zipping up the last suitcase, Steve called from the library, where he spent most of his time.

"I should be home by two," he said wearily.

"Not to worry," I told him. "I've already packed for you."

"Packed?"

I laughed. "Your clothes, Mr. Absentminded Professor. Never mind, I'll remind you of all the details when you get home."

Unable to sleep, I decided to wait up for Steve and repack our clothes in a more efficient, wrinkle-proof way. My clients liked it when I gave them tips on packing or organizing briefcases. Now that I helped professors sort through their papers as well as their closets, I had started calling the people I worked for *clients*, a word that made me feel more professional every time I used it.

First out of the suitcase were our new swimsuits—mine a black bikini. For Steve I had chosen a bright yellow Speedo to remind him that he was on vacation. As soon as we got to our hotel, we would go swimming, which should put him in the mood for the black negligee—a total indulgence on my part, but I'd walked through Lingerie on my way to Swimsuits at the department store and couldn't resist. On seeing the filmy black lace now, I couldn't resist trying it on again. Part of me felt old, an ancient twenty to be exact, but in the negligee I felt like somebody else, someone with potential. I would have liked to have had the gown to go with it, but spending more money was out of the question. Besides, maybe it was a little sexier this way. Or I could put on my new black teddy, nylon but soft as silk, I mused, rubbing it against my cheek.

I next pulled out my sundresses and Steve's sport shirts, our shorts and sandals, khakis and deck shoes. After repacking our new goodies in tissue and moving our shoes for better distribution, I crawled into bed and set the alarm for five-thirty A.M.—only three hours away.

Steve came in at 3:05. Disoriented, I leapt to my feet out of a sound sleep. "Don't get up," he said, but I was already hugging him. Since he had nursed me back to health, I missed no opportunity to show him affection, which wasn't easy because affection was something neither of our families had been any good at. It just wasn't in either of our bodies' vocabularies except when I'd been sick and we'd been scared.

"Poor guy, but you can sleep on the plane," I assured him.

"The plane is out. Sorry." He hugged me back wearily.

To my amazement I drew back and slammed my fist against the wall. "No!" I wailed. Adding to my misery, my fist now throbbed with pain.

"You'll wake the neighbors."

"Screw the neighbors! Screw you! It's not fair!"

"Don't cry," Steve pleaded. "Professor Langhorn is working on an important brief and he asked me to help. You can't say no to something like that. When he asked, I honestly forgot about this trip. I'm so sorry. Don't cry." Steve's mother was a crier, manipulated the whole family that way. He had told me this more than once. Marrying into a family of non-criers had pleased him.

The big suitcase I had packed so carefully stood waiting forlornly by the door. "I had so many plans," I said, catching sight of it, holding back tears as my face contorted. "Can't you take your research with you?"

"Look, this is my career—our life—I'm working toward." His voice soft, coaxing. "I want to go as much as you, Michelle. I'm exhausted. A break would be wonderful, but I can't. Later we'll go on a hundred wonderful vacations. Okay?"

I nodded.

He pulled me close and we dropped onto the bed. His hand reached under my gown for my belly and he fell instantly, deeply asleep. I cried myself to sleep.

At the time I thought I had pulled the disappointment back inside or killed it entirely. The intolerable hunger was too keen for me to do anything else.

NONE OF THIS, mind you, excused in any way what I was doing with Wilson. If Steve had been the most attentive man in the world, I still would not have been able to resist Wilson. Even so, I was surprised at myself for not feeling more guilty. I needed how Wilson made me feel—sexy and special. I needed him. On some level I felt I *deserved* him, and whatever contortions I had to go through seemed well worth the price. I decided to convert my three-week vacation in Southeast Asia into a Texas sojourn. My New York staff was not expecting me to be around and they all knew how badly I needed a rest. I would tell them that Texas was as good a place as any to recharge my batteries.

"THREE WHOLE WEEKS? And I'll have you all to myself?" Wilson grinned his loopy grin.

"If you want me," I teased.

He swung me around. We both knew the answer, and he sealed the deal with a kiss so fierce, I thought maybe every bone in my body would dissolve with pleasure.

Now that I had proposed this venture, I resolved to do my best to ingratiate myself to Helen. I took to hanging out in the kitchen and asking respectful questions, and finally she relented. Thus began my next challenge: cooking lessons when I was in town.

One Saturday Helen demonstrated how to flute the edge of a pastry crust. Before Wilson, I regarded homemade pastry as a waste of time and energy. In this new life, however, I not only wasted hours this way, I endured the humiliation of my own ineptness for the insane reason of wanting to present Wilson with a pie I had made with my own hands.

Although still highly suspicious of me, Helen began to convey a generous spirit when it came to my culinary skills, appalling in their absence even after her lessons. "I should have paid more attention growing up," I said by way of explanation, or apology.

"Not everyone pays attention to the same things. Me, I just got a knack for doughy stuff. Mama says I was born with light fingers, good for a baker or a pickpocket." Until I saw the trace of a smile, I wasn't sure Helen was joking, and by then it was too late to laugh. Since she delivered all her lines in a flat monotone, some meant to be funny, some not, navigating her sense of humor required skill.

As Helen looked on, I tried to roll out another glob of dough that kept sticking to the rolling pin even though I had dusted it with flour. Despite her newfound patience and generosity, I suddenly became irritated by Helen's presence and I snapped, "I'm just a little slow when it comes to pastry!"

Helen shrugged. "Who's to say what's slow? But I am wondering why you are fixing so many pies."

"I'm just looking to make one perfect pie, that's all. Just one!" I smacked the countertop with my flour-covered palm.

"Forget perfect," Helen answered, and walked out of the kitchen.

ONLY WILSON was perfect, I thought the next night after he brought me to climax three times before attending to his needs. More than a little satisfied with ourselves, we listened to the distant rumble of the night train and the faint gurgle of the creek. I turned toward him and put my hand on his cheek.

"Are other women as easy to pick up as I was?"

"I didn't pick you up."

"Yeah, you did."

"If so, it was the most painful pickup in history. There has to be an easier way." He smiled and propped his head on his arm.

"No pain, no gain," I teased.

"In one swell fall, I gained the world, and I don't ever want to lose it." He picked up my hand to kiss my fingertips. "That's a roundabout way of saying I never want to lose you, Mickey. I didn't know I could be this happy."

"I'm happy, too," I murmured.

"Happier than you've ever been?"

I nodded yes and meant it, then found myself saying, "Tell me about Connie. Didn't she make you happy in the beginning?"

Even as I asked, I knew parts would come back to haunt me: that she carried herself with the elegance of a dancer, that he'd been taken by her brown cropped hair and olive skin. But they had never had the right sort of give-and-take between them, he said, speaking quietly. No humor or real passion.

After taking a few landscape and horticultural courses at the local college, she started a landscape consulting business, which she tried to keep to a part-time occupation but it grew. She did love the farm, too, at least at first, and her enthusiasm had been a blessing for Wilson. They never quarreled, and he mistook her satisfaction with her work as satisfaction with her life. The very fact that Connie did not make emotional or physical demands on him should have told him something. Too much ease in marriage is as treacherous as too much turmoil, he now knew.

Steve and I had a similar problem, I realized. Maybe all that civility had worked against us. Connie had been civil. And Connie had left.

That's what Wilson was saying now: One day she ran away with a characteristic lack of fuss, leaving behind a pot of chili on the stove, a note exempting him from blame, and a cellar full of the wine she'd ordered. Since then he hadn't seen anyone who really interested him. "Until you came along," he said, holding me tightly. "Now I have a song in me, and the words go, 'Mickey, Mickey, Mickey. Oh, how I adore you, Mickey.'"

A SONG IN WILSON; a whole symphony in me, new notes I had never heard before. After the initial shock of *owning* Mickey, I passed whole days dappled in happiness. Wilson proved a lover in every way. He asked me all kinds of questions, like what did I look like when I was young?

"Skinny, gangly, freckled, with bangs that almost covered my eyes," I told him. "The kind of girl that nobody gives a second look."

What was my favorite city?

New York, for its kaleidoscope of different worlds and its energy.

Wilson said he'd take my word for it. He hated New York, didn't like most cities.

Did I like movies? What kinds of books? Art? Our reading habits differed: I shared Steve's love of nineteenth-century novels and was otherwise eclectic; Wilson preferred history—World Wars I and II and books on Texas were his favorites—along with books on birds and nature. In my cherished nineteenth century, he would have been a well-read naturalist. It turned out we both liked the same films—black-and-white movies of the forties like *Double Indemnity* and the splashy Technicolor musicals of the fifties, *Singing in the Rain* taking first place with both of us.

"You weren't even born in the forties," he teased.

"Maybe that's why I like the movies so much," I said.

My answers sometimes surprised and alarmed me. I had already told him that I was divorced, but later, feeling guilty and superstitious, I volunteered that the divorce was all my fault. After that disclosure I tried to be more careful, but I was definitely enjoying the attention, the fact that Wilson hung on my words, that he cared for my opinions. In fact, his interest overwhelmed me at times, and I often had the urge to cry.

One evening at the Raptor Center, we were watching over a little brown owl with a damaged wing. A farmer's wife had discovered it sitting in the corner of a shed and brought it to Wilson. Patiently Wilson kept waiting to see if the little thing would eat the live worm or dead mouse he had placed in its room. No luck.

"Why don't you feed it yourself?" I finally asked as we sat

on a bench looking into the room where the owl perched, a slow-motion blink its only movement.

"Oh, Mickey, I've got to do everything I can to keep that owl from becoming too dependent on me," Wilson said. He had on one of his rumpled blue work shirts with a white undershirt showing underneath. His hair curled around his ear, the way I liked, and he looked delicious to me. "Like I told you, I hope those wings fly again, but that won't matter if the owl can't forage for itself."

Wilson took my hand in his large one, and I leaned over to kiss a sunspot that I hadn't noticed before. He grinned but soon the grin faded. "But I don't want you too independent, Mickey. I want you to need me. I feel like . . . I feel . . . I know that I'm in uncharted waters with you." He shook his head in wonder. "I don't know what to do."

I stood in front of him, his face in my hands. "Thank you," I said.

"For what?"

"Those waters." No one had ever loved me this much. No one had ever cared like this. But I didn't know how to tell him that and keep afloat myself.

MUCH TO MY AMAZEMENT, my hands soon felt at home in dough or on raw meat. Helen and I worked together in the kitchen, often at the big pine table, where I'd help prepare the evening meal. So far, she praised only my skill at peeling potatoes. Most of the time I could see her bite her lip to keep from saying anything. One day, in a rare fit of frustration, she asked, "Didn't your mother teach you anything?" We'd spent thirty minutes rolling okra in cornmeal, which I then burned in the skillet.

I laughed. "Not much. I remember wanting to try my hand in the kitchen a few times, but my big sister scolded me for making messes and my mother said she didn't have time to fool with me. They couldn't be bothered, and before long I decided I couldn't be bothered, either. To be honest, by the time I was twelve, I was grateful that most housekeeping duties were foreign to me." As I talked to Helen and smelled her cornbread in the oven, I wondered how I would have turned out if someone like Helen had been my mother.

Daisy Strait wouldn't admit interest in any of these domestic tics, of course, for it was her destiny to point to the exit door for poor souls wandering lost in their overwhelming gourmet kitchens. It was Daisy's duty to help them feel virtuous about not spending time with all those gleaming appliances. Simplify your life—give up the rolling pin and the pasta maker, for that kind of equipment either obliges you to use it or feel guilty when you don't. In all candor, practicing what I preached had saved me from some uncomfortable moments.

In Rollins, Texas, though, I discovered that domesticities struck me as sexy. Though I had come to cherish Helen's companionship, I didn't mind that she usually left just before lunch, returning in time to prepare dinner. Having the house to myself felt wonderful. I roamed about in Wilson's home, familiarizing myself with his belongings, memorizing every nook and cranny for my absences ahead. I came to love the dark pictures in the gilded frames, the faded green walls in the bedroom, the yellow pillow on the old orange velvet sofa, and the wooden red chair that sat next to it without any rhyme or reason. I loved the hodgepodge and slapdash mixes of color. Oftentimes, when Wilson was at the center, I would catch myself at the window looking for him instead of returning e-mails or shaping Daisy's next lecture.

After lunch together, I would spend an hour going over the fifteen-minute conversation we'd just had. It was ludicrous, since our talk was no more than an update on the TV deal or the gossip he'd picked up at Barley's Café, the adult male equivalent of the corner beauty shop. I blamed this bizarre turn of events on some atavistic impulse on my part. I certainly didn't mind, though I couldn't quite squelch the anxieties lurking in my other worlds. Even on vacation, as much as I wished otherwise, I still had to contend with my business and my columns. Fortunately, I kept two or three months ahead on the column, but I still had to review each one and make sure it remained timely. I also had to keep writing them if I wanted to maintain that safety margin.

I also had my e-mail. Since I hadn't done anything about Pam, the disruptive newcomer in my New York office, I ended up writing notes to assuage the mightily ruffled feathers of my staff. Then one day, in a fit of cowardice, I fired her via e-mail, without the courtesy of a phone call. I was not proud of myself, but I was also irritated with everyone else involved for forcing the issue.

The obligations in my private life didn't go away either, though I thought of them as Michelle's obligations. Thinking of myself as the New York Michelle alarmed me. I mean, I was Michelle. Mickey was not only a nickname but a recent and temporary one at that. I was having a romp, an affair. I fully expected it to play itself out. My delusional sense of control remained boundless.

Once or twice, I caught myself panicking that Steve might go to Dallas on some kind of legal business. I didn't quite have the scenario down, but in my fantasy he was asked to take a crucial meeting there. There was no time to call or e-mail me. The plane was being held for him. Landing in Dallas, eager to see me, he arrived at the Adolphus Hotel, where he knew I stayed when I was in that city, only to be told that Ms. Banyon had a room but had not been in the hotel for *weeks,* not since she was seen holding hands with a rangy-looking stud in a blue denim shirt.

I knew it was ludicrous, but a little voice in my head kept saying, "Life is stranger than fiction." The real cliché that terrified me was: "You may live to regret this."

I also regretted that Dottie and Wilson had appeared in my life about the same time, a wrinkle I could have done without. Occasionally, I regretted not taking a few of my vacation days to spend time with my niece. However, all regrets and anxieties were nothing compared to the fun I was having. Almost everything amused Wilson and me in one way or another.

On walks around his farm, we'd take turns humming songs from Broadway musicals and making the other guess which song it was. I stumped him with "Gimme the Ball" from *Chorus Line,* an innuendo that led like so much else back to his bedroom. We rented old Katharine Hepburn and Spencer Tracy movies, and some mornings when we woke we'd riff on their dialogue. "The calla lilies are in bloom again," I'd say to Wilson, my voice wavering, and he found my Hepburn imitation hysterical. I became proficient on Wilson's tire swing over the creek, and like young lovers, we'd squeeze in together, then fall into the cold creek, running and laughing all the way back to the house.

I'll admit I didn't find my attempts to mount a horse nearly as funny as Wilson did. "Swing that leg high. Just swing the leg," he said, pushing my butt up at the same time. On one "just swing," as I grasped frantically for both the horn of the saddle and the horse's neck, Wilson began to snicker, then to laugh, then guffawed until he had tears in his eyes. To my relief, he didn't insist on any more riding lessons after that.

He got his comeuppance a few evenings later, though, when we discovered Helen's bag of bubble gum, her some-time substitute for a cigarette, and we decided to find out who could blow the biggest bubble. After a while, in a fit of inspiration to create a new sensation, I thought I'd give him a blow job with the help of a bubble. The blow job came off rather well but not the gum. As we tried everything from soap to alcohol to ice, Wilson panicked. "Don't worry," I told him, "I'll save you from a sticky dick." Then I burst into laughter. He tried hard to see the humor, but, as he said, it kept eluding him.

AFTER THIS GIDDY WAVE, I began to settle into the rhythm of the farm. Then, close to the end of my vacation, I became restless. My pride in a tasty meal, my fussiness over a pretty dinner table, my puttering about the house—all began to get stale. Unused as I was to so much unstructured time, I began to realize the imperative of a framework. To be a self-starter within a framework was entirely different from having a whole day without consequence and with no clue as to where to focus. I ended up writing a very good column on "Coping When Days Yawn Back at You." I'd never before considered what it must be like to be alone in a house in the middle of nowhere, day in and day out.

Yet no one could wish for more, I reminded myself silently one evening after dinner as we sat in Wilson's now-homey kitchen. I sipped hot lemon-water while he finished his second slice of pie and filled me in on the condition of a new baby hawk whose mother had been shot. Fortunately, the baby was responding well to her blind surrogate mother. Watching Wilson's face when he got excited over one of his birds was a favorite amusement, but when he brought up that blind hawk, I thought of Dottie and how remiss I was in my own surrogate duties.

Earlier that day when I checked my home phone, I'd heard a message from Andrea saying that Dottie had pneumonia and had checked into Mt. Sinai Hospital. On the voice mail, Andrea had insisted everything was fine, but I felt awful for not being there. I immediately tried the hospital, but no one answered in Dottie's room. After pacing up and down the hallway, I resolved to return to New York. I wanted to see my niece.

Besides, I thought, as Wilson talked about the baby hawk, I needed some distance from this lover of mine. I'd become aware that I listened raptly to everything he said, a little too raptly. *Raptly, raptor, raptness.* It was genuine—it had to be, I had no experience faking such a sensation—but, real or not, I didn't like it. I was becoming far too attached to this man.

Suddenly, as if just remembering, he smiled, pointed to the rest of his pie, and said, "This is fantastic, sweetheart." I smiled and accepted the compliment but then, without warning, I felt all my recent domestication rise up in a smothering wave. I could hear Daisy scolding me about succumbing to traditional roles and betraying every woman in the free world.

"Oh, shut up," I silently told myself as I rose from the table, tugged on Wilson's chair, and pulled him to the kitchen floor. Disbelief and delight spread across his face. This is self-definition, too, I thought as I unzipped my pants and drew him to my crotch.

Later, as we lay spent on the floor admiring the ceiling tiles of the kitchen, I told him I had to leave town, just for a bit.

"But you promised," he said, bristling, an injured look in his eyes.

"I'm sorry," I said. "It won't be for long." I kissed the faint scar on his forehead from that fateful fall. I wished I could tell him why I was going, but I needed to keep my New York life separate.

chapter 8

THE TRANSITION FROM A CONVENTIONAL AND SLIGHTLY repressed wife and single-minded career woman to a lust-driven adulteress was dramatic enough, but returning to New York to reclaim younger-sister status all but undid me. My sister, Andrea, petite and proficient as ever, stood waiting for me in the Mt. Sinai Hospital lobby in New York.

She looked just like our mother, including the no-nonsense set of mouth and the quick-moving eyes, ever ready to judge. Her dark honey-colored hair was short and brushed back, and she wore a shirtwaist dress just like our mother had. Where did she find those awful dresses? I wondered, and then without warning I experienced both revulsion and sadness with such force that tears welled in my eyes.

Clearly startled by this emotional display and mistaking its meaning, Andrea backed away from me and warned: "We are nothing but cheerful in Dottie's presence, and her pneumonia's responding to treatment. She will be fine."

"Never occurred to me otherwise," I said tersely. It was a record. In less than three minutes the scratchiness between us had begun. As far back as I could remember, Andrea had a knack for denying all things bad. Then again, so did I—sometimes.

"She looks like a waif," Andrea whispered just before we pushed open Dottie's hospital room door.

Actually, I was taken aback every time I saw Dottie. I always thought of her as a round-faced cherub of a child and was surprised from one visit to the next by how thin she'd become. Seeing her now, I realized that she'd lost even more weight. I kissed her on her cheek, a gesture both natural and foreign. As I have mentioned, we were not an affectionate family. Touching had never been a Harmon trait.

"Hi!" I said.

"Auntie M," Dottie answered with no inflection. I loved when she called me that. It allowed me to believe I could be the kindly aunt of make-believe, a fairy godmother over the rainbow for this Dorothy.

I patted my niece's head in the same awkward manner I patted the pets of doting owners. Andrea was fidgeting with the covers at the foot of the bed.

"A lousy break, huh?" I said. Dottie shrugged her shoulders and said nothing. I felt she might talk more without Andrea there, and, as if mind-reading, my sister abruptly excused herself, saying she needed to have a chat with Dottie's doctor.

I sat in a chair close to Dottie's head. "Your mother tells me you've had quite a bout."

"What would she know about anything?" Dottie's voice was apathetic and tinged with surliness. Her mood mystified me. "I wish she hadn't come; I want to be left alone."

"I don't want to leave you alone." I pulled at my fingers. "I haven't had much experience with being an aunt."

"That's for sure," she said, surprising me, but then she broke into a beautiful grin. I hadn't seen her surly side, but I liked that she didn't always need to please. I wished I was more like her.

"I'm sorry, that was mean," Dottie said. "You've been great

when I visit and this past winter, too . . . when I've seen you. Really."

"No, I'm sorry. It's true I missed too much of your child-hood. Then you move here and I'm always leaving."

Dottie readjusted her covers. "Oh, never mind. I'm just in the pits, which is why my mother got you to come. I'm sure she wants you to bear some of the burden of my illness—a great way to get back at you."

"I'm the one who insisted on coming," I began as the door flapped open and Andrea returned with cups of coffee. I would have to wait to find out why on earth my sister thought a payback was due.

THE NEXT FEW DAYS with Andrea in the city went pleas-antly enough, considering our track record. We seemed to have come to an agreement without speaking—we avoided the hard topics and kept things light. Though she stayed at my place, I worked all day and we spent the evenings at the hos-pital. While both Dottie and Andrea knew about Daisy Strait Enterprises, neither asked about my business. This came as no surprise but hurt my feelings all the same, even as I attributed Dottie's indifference to her youth.

I would have liked my family to share my pleasure in what I do. I remembered one rare afternoon, when I was about eleven, practicing my tennis strokes on the side of the garage. My father had just come home and stood watching me. "Remember, Michelle," he said, "keep your eyes on the seam. Get into a rhythm: seam, hit, bounce."

Then he came over, clasped my arm with his tanned hand, the light hairs on it bleached white by the sun, his will focused in his grip as if his own power would ensure ability in me. With one fluid motion, he extended my arm high and back, then guided it across my body for a more complete follow-through.

"Loosen up," he instructed, and on the third try I did, our arms in a duet, reaching back, swinging through. The rhythm, the sway, my happiness in his attention. In that moment, I remember feeling so sure that I could do anything.

TO MY DELIGHT, I received a warmer welcome from my staff than was customary. Though they were loyal, Beth and Gloria could also be remote, albeit for different reasons. Beth, my executive assistant, was shy and sensitive. I had lucked out when I hired her, since she turned out to be a lifer—one of those people with no real aspirations of her own but committed to the well-being of her boss. In her early forties now, she wasn't vain in a usual way. She wore faded, unflattering cotton suits that she pressed herself, wore no makeup to mitigate her city pallor, and probably didn't wash her brownish-blond hair often enough. In her effort to suppress the inevitable wrinkles of age, she had simplified her expressions down to the occasional smile interspersed in extreme circumstances with a mild pout of her lips.

My scheduler, Gloria, a single mother with two young children, was necessarily tougher, and good at her job. Compact and efficient, she was not a person given to compliments, but now she commented on how well I looked and took the unusual step of smiling, although awkwardly. Beth, of all things, hugged me. When these two thanked me for firing their "albatross," I realized the reason for my popularity.

"That bitch stirred up more trouble than there were problems to multiply," Gloria said indignantly. "She called us willing participants in a dysfunctional corporate culture. She called us *dysfunctional!*"

Suddenly I was all Daisy. "What? Why didn't you tell me this sooner?"

"We tried," Beth replied in her unassuming, soft-spoken way.

"I'm sorry I put you through that," I apologized before suggesting that Gloria give me a quick rundown of the weeks ahead. Beth's edit of my latest column was on my desk, along with my correspondence. My staff needed some extra attention, and a few days later, I apologized again, adding for good measure, "I hope each of you knows that I have complete confidence in you as individuals *and* as a team."

"Thank you," Gloria said in a flat tone that belied one bit of thanks.

Beth was the first to relent. "You have a lot on your mind— your column . . . your lectures."

"Yes, yes, I do," I agreed, "and it feels good to be back."

DOTTIE'S SPIRITS IMPROVED along with her health. My niece turned out to be a fine mimic of her roommates—one from Brooklyn, the other from Louisiana—both of whom pretended not to understand the other. After five days, the doctors said she could leave the hospital, and I suggested she come home with me until she felt better. But Dottie insisted that she needed to get back to her dancing and that she preferred to go back to her own place in Brooklyn. She also let it slip that her old boyfriend was still pressing her to return to

Indiana. I had a feeling she was considering it and wanted to yell, *Don't go back! Don't play it safe! It's time to move on.* Yet who was I to talk? I, who turned caution into a fine art. My interlude with Wilson was my first and only attempt at pushing my well-guarded boundaries.

If Andrea knew more than I did about what was going on in Dottie's life, she didn't tell me, and I knew better than to ask. We'd done much better than I expected together. When she left, we even hugged each other good-bye. Still, I worried about Dottie and had imaginary conversations with Wilson about my niece. Because he instinctively knew things about me that I didn't, I thought perhaps his insightfulness might apply to others as well. After all, his son was in his early twenties, so he was familiar with teenage problems. Thinking of Wilson made me happy; thinking of seeing him soon made me happier.

For now, however, I had my New York life to contend with, though Steve was not part of this visit. *Hong Kong has me for at least another month,* he wrote last. *I'm sorry, honey. Would much prefer a good dinner with you. How is Dot? I promise you both a night at the ballet. With maybe a celebration thrown in. Maybe. Stay tuned. Hugs and kisses, Steve.*

I smiled reading it. I had to give Steve credit. Sure, he had difficulty tuning in to me, but he always stood by me, especially during the hard times. In the beginning of our marriage, he'd helped me to see that the rebuffs of my mother and sister weren't my fault. He also had taken it for granted that there could be a more worldly me, and I didn't disappoint him—often, anyhow.

But a worldly me wasn't what I needed right now. A hard-working me was more like it. In the upcoming weeks, I had speeches in the Midwest lined up, and I liked to target my talks to the specifics of each group. This took some extra work, but I didn't want anyone going away feeling they'd heard a warmed-over talk.

As the days passed, I daydreamed about Wilson more and more and realized I had to stop pretending that this was a temporary romp. Mornings when I had my grapefruit and coffee, I imagined him at Barley's Café, eating his two eggs over easy, hash browns, and bacon, trading stories with the other regulars. While he didn't go to Barley's every morning (he swore some of the guys showed up even on Christmas and New Year's Day), more often than not he could be found there. I didn't know that in the beginning, though. Our first few mornings together, he stayed and had an extra cup of coffee with me in the kitchen. We sat and swapped parts of the *Dallas Morning News*, holding hands from time to time and savoring the morning light and the high call of a mockingbird.

But one morning when I came downstairs freshly showered, he was already outside. I stood at the door and admired his strong, solid legs with contentment as he climbed into the cab of his truck. I thought he was headed to the barn, but he waved and turned toward town.

I didn't wonder where he was going—well, maybe I did a little—but why didn't he want to stick around longer? And why hadn't he kissed me good-bye? For one crazy moment, I thought he'd grown indifferent. *Seam, hit, bounce*—that stupid refrain in my head. But my father had not been indifferent. He had watched me practice as the late-afternoon sun warmed our faces, his khaki sleeves rolled, his light hair glistening in the light. "Look at the seam, Michelle," he said. "Hit the ball." *Seam, hit*—I loved the rhythm and didn't ever want to break it—*bounce.*

Okay, I knew Wilson wasn't leaving me and that my attack of insecurity bore no relation to reality. When he returned for lunch, I heard his whistle. As he removed a new water hose from the truck bed, I felt foolish but also realized for the first time how quickly I'd become dependent on him, how frightened I was by the thought of losing him.

Later, when I teased him about forgetting to kiss me good-bye, he apologized and said he thought he had. "I'm sorry I left early," he added. "The guys were beginning to wonder what happened to me."

The next morning Wilson came to find me. "Anything you want from town?" he asked as he swung me off the ground. I volunteered to go with him.

"But I'm going . . . well, I'm going to Barley's," he said, as if that explained everything.

"So I'll go, too. I've never eaten pie in the morning."

"You're kidding!" A real look of pity crossed his face and then he gave me a bear hug. "I'll bring you three different kinds." His effusion, I couldn't help noticing, had not included an invitation. I repeated my desire to go while gently pulling away from his arms.

"Women just don't go," he said, zipping up his jacket.

"Why not?"

He shrugged. I suddenly knew he would give up going rather than take me, and I let him off the hook. His generosity in bed made me willing to forgive a lot. I was insatiable.

·   ·   ·

confessions of a bigamist

MICHELLE, YOU'RE NOT in Texas anymore, I reminded myself. I shook my head and looked around my New York office, the heart of Daisy Strait Enterprises, which I needed every bit as much as it needed me. In this space I felt a surge of energy, a sense of satisfaction. Daisy Strait meant escape, independence, power. To stay strong, I had to focus on the pressing problems of the day. There would be time enough for other pleasures.

chapter 9

WILSON'S FRIENDS WANTED TO MEET ME. "A DINNER at 'the club' on Friday," he told me on my return. I had nothing to wear, I insisted, scrubbing the new potatoes for dinner with extra zeal.

"They're not fancy-schmancy, Mickey. They'll love you, no matter," he said, taking the vegetable brush and hugging me close.

Actually, I was pretty sure I wouldn't be loved whatever I wore.

As I dressed for the evening, Wilson sprawled on the bed watching. "I love your hair that way," he said. "It's so much more you than that straight stuff." Since arriving in Rollins, I'd let my hair revert to its natural state—curly and full.

"You like me wild, huh?" I asked, gyrating my hips as I put on lipstick and heard the Michelle in me say *fool*.

"You're such a girl," he said, admiration running through his voice.

"No, I'm a management consultant," I answered, reminding him once more how we were going to explain my career. Wilson protested that this was all so much folderol. Why couldn't I just say I was Daisy Strait? he wanted to know. "Why, I'll bet they've heard of you."

He was probably right. But I'd managed to keep my professional and private lives separate this long, and I wasn't about to blow it now, especially not now. "I want them to get to know me as Mickey Banyon." I added, "Daisy would dominate everything, trust me," and Wilson did.

I EYED THE three other couples sitting around the white-clothed, candle-sparkling table and wondered just what lay in store for me this evening at the only country club in Rollins. As I suspected, the men were wary; the women, proprietary. Making matters worse, Wilson was seated next to a willowy brunette, recently divorced, who had come with her brother-in-law since her sister was sick. No odd numbers at this club. The only person to welcome me with any relish was Brian Samuels, Wilson's doctor friend.

Immediately I was out of the conversation loop: The discussions leapt from school-board policy to the shenanigans of some local minister to state politics to remembering a hurricane that had ruined a beach trip they'd all taken together—all in an indecipherable verbal shorthand. If this group divided into teams, I would be the last person chosen. Only Wilson beamed at me—and my ruffles—while I sat there mute.

Yes, it was that blouse—Wilson wanted me to wear it. Having decided to play myself down to fit in, I added a frumpy dark gray wool jacket and skirt bought in a nearby shopping mall. It was a hokey combination. I should have gone for the little gray sleeveless silk shift lying folded in my bag, but I thought it'd be too haute couture for his friends. I was wrong, though. These women wore simple cuts, more colorful than my Michelle clothes, but with just as much taste. I would have felt right at home.

Meanwhile, high-cheekboned, pert-nosed Lindy, the animated divorcée, chattered away at Wilson, who listened with attention. Why had I lived such a single-minded life? I'd never learned to flirt like that. Maybe it was a Texas thing. Maybe Daisy could do a lecture on how not to feel dowdy and dull in a simple life. Then again, what did Daisy know about entrancing a man?

"Mickey." Brian Samuels spoke my name—one of my names—and asked me something about Wilson being a good patient.

"She's a terrific nurse. Best I ever had!" Wilson jumped in, eager to sing my praises and draw me into the conversation.

"The last time you had a nurse, you were twelve years old and had your tonsils out," Brian's wife, Hillary, teased. Hillary had black hair in a flapper's bob, and voluptuous cleavage.

"He wasn't so healthy when he hobbled into the emergency room," said Brian. "I couldn't tell if Mickey here was a good Samaritan or a lady wrestler—or both." He winked at me.

"An *invigorator* is what I'd call her," Lindy's brother-in-law, Wendell Jackson, said. "I thought Wilson had his hands full with that TV business before. Now he's really gone on a tear! That gal will wear you out, Will Collins." Wendell feigned wiping sweat from his brow. He had thinning gray hair that he combed straight back from his forehead.

Brian Samuels laughed lightly; Wilson looked half-embarrassed, half-pleased. The women glared. I cut my beef filet into tiny bites. An uncomfortable silence ensued until Lindy politely asked if I was really a nurse. She looked more determined than at ease in her vivacity, I realized.

"I'm an efficiency consultant," I replied truthfully. A Transformational Adviser is how I liked to think of myself, but I'd never said that out loud to anyone. Those willing to pay for my help were looking for real change in their lives, I felt, whether they knew it or not. I just held their hands as they took their baby steps into a new way of being.

"An efficiency consultant," Hillary Samuels repeated, her bob swinging my way. "How interesting," she drawled.

THE NEXT MORNING Lindy, the divorcée, called to invite me to an afternoon horse show. I accepted but not without trepidation. "She's checking out her competition," I told Wilson as I plopped a plate of bacon and eggs in front of him. Any day now I planned to upgrade his eating habits.

"Lindy's not that way. She likes you," he said, slicing happily into his egg over easy. "When you talked to her, she lit up."

"She was plenty alive talking to you." I sat down to my toast and grapefruit.

"That's pretend. That's just Lindy."

That he understood her behavior amazed me.

"Do you know what kind of coffee this is, sweetheart?" he asked, sniffing and sipping as if he'd never tasted it before.

"The same you've always had, I'd guess. Folgers?"

"It would be nice if Helen bought our coffee from one of the small organic farms in Mexico."

I waved my hand in front of his eyes. "Wilson? You dreaming or what? There are no organic coffee beans in Rollins, let alone from small Mexican farms."

He shrugged his shoulders and continued eating without further comment, but after a few more bites of toast, I couldn't resist: "Why?"

"Those farms replicate rain-forest ecology. Migratory birds

love them but the farmers barely scrape by." He ticked both reasons off on his fingers. "I thought you'd never ask," he said, and smiled. "Wouldn't it be something if we could create those ecological conditions at the center? Think of the kinds of birds we could have then."

"But drinking organic coffee won't help create a coffee farm."

"It would help support the farmers and the environment," he answered, as if I were the illogical one. We sat there drinking our now–politically incorrect coffee until Wilson spoke again: "Wendell Jackson thinks you're great."

Wendell Jackson, who crowned me the Invigorator, the superhero who would wear Wilson out.

"Wendell Jackson said two words to me last night."

"He's no fool. You were fun to watch last night, the way you moved, the way you took in everything. Talking to you isn't the only way to figure things out about you."

"It's highly efficacious, I've found," I answered, grinning at Wilson's sweet paean to me.

He put his hand between my legs. "How 'bout this, lady? This efficacious enough for you?" The question struck us both as hilarious.

"They don't call me the Invigorator for nothing," I gasped.

BEING IN TEXAS, I assumed Lindy Akers was taking me to something akin to a rodeo. Instead, we watched young people decked out in riding habits put their horses through jumps in a most decidedly English manner. Rollins, Texas, I learned, supported two English tack shops and year-round fox hunts conducted under the tutelage of a colonel. The dress code for his riders did not permit sunglasses or any other deviation from British standards. All this was fine, but I experienced a twinge of disappointment. I wanted to see some bucking and calf-roping, some of those rodeo clowns.

Lindy, however, was not a disappointment. Maybe her need to hide under a patina of stiff-upper-lip good sportsmanship made her particularly adept at burrowing through my layers of fraud, deceit, and newly excavated insecurities. At any rate, we both recognized that we were kindred struggling souls underneath, no confessions needed.

"I had a horse just like that," she said as we watched a particularly graceful rider jump. "And a face like that young girl's. Look at her expression—sheer satisfaction. She has the day, the thrill of a good jump, the perfect rhythm with her horse— it's like dancing with someone so good that you lose yourself in the music."

I nodded, thinking of Wilson in bed.

"That girl believes her pleasure today will transfer to the rest of her life," Lindy went on. "She doesn't have a clue about the muck that's creeping her way."

At her age, I wanted to say, I already understood that muck. It wasn't too far-fetched to say that I'd created my business to help me cope with life's debris. Now, though, I had come to think of Wilson as my own special amulet that kept the muck from intruding.

YET INTRUSIONS THERE WERE. *Hey, Daisy Mae,* Steve wrote. *Texas sounds like it agrees with you.*

Three A.M., another e-mail said. *Am pulling an all-nighter. Eyes are spinning.*

And another: *Hope to see you before Thanksgiving—kidding, of course. Hope to see you soon. Good night, sweetness.*

I went into a frenzy of guilt—long overdue, I suppose. At the same time, I also became furious with Steve for everything he'd ever done to upset me. Angry and irrational, I even blamed him for not insisting that I speak up more about Daisy, though, in truth, this wasn't his fault, just as it wasn't his fault that I'd become hungry for a veritable stranger.

Despite my lust daze, I didn't shirk my Daisy duties. I had my columns to write, and my Texas life was a great source of new ideas. I spent the usual amount of time in contact with my New York staff and worked hard at getting the Dallas office up and running, too. I had chosen wisely with Amy Ward—she proved invaluable at putting me in touch with a variety of businesses and establishing my presence in the Southwest, not only as a speaker but also as a consultant to companies. Of course, I was also still out on the lecture circuit elsewhere, running constantly from different cities back to Rollins and New York.

As you might expect, by this time I had developed a system for my travel transformations. Chameleon that I was, I now had three wardrobes to contend with. For starters, I needed Mickey's sneakers, Daisy's practical walking shoes, and Michelle's high heels. The Mickey look, which was the simplest, required a pair of jeans and, her world being Texas, pastel T-shirts or sweaters. Sometimes I included a starched blue-denim work shirt that I wore with the collar turned up and the shirttail tied at my waist. Always I included an ensemble of Daisy's wrinkle-free pantsuits and skirts and jewel-toned blouses—ruby and sapphire—not unlike the bright colors that female politicians wore in order to stand out and to pep up the crowd. Of course, Daisy's black or navy suits wouldn't do for Michelle—the fabric was too cheap and the cut too boxy. As Michelle, I leaned toward Armani—silk or lightweight wool—expensive suits and dresses that hung beautifully on my body.

I also packed a hair dryer, large rollers, and hair spray to keep my hair straight when I was working on the road or going back to New York. Being the right person at the right time was getting awfully cumbersome, I thought more than once as I sat on top of my suitcase, tugging at the zipper and stuffing in stray bits. My life was expanding, all right, but in a limited canvas box. It was worth it, though. And somehow I got it in my head that if I kept all my lives separate, at least in appearance, Steve wouldn't catch me out. More than anything, I dreaded someone Steve and I knew seeing me in my Mickey garb. I know my fear was not rational, but my anxiety about Steve's finding out about Wilson certainly was. Even as Daisy Strait Enterprises was roaring along, I longed to keep the world from encroaching on Wilson and me.

Unfortunately, when I was in Rollins, Wilson Collins wasn't exactly interested in pulling up the drawbridge. As much as he enjoyed our time together, he had his other passions—his birds, the TV deal—and I had a hard time containing my jealousy of these other loves. Even my jealousy was an annoying intrusion on what I persisted in thinking of as an idyllic interlude—no matter that all sensible evidence pointed to the contrary.

To be close to him, I helped Wilson with his schemes to seduce the production company on one front and the whole town on another. I drafted press releases for the newspaper and wrote up a couple of speeches for him to deliver to community organizations. "But we're not publicists—or event organizers," he protested.

"Trust me," I said, and once again, he did. This time I felt a bit of shame for daring to ask him to trust me. I surely didn't.

TO STAY MYSELF A LITTLE, I made time on my next trip to New York for a visit with Dottie, who, as far as I could tell, hadn't rallied very well. We spent the weekend at my place watching reruns of old sitcoms and listening to music, lapsing into a surprisingly comfortable silence. We read our respective magazines and books, and only sometimes talked.

About her parents, Dottie had nothing but scathing words. I remained carefully noncommittal, knowing that any derogatory remarks could be flung in their faces in her battle against them. At the same time, I wanted her to know that I, too, had struggled against conventionality. In the long run, though, it occurred to me that I had merely traded one set of conventions for another. Affairs were pretty conventional, weren't they? Of course, we didn't speak about that, but Wilson was always in my thoughts.

Then on Sunday afternoon, at the last possible minute when people seem to say what is really on their minds, Dottie brought up, of all people, my father. "Mother says he shirked his family responsibilities," she said hesitantly.

I fluffed the sofa pillows. "He cared for us. The army came first, but . . . well, we were a family of shirkers." I punched one pillow hard in its soft center. "Of family responsibilities, I mean." I wanted to say that I was the family responsibility they shirked, but that sounded pretty whiny for a forty-seven-year-old to say to a twenty-year-old.

"My mom never mentioned anybody but my grandfather."

"Oh. Well, if he hadn't cared, why did he always come back?" I couldn't tell Dottie that her mother and grandmother were the ones who pushed him away, and only his caring kept him from leaving us altogether. "I don't think he felt particularly welcome at our house. It's no wonder he signed up for long tours of duty. But he always wrote and always asked about school and friends and . . . you know, the usual." *He loved me*, I wanted to shout, *and I don't want your mother messing with my reality!*

Keep your eye on the seam, Michelle. That afternoon my father had watched me practice my tennis until twilight when my mother called him in. Through the screen door I could hear her shouting. In a few minutes, he was yelling back and all hell broke loose, and then he stormed outside and took off in the car. I felt responsible then, though looking back, I doubt that I was. After that, I devoted myself to tennis. He had proven that he cared about what I did. He had stayed to help me as long as he could.

"But that was a long time ago." I sighed, and smiled. "How would you like an ice-cream cone?"

Dottie agreed but then blurted, "Did you know my parents hate anything not ordinary? They smother me with ordinariness and I am not ordinary. And I am not an ordinary dancer!"

"Of course you're not." Cursing our family's history, I put my arms around her slender shoulders and rocked her back and forth. "And to prove it, let's do something extraordinary."

"Right now?" Her eyes glistened, and I nodded my head

yes. And then I initiated Dottie into one of those true New York pleasures, and we walked from my place all the way downtown—more than a hundred blocks—for ice cream, and she danced on every empty sidewalk.

I AM NOT an ordinary dancer. I thought about Dottie as I peeled a Vidalia onion under running water in the kitchen in Rollins. I was helping Helen make black-eyed peas and ham hock. "This was one of my father's favorite dishes," I told her. "My mother used to cook it for him all the time."

"My husband, Ben, loves it, too," volunteered Helen—it was the first glimmer of her private life she'd offered me. "Were they Southern, your parents?" she asked, taking one more drag on her cigarette before putting it out to shell more peas.

"Yeah, is it a Southern dish?"

Helen shrugged. "I wouldn't take you as Southern, the way you've got everything so streamlined around here."

"Strictly speaking, I'm not. Do you think Wilson minds me putting his stuff away?" I asked, addressing her implied criticism of my "tidying." "Anyway," I went on, "I don't associate getting rid of clutter with any region."

Helen shrugged again and I peeled and she stewed sweetened tomatoes in silence.

"I was always this way," I confessed. "While my mother and sister made a great to-do over cooking and cleaning, I liked to keep our things simple and uncluttered." I stopped peeling and laughed. "Once my mother assigned me the chore of keeping our living room dusted, so I stashed all her gewgaws in a closet. The room looked better; my work time was halved. When she saw what I'd done, she had a fit and grounded me a week for cheekiness."

"What did you expect? You were rejecting her, weren't you?"

"I never thought of it that way." I picked up another onion. Again we worked in silence. "My father was around, one of the rare times," I went on. Helen already knew about the army posts and his absences. I liked telling her what I could. "He didn't comment on what I'd done, but he seemed amused by it. I remember we played cards together—we did that once, I know." I wiped my eyes. "The onions have made me cry."

"Memory is a sly trickster," Helen said, and sighed.

GUILT IS A TRICKSTER, TOO. In the Dallas/Fort Worth airport I saw Sonia Sartin, my Fort Worth hostess, coming toward me, and I froze. My mouth went dry. I even became a little woozy. People fly, I reminded myself. I'm not the only one who travels.

Sonia shook my hand warmly. "Wilson tells me that you've set up an office in Dallas. I had no idea I'd be the catalyst for a blooming romance," she said, and smiled so warmly and naturally that I decided she had no idea we were talking affair here. "And Lindy Akers tells me the two of you have become friends."

"You know Lindy?" I asked lamely.

"I'm related to her former husband's family, but she doesn't hold it against me. Why don't you come with her to lunch soon?"

I accepted her invitation, and we each hurried on to our gates. I mulled over our brief exchange. Lindy must know I was Daisy Strait. Had she told everyone? Or was she respecting my ill-conceived need for privacy? I wondered how so many people managed the stress involved in an affair. If I was going to live the life of an adulteress, I would have to get used to this sort of situation.

I wanted to stay in a make-believe world, what was left of it. I wanted to savor it. I began to steer my conversations with Wilson back around to the topic of us, our reckless beginning, our plunge into such uncharted emotional depths. I wanted to return to the beginning, as if that could keep the middle and eventual end at bay.

I watched Wilson play-wrestle with Luck on the grass with joyous abandon—the same abandon that fueled his passion for his causes and his love for me. He had lost so much, this man, and now he was willing to risk losing again. If he had fears, he didn't flinch—all the more amazing. Luck flopped on top of Wilson, who grinned up at me, and I finally realized how helplessly, hopelessly I'd fallen in love. In that moment, my infatuation and lust ripened into something abounding and inarticulate, which I expressed by joining the fray and heaving myself onto a startled dog and his more startled master.

After that, in as many ways as possible, I tried to convey to Wilson the enormity of this new feeling, its uniqueness, its terror and triumph. At times my newfound effusiveness might have been somewhat more than Wilson expected, but I didn't care; I was so happy for the release.

That I had always considered romantic love an untidy and rather inconvenient illusion no longer concerned me. If the Daisy in me had her way, romantic love would disappear altogether on the grounds of complications and obstructions to a simple life. But Mickey was brave. Mickey was a believer.

Had Wilson felt this way before? With Connie? Before Connie? I asked one night as he knelt on the bed, my leg on his shoulder as he stroked the soft skin inside my thigh. Of course, he said everything I wanted to hear. He had never felt this way, either.

"Do you mean that?" I asked. "Or do you just think you do? Do you think it's like an old injury that you forget about until the weather changes and the pain comes back? Is what we have really different?"

"Hush," he finally whispered, licking the arch of my foot, and I finally did.

THE WIVES, as I thought of them, proved to be more good source material for my columns. After that first awkward dinner at the country club, Annette Jackson, the absent wife that night, called: "My sister Lindy told me our friends were less than welcoming to you. Wendell claims to have noticed nothing out of order. What do you think?"

"I think Wilson's friends had planned to save Wilson for someone they know and trust a little more," I said, "like your sister Lindy."

Annette laughed. "Well, yes, we did, but Lindy lectured me on that, too. She made it clear that if and when she is ever ready to date again, she will inform us herself, thank you. Meantime, we're to mind our manners. Can we start all over? Lunch at my house tomorrow? Lindy will be there, along with the others."

ANNETTE'S LARGE contemporary house, placed in the middle of an acre of farmland, was graced with stunning outdoor views. The larger windows at the back and east looked out on a wooded area about fifty yards from the house; the west side butted up against a garden of formal hedges sprinkled with rosebushes, two wooden benches, a stand of bamboo, and a few large clusters of pampas grass. Someone had made this eclectic assortment of plants look as if they belonged together.

"Annette designed the garden herself, her first effort," Lindy explained as she conducted an envious me on a brief tour. "A few years ago she opened a nursery and now has so much business, she hardly has time to breathe."

I wondered if Annette and Wilson's ex-wife, Connie, had worked together in the landscape/nursery business, but I didn't want to ask. Maybe I didn't want to know.

"She's certainly got a flair," I told Lindy, whose light brown hair swung casually about her face. Annette walked up with a tray of glasses filled with cranberry juice and thin slices of lemon. She had the same coloring as her sister but had shorter, fuller hair, feathered back and tinged with red. She was also heavier and more wrinkled, the sun showing in her face.

"What a beautiful place you have," I said. "I appreciate your taking the time to share it with me."

When I offered to help with the lunch preparations, I was given carrots, green peppers, and onions to dice. My dicing skills had not improved much, and I began to chop one way and then another on the same onion. My effort was painstaking and slow, but by the time Hillary showed up, I had lost my self-consciousness. Except with Wilson, and then mostly in intimate moments, I had never let myself just be. My awareness of others' expectations never left me, even with Steve. Maybe if Steve and I had spent more time together just hanging out . . . but we didn't. Though it was all the rage to live in the present, I had never quite figured that one out. As I cut those vegetables every which way, listening to the women and not worrying about mistakes, miraculously, all the disarray in my life ceased to exist. This is real life, I thought to myself.

Hillary Samuels, I discovered, taught seventh grade, but was on spring break. "I'll be glad when my class comes back," she said. "As it is, I'm running errands for Brian's mother and my stepmother and spring-cleaning and fixing leaky faucets and helping my son decorate his new apartment in Dallas and doing whatever else I have no time for when I'm teaching. Give me those seventh-grade hormones anytime. They're predictably random." She did not look the least bit worn out from all this activity; nor did she treat me as an outsider this time around. She just assumed that I, too, understood the busyness of family life. With her lovely high breasts, flat stomach, shapely legs, and firm upper arms, she had a shapeliness I couldn't help but envy. The women her age in New York who achieved her look spent hours a week exercising, but I suspected Hillary came by her look naturally.

"Why is it we're busier now than when our kids were young?" Annette asked nobody in particular as she ushered us to the table.

"We have obligations, jobs, family, church, community. If we're lucky, we also stay involved with our children and grandchildren," Hillary said, and Annette picked up the litany: "Not to mention parents and friends breaking down a little more often."

"Plus, we've never learned to look after ourselves," Hillary said.

"Hillary was our radical feminist in the seventies and thinks we haven't learned our lessons very well," Annette explained.

"I was a feminist for all of two minutes," Hillary said, laughing, "I admit it. But I didn't have the right temperament—or was it the right husband? The only one of us to take the lessons to heart was Connie Collins."

"Yeah, and look at the wreckage she left behind," Annette said.

An awkward pause followed until Lindy turned to me: "We lived vicariously through her exploits after she left, you know. By Rollins standards, her life got pretty wild." She dabbed her mouth with her napkin. "She left ostensibly to be some kind of ascetic, but in California she had flings with both sexes according to a cousin of mine who met her out there."

"Oh?" This story didn't exactly jibe with Wilson's. My guess was that the women had it right. Probably he'd convinced himself his version was true. Unless my beloved embroidered the truth the same as I, in which case I shouldn't be shocked, but I was.

Hillary elaborated, "In all fairness to her, those were the beginning years of the Raptor Center. It turns out that marriage is a work-related casualty in that field like so many others. Wilson was always preoccupied with one thing or another."

"Still is, but, Mickey, you're changing all that. Wilson is crazy about you," Lindy said as she passed around glasses of champagne, then lifted her own to me. "Welcome to Rollins."

"Yes, welcome," Annette echoed.

"And so long as you don't hurt him, we'll be crazy about you, too," Hillary tacked on. Smiling, the women all raised their glasses.

I made nice back, but I wasn't sure if I'd been extended a welcome or a threat.

AS I GOT out of the car, Wilson rounded the corner of the house. "How did it go?"

"Fine. Least I think so."

He continued to look anxious until I amended: "I can see myself spending time with them. Everyone was on her best behavior. All of them are very protective of you, but we're going to do fine. Really."

When he grinned, I realized I would have said almost anything to get that sappy look back on his face, the one that announced to the world his happiness. I didn't care why Connie had left or if he'd lied about it or lied only to himself. Grabbing his hand, I pulled him toward me. "Let's make love outside," I suggested. "How 'bout under that tree right there?"

All right, so I was a fool for romance. So what if Daisy abhorred its inefficiency? Somehow I had veered off into a life of instinct over analysis. Perhaps responding to love was like responding to a sunset or a waterfall or the first autumn morning. You could consider the principles of physics and psychology and physiology and break everything down to neurons or light speed or whatever. Or you could bask in the whole of the experience. Deconstruction is way overrated, if you ask me—you don't want to ruin the moment with a graph. That tree thing was fun.

chapter 10

UNFORTUNATELY, LOVE AND LUST CAN'T FIX EVERY-
thing. A few nights later I announced to Wilson that I needed
to leave yet again, for two weeks or longer. "Damn it, Mickey!"
he said, standing stark naked in the center of the bedroom.
"You flit around like some damn butterfly."

"I thought you liked butterflies!"

"Don't change the subject!"

Though I expected disappointment, I hadn't reckoned on
his opposition. I hadn't planned on leaving so soon, but Steve
in an e-mail had said that he was coming home two weeks
early. Wasn't I supposed to be in New York this week? Maybe?

That plaintive *maybe* undid me. That was as close as he
could, or would, come to saying he needed me home. Wilson's
signals also didn't take a mind reader. He stared at me in disbelief.

"Look, darling, I hate this as much as you do," I said, and at
once realized my mistake. I'd never called him "darling" and
probably sounded too glib, too sophisticated, especially the
way I'd said it. Patting the bed, I tried again: "Sweetie, please
come talk to me."

"But why?" he asked.

"I don't want to leave with you so upset."

"I mean why go?"

"Because ... I've already told you ... this is a crucial time for my business right now. A crisis came up. ..."

"They shouldn't be able to order you around like this. It's your company!"

I burst out laughing, went over to him, and tucked a lock of his hair behind his ear. "We all get ordered around one way or another. Your taskmasters are your birds and this farm—mine are my minions, as you know perfectly well." I dragged my fingers lightly down his spine and lingered on the curve of his butt. I could feel him stir, a low rumble in his throat.

An hour later, on the verge of a delicious sleep, I heard him mumble something about cutting back on my work. In response I threw one leg across him.

"I'm serious," he said.

I snuggled closer and kept my eyes closed. To stop him from speaking, I murmured, "Can't, sweetie, I'm paying off my company's debts."

The bed underwent a small commotion. He raised himself to a sitting position, his voice an accusation: "You didn't tell me you have debts!"

"Everyone has debts," I answered calmly. If I didn't open my eyes, he would settle down.

"That's pretty important to keep from me."

My eyes opened. "I wasn't keeping anything from you. Anyway, you've got enough troubles of your own without worrying about all my sad stories." A debt-ridden business made for a better excuse than a lonely husband.

Wilson ran his thumb across my forehead. "Don't you understand? I want you to share everything—all your life."

"I will, I do."

"Oh, Mickey," he said between light kisses all over my face and neck. "I was afraid you wouldn't . . . living on a farm . . . and . . . another kind of woman . . ." He leaned back, taking me with him. "But you're not another kind of woman. You are my one-of-a-kind girl, that's what you are."

I looked up at him and smiled wanly. "I hope that's good," I answered, my verbal faculties failing me. What did he think I'd agreed to? On complete alert, I started to protest but he put his hand over my mouth.

"Believe me, I can afford you—and your debts. Once we're married, you can stop worrying."

"*Married?*" I tried to laugh it off. "What do we need marriage for? Why mess with something this wonderful?"

"Because that's what two people do when they're in love. They get married. That may be an old-fashioned notion, but I want to be with you all the time, not just when you can work me into your schedule."

"Separations add spice and keep us from taking each other for granted. Married or not, I want to work. I love it." Finally, a true pronouncement.

"Couldn't you find a way to make it less demanding?" he asked. "I don't even know where you live!"

"New York. You know that."

"And you know that tells me nothing. Why are you so damn secretive?" He extracted himself from me and rolled over on his side.

I tried to snuggle up to his back but he remained tensed.

"Sweetheart, you know I share an apartment," I cajoled. "You know I'm seldom there. You have my cell number and you always know you can reach me. You also know I told you when we met how I structure my life, my need for certain routines." At which point, Wilson got up and started putting on his clothes again. "Where are you going?"

"Outside." He made an enormous racket slamming drawers and opening and closing doors.

My own anger grew as I considered the injustice of his. I had an intriguing job I loved. He had no right to ask me to give it up. What age did he live in, anyway? What kind of dinosaur throwback was he, wanting to deprive me of excitement and stimulation just so I could make a bunch of damn pies and put flowers in the house? I heard Wilson stomp down the stairs. Even while I lay there fuming, I felt ashamed of myself.

Unable to bear his anger another minute, I finally dressed and found him out by the barn stacking wood in the moonlight. "I'm sorry, but I wasn't expecting a . . . a . . . proposal," I apologized. "We haven't known each other long enough. . . . We've been impulsive but . . . this . . ."

"I guess I don't understand you," said Wilson, his face strangely silver. "I thought we wanted the same things. I'm sorry about what I said about your job. And I am too impulsive. I was way off base, I—"

I kissed him on the lips. "Oh hush, let's go back to bed."

He shook his head.

"I don't mean that way," I said. "I mean to cuddle."

Softening, he kissed the tip of my nose. "A wild tiger in bed and a sweet kitten out," he murmured. "I don't want you to worry ever again about anything." Except for the fact that he stroked my stomach lightly, Wilson seemed to be talking mainly to himself.

I smiled and closed my eyes. A sweet kitten, surely not a

definition anybody else would associate with me, including myself. Of course, I had been many things to many people in my life. A chameleon—that fit me best. I was a sure-footed, quick-changing, often-opaque creature. What was to become of me?

chapter 11

AT THE AIRPORT, I CHANGED OUT OF MICKEY'S bright blue blazer and jeans into a gray Chanel suit, a Michelle outfit if ever there was one. Not expecting Steve until early evening, I planned to drop my suitcase with our doorman and head straight to the hairdresser for a cut and manicure. Steve would be shocked to see my hair, not only this long, but disheveled and curly instead of sleek. I also wanted to avoid going directly home—from one nest to the other, so to speak.

When I finally stepped out of the elevator doors into our pristine living room, I inhaled the familiar starkness—a healing white that banished impurity, and confusion, the simplicity of white that protected against chaos. I touched the walls, straightened a lamp shade, admired a Saskia Weinstein sculpture. Reassured that these objects were indeed real, I marveled that in the course of a few weeks I could forget the hold this place had on me. And the view! The reservoir in Central Park gleamed like an eye amid the lush trees. A long time ago I had fallen in love with this view. And the shifting, restless light—even on a rainy day it pleased me.

"I could be happy here," I had told Steve when the real-estate agent left the room. I twirled around. "I could definitely learn to fit this space!"

"Then we'll take it," he answered.

"It's really out of our league."

"We'll manage," Steve said. By then we had been in Manhattan for a year and were looking for a place to buy. In a piece of good luck for us, the housing market had plummeted. On a whim, the agent had shown us this, and on a whim we bought it, a rare impulsive act.

TRANSFORMED—MY HAIR SLEEK, nails immaculate, body buffed and polished and adorned in black slacks and a white silk blouse—I stood in the doorway and waited for Steve with open arms. My momentary dread vanished as we held each other tightly. "Welcome home," I said.

"I've never been so glad to be here," he said as he carried his suitcase into the bedroom. "Did you bring this good weather with you?" he asked. "If so, I certainly appreciate it—and you." He turned around to smile.

"I hope it holds," I answered, and made a fervent wish for it—and me—to do just that.

By the time Steve had changed his clothes and splashed water on his face, I had drinks, fresh vegetables, and his favorite low-fat black-bean dip waiting on the marble-top coffee table, the marble almost the exact stone color as the pale linen fabric on our sofa. As we sat side by side munching on the crudités and sipping vodka and tonics, we began our ritual catching-up, although this time, after such a long absence, we had more than usual to discuss. Needless to say, I let him fill in a lot more of his blanks than I did mine.

Chiang Mai, he said, was stunning. "I walked three hundred steps—three hundred!—up to a temple on a mountaintop. The others barely made it." Steve laughed, remembering, but his laugh was more like a short bark. While he went on about the side trip to Thailand with his clients, I studied him closely. In khakis and a white polo shirt, he had a fresh, crisp appearance—so unlike Wilson's rumpled way—that belied a twenty-four-hour plane trip. I couldn't help marveling at how, working as hard as he did, he managed to keep himself in such good shape. His trimness—I'd forgotten about his trimness—but he looked weary.

"Is everything all right?" I asked.

"What do you mean?"

"Nothing . . . I don't know. It's just so unlike you to come home . . . unexpectedly." I smiled.

Steve took a gulp of his drink. "I wanted out of that place. Catch my breath. Didn't mean to worry you, but I don't trust the corporate snoops with my e-mail."

"Your office spies on you?"

"Mine, theirs, who knows?"

Sooner than usual he moved to the opposite end of the seven-foot-long couch. This was when we usually turned our attention to any business problems we were having. Steve, as always, did most of the talking.

"Millions ride on this deal, Michelle," he said. "If I can carry it off, the telecommunication venture I'm representing will hit the jackpot. To put it in its simplest terms, they'd have an exclusive license to electronically disseminate all Asian financial market information and data throughout that hemisphere."

"My God!" I had had no idea of the scope of Steve's project in Hong Kong. Maybe I was as guilty as he was of not paying enough attention to my spouse's work life.

"My god right now is one Bill Brisco. If our negotiations are successful, he promises he'll ask the firm to make me the partner in charge of the whole account. That is, if he replaces his present CEO. Turns out Jones plans to retire next year. Then Brisco will move up, but only if the joint venture is in place."

"And then Brisco rewards you!" I finished triumphantly, his good news unexpectedly mitigating my guilt.

"Only if the deal works out. But if it does, I jump to the top of the class and become as healthy, wealthy, and influential as all the old Turks in the firm."

"Steve, that's wonderful." I reached over to pat his leg. "Isn't it wonderful?" He hadn't smiled once since he'd begun talking.

About this time, Steve usually refreshed our drinks with ice cubes, and if we felt really crazy and wild, he would pour in another splash of vodka. He got up in search of the bottle.

"I don't know anymore," he said irritably. "I'm sick of the whole thing—the jockeying, the lack of sleep, our idiocy, their idiocy—you name it." He poured more alcohol into his glass, a lot more alcohol, before he sat down again.

"It's no wonder. Between the pressure and frustration, you must be exhausted." I moved closer to knead his neck. "You need rest, rest, and more rest."

"In about a year maybe," Steve answered before draining his glass and reaching for the vodka bottle again.

That he'd brought the bottle into the living room was unusual enough; that he was pouring himself yet another drink was unheard of. The only part of our usual ritual that he observed was to put his arm around me as I swung my legs across his lap. Usually we talked another thirty minutes about anything else of interest we had done or seen on our travels, but not this evening. I should have felt relief that at least I didn't have to discuss my comings and goings, but I couldn't stand to see Steve so ragged out. All I could think about was how to make him happy, and I resolved to be upbeat.

"Since when did you not enjoy a challenge?" I asked, gently massaging his hands. His fingers were long and narrow. He didn't seem to mind my touch.

"Since my whole career could hinge on it. Since greed overtook me," he told me. "Since negotiations got more drawn out. Since I can't control global economic conditions. And, not to be forgotten, since lawyers on both sides get paid by the minute." He grimaced. "I can't control that either."

"But can't you make your side get on with it?"

"Except for me, the longer it lasts, the better off the firm is, and that's just our side. Now, enough shop talk," he said, drawing our conversation to a close at the same time he usually drew our conversation to a close. Evidently our routine was back on track.

This signaled that Steve was ready to start nuzzling, and "Voilà!" as he was fond of saying, we would end up in bed for the next twenty minutes or so, our catching up completed. Afterward we'd wander out to a local restaurant. Though I accepted long ago that Steve was an inveterate stickler for habit, tonight his predictability bothered me.

"I wish you'd told me about this sooner," I said, though part of me was glad he hadn't.

"It didn't become this big a deal until the last couple of months. I don't trust phone lines or e-mail or even letters anymore. Let's drop the subject. Come here," he ordered as he rose and headed for the bedroom.

Wanting to stall, to express sympathy, and, all right, to show off, I announced that I would cook dinner. "An omelette, maybe," I said, warming to the idea. This might be fun, our working together in the kitchen.

Steve stopped and laughed. "Thanks, but no thanks." Without wasting more time, he kissed me. Because of our frequent absences, I had always looked forward to sex with Steve. But now, while kissing, I began to worry in earnest: What if, overcome by guilt, I should burst into tears? As he unbuttoned my blouse, I worried that I wouldn't respond to him properly. He unhooked my bra deftly, then cupped my breast and ran his thumb across the nipple. Would he suspect? Would I confess? I stroked the back of his head as he leaned down to kiss me.

Unexpectedly, as soon as we lay down, my body kicked in, clearly pleased to do what it had only recently learned to do so much better. My enthusiasm whetted Steve's desire. The vodka, my need to compensate for his troubles, and, weirdly, my adultery caused even less restraint, turning me into more Mickey than Michelle. This new freedom of mine wasn't going to disappear so quickly, I discovered happily. Steve responded well enough until, carried away, I bit—not hard— his bottom. He turned over and pushed me away. "What's with the rough stuff?" he asked, sitting up.

"Rough stuff?" At first I honestly couldn't figure out what he meant. "I guess . . . I suppose I got excited." I pulled him down. "Come on, let's don't quit now." Michelle did not say things like that. That was Steve's role, and he was having no more rebellion in the ranks. Laying me on my back, he took up our usual routine, not a bad one, mind you, until other habits also intervened—the phone rang. Just when we were coupling in earnest. "Don't be too long," I said, face flushed, as

Steve stretched to answer it. For good measure, I continued to stroke him. With his free hand he did the same for me.

"Sorry, Leonard, I've got someone on the other line, could you hold a minute?" Steve then turned to me: "Sorry, darling, we'll have to speed this up." Exactly sixty seconds later, he resumed his conversation, a satisfied man. He did promise to make it up to me later, though.

AT THE OFFICE, my staff waited with updates, some of which were important, the importance lying not so much in the reports as in Beth's and Gloria's desire to establish contact, to stay near the center of the circle. I readily admit I basked in their attentions and would, if possible, have spent more time listening and encouraging each with words.

I also knew that often my visitations created more commotion than direction. The fact is my office ran best without me. I threw off everyone's routine, including my own. Beth and Gloria didn't come right out and say so, but that was the truth of it. I kept asking questions about matters they had already checked off. I was a second-guesser and liked to weigh options as long as I could. I attributed my meddling to my early days in the city when I'd been strictly on my own.

Back then, when I first arrived in the Big Apple in the late seventies, a young doctor asked me to help her organize her still-modest worldly goods in her new apartment. She'd heard of me through a mutual friend from Michigan. Impressed by the manner and dispatch with which I arranged her possessions and, not incidentally, a good portion of her life, she promptly found me six more clients. I printed up business cards. Calling myself a business was terribly exciting, and I spent two weeks trying to design the perfect card. Finally, I asked Steve for help.

"I need a name for my business," I told him over pizza. "Something inviting but no-nonsense and not too forceful." We were eating at our living-room coffee table, about the only place in our first New York apartment to eat. "Prospective clients might not want me to wallow in their private papers or underwear if I intimidate them."

"What about Regular Not Deep Dish?" he suggested, his mouth full.

"Steve."

"Call yourself a flower," he suggested, looking over my shoulder at the O'Keeffe poster on the wall.

"I don't know the names of flowers," I protested.

"Well, there's a calla lily right there," he said, pointing. "Roses, violets, daisies, irises . . ." He ticked them off, then took another bite of pizza.

"Daisies. I like daisies. I'll be Daisy Banyon and call the business Daisy Banyon, Personal Coordinator." Pleased, I cut another slice for each of us.

"Just be Daisy," Steve said. His curtness stung a bit. Maybe because my first payments had been in the form of tuna casseroles, my work didn't exactly fit into his picture of the young hotshot attorney and his more or less elegant wife. Looking back, though, I think I was the one having trouble coming to grips with who I was and who I thought I was supposed to be in New York. Steve was only trying to help me establish an image of my own in his usual terse way.

And establish an image I did. Having a new name opened up all sorts of possibilities for me. Daisy would be my alter ego, my confident, professional self, the one who wouldn't mind rolling her eyes and telling a client to throw away every one of those ten-year-old dresses and that closet of unwanted and outdated camera equipment. I had already noticed that the more sure and competent—the bossier—I acted, the better clients liked it. I just wasn't always good at it. Daisy would be.

The next day I came up with Daisy Strait. "Because organizing is straightening, at its most efficient," I explained to Steve, this time over peanut butter sandwiches.

"Good idea," he answered, but his mind was on the brief he was reading. His mind was always on briefs he was reading.

"Daisy alone isn't substantial enough," I said. "I'll be Daisy Strait Enterprises. Daisy Strait says it all," I announced as Steve continued to read. I threw our paper plates in the trash.

Daisy Strait alone, however, proved to be plenty substantial. To both my surprise and dismay, I began putting in sixteen-hour days. I was in demand. Nobody in New York had time to look after their own things. Men didn't seem to mind a woman rummaging through their most private messes one bit. They all had had mothers, if not wives. Within a year I hired Beth to help me with my paperwork. In another year, I rented office space in another building and employed a bookkeeper and got a student to help with the grunt work. Thus began Daisy Strait Enterprises, my baby to fuss over. Now my staff fussed over me, and I liked it.

On this trip Beth had waited until I walked into my office to give me potentially good news. "A freelance reporter called the other day wanting information on your business. She has in mind a story for that home magazine, *Serendipity*."

Now, this pleased me. Except for my column, we had never had play in anything other than the local papers and TV stations at the towns where I spoke, and to be honest, not much in those. My business was acquiring new momentum, for which I was grateful, sort of. Juggling Wilson and work and Steve was hard enough at the present pace. I let out an audible sigh but prepared a perfect Daisy Strait smile for Beth's benefit, and maybe, just maybe, mine, too.

BY THE END of the week, Steve's voice wasn't so tight and the knots left his neck. By the end of the second week, he was back to one vodka and tonic an evening, and his understated swagger returned. Friday we were joining Roberta and Buzzy Simpson and Merin and Jack Gamble at the theater—a hot import from London's West End, the kind of event I usually looked forward to, but I was a little worn out. I had worked extra hard every day to free my evenings for Steve. And thoughts of Wilson kept popping into my head, especially at night.

Although he and I talked once or twice a day on the cell phone I'd bought to use solely with him, neither of us brought up anything about our last conversation before I left. The unspoken tension weighed on me, let alone the absurdity of contemplating marriage to another man even as my husband lay sleeping beside me. So much for the simple life!

So much for the play, too. Steve had to nudge me twice when I dozed off. In the rest room at intermission, I splashed my face with cold water and jogged up and down in the toilet stall to get my circulation going before catching up with my group in the lobby. Fortunately, they had finished discussing the play's first act.

"Have any of you seen the Baileys' new place?" Merin was asking. "I hear it's so grand it's gaudy, a throwback to the over-the-top eighties."

"Grand proportions, but not overdone," Roberta countered. "I think Judy has a good eye. Her porcelain collection is to die for."

"Yes, it is first-rate," Merin acquiesced.

"Grand proportions," I repeated, only half listening but trying to participate.

"I wouldn't want that woman's stuff in my home," Jack said. "There's no place to put a coffee cup."

"My husband has the taste of Attila the Hun," Merin said through her teeth as she smiled at Jack. Fortunately, he seemed to thrive on her put-downs of him. With Merin's exotic dark looks, she could get away with anything. Even her too-early and too-strict face-lifts, although they had aged her. His first wife had talked to him as grievously. Because both wives treated everyone else with respect, I'd decided this disparagement must be something he encouraged somehow—consciously or not.

"I think the Baileys' place is more Gilded Age than eighties," I offered. I thought of Annette and Lindy in Texas and the comfortable but modest way they lived.

"Smart girl!" Jack said.

"She has this neat and tidy thing, you know," Steve explained as the intermission came to an end.

"Would that we were all more like Michelle," Roberta said for me, and I remembered why I liked these people. Whatever else, they were loyal. That we weren't exceptionally close had more to do with the pace of our lives than anything else, except perhaps, in my case, my prized privacy, my deliberate reticence. In Rollins, though, among Wilson's friends, I spoke up more often. Here in New York, I continued to edit myself because I wanted my thoughts to seem fully formed. All right, I wanted to appear more mysterious, too. Except now I really was a woman of mystery.

After the show, we regrouped over drinks, and I heard Jack ask Steve the name of some exotic dish that they had tried together in Scotland. "You know, in Edinburgh, that fancy restaurant we went to that Merin liked so much?"

Steve and I had never been to Edinburgh.

Steve shook his head. "Escapes me this minute," he said, an atypical Steve response. He glanced at me. Maybe he had taken that trip—without me. Not so unusual, I reasoned; I didn't bother to tell him every little town I went to, although I did tell him about pleasurable places—not counting Rollins.

"Sounds like y'all had some fun," I said.

Steve gave me a quizzical look.

"Roberta and I didn't go, either," Buzzy sympathized, and took a handful of peanuts. "Damn shame. Heard the golf was wonderful."

Did Steve feel guilty, not about going but about not telling me? As guilty as I felt at this very moment?

Buzzy somehow managed to turn the conversation to the quality of his children's education—his son had ended up at Little Red School House, and Buzzy and Roberta weren't sure about its less traditional curriculum. Even though he and Roberta were both in their mid-to-late forties, their children were only ten and thirteen. My Texas friends, who weren't more than five or six years older than these women, had grandchildren.

"I'm so glad Jack's kids are in college and into their own friends; no extra baggage for the holidays and all that," Merin said. Now it was Jack who looked uncomfortable.

"That's probably good for everyone," Roberta offered. It was hard, she added, to pay proper attention to her children's schoolwork, hold down a full-time job, and attend to the health and beauty maintenance needed to keep up with the younger colleagues in her position as a senior partner in a high-powered public relations firm.

"And then there's Steve," Jack said. "Great legal mind. Looks like a kid. Keeps in shape. Away half the time and still knows more about what's going on here than the rest of us."

Steve demurred. "When I'm involved in marathon negotiations like now, the Internet is my only bedtime recreation."

I thought of our *coitus quickus* the night he arrived home and frowned. Maybe I should become a laptop.

"Sounds like great bedtime recreation to me," Buzzy said.

"I'm talking about the *New York Times,* Buzzy, not online sex!" Steve protested. Everyone else laughed as if they'd never considered it a possibility for Steve. Maybe they were right. I was getting less and less sure of things.

Jack roughed Steve's shoulder. "Yeah, but online you can be anybody."

"We all have so many masks," Roberta commented.

"Yes," I answered. "Different faces, emotions, sometimes even different bodies, and each with private and public parts, all equally real, all giving witness to something . . ." I shook my head, puzzling over what that something might be until I noticed everyone looking at me. Then Buzzy mumbled about how I was as deep as still water.

I looked forward to Monday at the office. I knew who I was there.

At two A.M. my eyes popped opened, a dawn of sorts: I'd used the expression "y'all."

THE THIRD WEEK at work proved to be not so great after all. My heart just wasn't in the fussing-about. Steve, his vigor restored, had returned to Hong Kong. I wished I didn't have to hang around, but Gloria had scheduled lectures for me in the New York area.

Caught up on my mail and columns, I became restless and daydreamed about Wilson Collins. This mooning about, coupled with erratic but unfocused energy bursts, played havoc with the staff. At least three times I had to apologize for snapping at Gloria or Beth when they merely asked questions. Probably a few more apologies wouldn't have been amiss. Daisy did not show impatience. I'm sure they noticed the change.

By Wednesday it occurred to me that I'd become a sex addict. I'd always shunned cocaine, cigarettes, and excessive use of alcohol, but who knew that inside me all along had been an addict monster, a ferocious one at that? I walked along the street and stared at men's shoes in store windows and thought of Wilson's feet and wondered if I had a foot fetish. On the way to work one day, I followed a sweaty jogger standing by me at a red light into a coffee bar because his smell reminded me of Wilson. Standing in line behind him, I became so embarrassed by my behavior that I turned and fled.

Horrified and gratified, I sat at my desk, eyes closed, a mug of peppermint tea in hand. Peppermint stimulates your mind, according to Gloria. If only I could stimulate my mind, to balance my hungry body. I jumped when Beth whispered, "Maybe you want to go over these appearance requests . . . before Gloria gives them a final no?" She walked so lightly, that Beth.

We both knew these were the kinds of requests they'd been handling on their own for years, but I looked them over anyway. Often Gloria knew better than I not only what would work in my schedule but what suited me best. Beth laid the stack on the desk; I closed my eyes again, but she didn't move. I roused myself enough to say thank you. She kept standing soldier straight.

"I'll let you know if I have any questions," I said. Having sounded too dismissive, I repeated, "Thank you."

"Could I be of any help?" she asked, a tentative catch.

"I said I'd—" My tea sloshed onto the stack of papers.

Beth dabbed at the mess with her cotton handkerchief, this hankie her rebellion against simple living. Why wash when you can throw away? the rest of us argued. To Beth's credit, she did not call forth the destruction of forests, only the survival of tradition. She'd have worn white gloves if they weren't so conspicuous.

"You haven't been yourself lately, Daisy," said Beth, quietly. "I mean, I know you're not Daisy, or not *just* Daisy, but you're always Daisy in the office. Except now you aren't, and it's worrisome to us all. We'd like to help." This was an extraordinary outburst for Beth—for anyone in this office.

The illusion of Daisy for my staff counted as much as the reality, even though they knew better, knew exactly who I was and what I looked like in my private life. But, in effect, they thought of me only as Daisy. Probably because I encouraged it. Suddenly Beth's offer of help overcame me. I put my face in my hands to hide my tears.

"Do you think you need a rest?" Beth asked gently.

I shook my head no. "I . . ." More time off would stick me here in New York, making it harder to duck into and out of Rollins.

"I think I should go back to Texas," I blurted out. "I don't think I've got that office quite up to speed yet. I could write and consult and . . ."

Beth looked puzzled.

"And I find that area . . . restful."

"Okay," she said. "You know, there's a medical supply company in Fort Worth that wants you to streamline their operations."

"Good," I said. "I could get Amy Ward to help me out with that one. I think more work is what I need. The very antidote to my . . . malaise."

Beth looked surprised, but I felt my usual energy puffing up, filling out, as a sense of joy welled up inside me.

chapter 12

THE LIGHTS IN THE OLD COURTHOUSE GLIMMERED. The high-school band played "Fire and Rain"—miraculously in tune. The party was working; I could feel it. Wilson beamed at me over the head of Ruth Raleigh, the television producer with Green World Productions, who was beaming at him. Ever since Ms. Raleigh arrived yesterday, she had managed to figure out a way to beam at Wilson while stiffing everybody else. In her thigh-high skirts and stiletto heels, she pranced around Rollins, tossing her black hair—worn well below her shoulders—to great effect.

I had a good mind to let loose both Michelle and Daisy on the woman, show her what strident efficiency and studied aloofness were really about, but the last thing I wanted was to frighten away these television aliens from Wilson's pet dream. Too much work had gone into enticing them here and making them feel welcome.

While I was away, Ruth Raleigh had finally agreed to visit the center. Meanwhile, Wilson decided that the original and now-unused town courthouse would make the perfect place for a welcoming party and, possibly later, for offices for the production company. He liked the idea of the courthouse, vacated a few years back, having another life. Both Wilson's enthusiasm over the television opportunity and the use of the old building were catching. As before, I threw myself into his problems and, as before, provided the kind of help he desperately needed, including transforming the large marble-floored lobby of the courthouse. For these abilities, I blessed Daisy. And I blessed those skills again this night as I beamed back at Wilson. I hadn't gotten that many beams from him lately.

BEING MICKEY AGAIN felt absolutely right. Michelle and Daisy were not hovering in the shadows as a kind of reprimand. Quite the opposite actually: I had achieved some kind of balance in myself, a compromise of sorts. When Daisy, I was more productive than ever—for Wilson as well as for Daisy Strait Enterprises.

The Michelle part of me did not roll over emotionally and play dead, either. I began an e-mail correspondence with both Roberta and Merin in New York, who both seemed delighted. In the past, we had only known one another alongside our respective spouses. It was a small but important shift for me. I realized how much my need for intimacy and my fear of rejection had been at war with each other.

I also made use of Michelle's excellent sense of understated chic to disguise the courthouse lobby with the help of my committee: Annette, Lindy, and Hillary. Annette and I rented and borrowed every palm and ficus tree to be found from florists and landscapers. We used up-lights to create a warm glow and draped sky-blue fabric all over to help both the acoustics and human scale. I gave the local caterers a simple menu to follow, for while I'm not much of a cook, I sure know what works at a party.

Through the Internet I followed the ups and downs of

Wall Street, especially the performance of media conglomerates, because the fate of the center as an Amazon setting would most likely be affected by the market. We needed to make an economic case for doing it, regardless. Following the market revived my interest in politics, too. These new activities made me realize just how deadened my old Michelle self had become.

Having such various lives filled me with a sense of power. And I would be remiss if I didn't confess to being caught up in the giddiness of all the identities and attitudes, including the last and best, sensual, dopey one. I pictured myself as a kaleidoscope of intensely colored stones. Each time I turned or jumped on a plane, the stones fell into another lovely pattern.

I told myself that one role seldom satisfied the diversity in our natures any more than one person satisfied all our needs. Complete fulfillment comes from the courage to act out several roles and appetites at the same time. And that is how I came to be happy for once and a little while. I didn't expect it to last forever, but a season, however brief, would do.

HAPPY AS I WAS, I avoided acknowledging Wilson's estrangement from me. It happened. My first night back, he had broken the marriage ice again. "Would you like to see my grandmother's engagement ring?" he'd asked as we stood by his desk looking at notes he'd received from Green World Productions. His hand hovered by a desk drawer.

My response was glib. "We've got lots of time for details like rings. Right now, let's concentrate on more urgent matters," I replied, grabbing his butt playfully. Wilson dropped the subject and walked away with his hands in his pockets. When he brought the ring up again, I again dodged the issue.

I believe I hoped he would tire of me, for I knew full well this romance would have to end someday, although I didn't want that. Mostly, I tried not to think about it. I was trying hard to stay in the moment.

Only gradually did I realize something had changed in Wilson. I suspected his brooding began in my absence, a weakening of his blind faith in our bond. While he appreciated my help with his projects and our sexual romps had not diminished in quantity or quality, his buoyancy around and about me disappeared. He retreated, pulled back, a nuanced but distinct distancing. Little things, really. He left earlier for Barley's in the morning. He didn't always remember to kiss me good-bye. His compliments grew scarce.

Helen had retreated a little as well. "He needs some bucking up," she had said to me a couple of weeks after the ring incident. This advice plus my own emerging awareness of his withdrawal sobered me enough to know I couldn't pretend to be in never-never land with him.

I was not proud of myself for hedging. In fact, I felt absolutely selfish about him. Every part of me craved Wilson Collins. Scruples be damned, I was determined to gorge on my delight. I wanted to wallow in this freedom as long as possible. I justified my behavior only by telling myself that the joy of this time together would be worth the pain of separation later—for both of us. But tonight he beamed, I reminded myself. Maybe he had only been working too hard and his moods had nothing to do with me at all. Without question, he did beam.

confessions of a bigamist

. . .

"SUNBEAM, SUNBEAM, in my heart today," I sang in my head as I let Brian Samuels guide me onto the dance floor. My hair curled wildly, the way Wilson liked it. It couldn't get too wild for that man. My new ritual after a shampoo was to flip my head over and blow-dry it that way, scrunching it for added measure.

"Wilson tells me we have you to thank for this extravaganza," Brian said as we moved our hands and feet in a stilted fashion, dancing in place. He was a better doctor than a dancer, and I was no Ginger Rogers, either.

I laughed. "Wilson exaggerates. Your wife, among others, worked as hard."

"Not what I hear. You get the credit. Wilson said there was a chickens-with-their-heads-cut-off approach until you returned."

It was nice to know Wilson's attitude had improved. Early on I discovered that Wilson didn't take easily to instructions. Besides the material I wrote for him, he only asked me what I thought every now and again, and every now and again I would tell him. But tonight he had beamed and I had beamed back.

Where was he now? Talking to shark-tooth herself, Ruth Raleigh, I supposed. And why not? She was younger, sexier, more glamorous, more predatory. She would probably jump at the chance to marry him; she would probably propose herself, that woman. Of course, in reality, I hadn't yet said a definite *no*. In reality, I was leading him on.

At the end of the set Brian danced me over to a table where

Hillary, Annette, and Lindy were sitting. Though Annette had worked on this party, her husband, Wendell, wouldn't come. He supported the center but hated dances and didn't want "all you women" telling him to get up and "shake his booty." No amount of pleading by the rest of us could change his mind.

Annette didn't argue with him. The pollination of marriage requires oblique approaches. "He was very torn when I left tonight," she said with a laugh. She'd camouflaged her wrinkles with makeup and accentuated her eyes with mascara. Spiffed up in a chocolate-colored cocktail suit instead of her usual gardening uniform, jeans and long-tailed shirt, she looked ten years younger. "What he wouldn't admit is that he really did want to meet the California glamorosi." She swayed to the music as dancers swirled around the room. "I think these TV people would be fools not to come here."

"Lindy, go ask that cameraman to dance," Hillary teased as she sipped on a glass of white wine and watched a cluster of townsfolk talk to a group of the Californians. "He's been watching you all night. Use your powers of persuasion for the greater good." Hillary had fluffed out her dark bob and worn a black dress that displayed her splendid cleavage to great advantage.

Lindy shook her head and shoulders to the rhythm of the music and artfully eyed the cameraman. "Not my type. Besides which, it's Mickey who has those powers." She smiled at me as I scanned the room for Wilson.

"Whatever else, Mickey, this ought to earn you some running-away forgiveness points," Brian said, only half joking.

"She has a job, Brian," Hillary chastised her husband.

"A job is one thing, leaving him alone so much is another." Brian grinned at me but I was still searching for the other subject of the conversation. "Why don't I try to find where that boy's gone to?" he suggested, and quickly left to roam.

"Ignore Brian," Annette said. "You're playing Wilson just right."

My mouth stretched at the corners, either into a smile or a grimace. I had not thought I was playing him at all—not in the way she meant, anyway.

"Women come at him too fast," Annette went on. "Marriage glistens in their eyes. He's spoiled—and shy. You play hard to get; most women have forgotten how."

"You don't know that," Hillary said to Annette.

"I know Wilson Collins. I've been reading him between the lines since my horrible crush in the third grade. I didn't play hard to get, either." When Annette spoke of Wilson, another twenty years dropped away and a girlish quality emerged, her expression sharing only a passing resemblance to that of the efficient woman running a successful landscape business.

"I'm not playing hard to get," I said.

"Hard to keep, then. I think he would marry you just to keep you down on the farm—literally."

"He loves her," Lindy protested. Lindy, the romantic, wanting love and fleeing so fast to avoid its possibility. Every time a man showed serious interest in her—and several had—she dropped them.

"Sure, but her reluctance has focused his mind," Annette argued. She tapped her fingers to the band's rendition of "Graceland." "I so wish someone would ask me to dance."

"Wilson may pout and act like you've been gone months, but he really is proud of you," Lindy told me, "and we're all envious."

"After tonight you had better be prepared for a full-court

press from the town of Rollins, as well as Mr. Collins," Hillary said, unaware of her rhyme until the rest of us laughed.

I certainly wasn't prepared for the whole town assisting Wilson with his wooing, but I appreciated their response and felt cocooned in their camaraderie. Just as I'd never known fantastic sex, neither had I known the easy camaraderie of women. As a girl, frequent moves made me reluctant to form close attachments; as a woman, my ambitions and need for privacy kept me distanced. Until now, I'd had no idea of what I was missing.

When I was away, I missed my new friends. Even so, I hadn't seen much of them during this stay in Rollins, even though they had helped me with the dance. I had assigned them tasks they could do from their homes—a phone call here, a phone call there—we were all busy. Most important, my time with Wilson felt fractured enough. Where was he, anyway? I made my excuses to the women and snaked through the crowd, looking for Wilson.

I should have taken the truly honorable course and come back only long enough to say good-bye. If only he would be content with what we had and not be so greedy, we could go on indefinitely. Forever, maybe, I concluded as he walked toward me. White shirt, white teeth, traditional navy blazer, gray slacks—he seemed sexier than ever, his clothes underscoring the strength of his body. He was beaming again and took my hand. Never had he looked more pleased, not even in the beginning.

"So? Have they said yes?" I asked as we stepped stiffly around the dance floor, his arm around my waist, mine on his shoulder. Traditional, this man was.

"Just about," he said, grinning. "Ruth Raleigh asked me to

go with them on a scouting expedition to the Amazon next week."

With this announcement, he swung me out from him, then pulled me back in with a snap of his wrist. For the first time in my life, I felt graceful. But I had to force a smile and exuberance: "That's fantastic! Are you going?"

"Of course I'm going." This time he twirled me under his arm.

"How wonderful for you," I managed, allowing myself to be led.

"And you," he said. Pulling me closer to him, he began, in earnest, spinning me around the hundred-year-old oak floor, his elegance making up for the dragging beat of the high-school band. Dancing had never been a part of my repertoire, but Mickey seemed to be a natural, at least in Wilson's arms. And I thought he couldn't dance! By the end of the song, I felt as triumphant as he looked. Then he whispered in my ear, "I accepted the trip for both of us."

ALL WEEK, WILSON prepared for the trip, too ecstatic to pay attention to the woman he professed to love. Miffed, as well as unenthusiastic, I buried myself in rearranging my work schedule and explaining my upcoming absence to my latest consult in Fort Worth (somewhat successfully), to Steve (more successfully), and to Dottie and my staff (who did not complain). I decided to give them all versions of the truth—I was taking a side trip, I needed to clear my head, why not the jungle. I worried that Steve or my staff might ask more questions than I was prepared to answer. This was surely not typical behavior from me. But then, what was anymore?

I hardly knew myself. In spare moments, I turned to my women friends.

One afternoon I stopped by Annette's to return some vases we'd used for the dance and found her weeding her flower garden. I volunteered to help. Helen had told me weeding was therapeutic, and I thought it made sense that what worked in a home or office would work in a garden bed as well.

"I underestimated you," Annette confessed as we dug into the earth. "Under that shined-up, agreeable face, you have a will of iron."

"I've never thought of myself that way," I said, tugging hard on two weeds at once.

"Those are lady's slippers, honey," Annette pointed out. She took them from my hand and replanted them without missing a beat in our conversation.

"Maybe I'm changing," I offered. "Maybe I'm turning into someone else."

"I doubt it. You've got a lot more determination than I gave you credit for."

"How do you mean?"

"You really do live your life on your own terms. I admire that. Just be careful."

I laughed and paused in my rooting and digging. "And how do you mean *that*?"

"You know. Now pull me up." Which I did; but I didn't know.

THE DAY LINDY and I drove into Fort Worth to shop for my Amazon wardrobe, she confessed that she understood my reluctance to marry Wilson, wonderful as he was. "I can't imagine marrying again. A lover, yes, but no more husbands for me, thank you. Not just because I was married to a major jerk, it's that husbands are too high-maintenance. A gender thing, I think."

"Men," I said. We laughed at that.

"Brian is right that Wilson hates to have you away," she went on, "though he doesn't say so—not even to you, I suspect."

I tried to brush this one off. "Not anymore. He is either getting used to it or happy about the upcoming trip together."

"How 'bout stopping for some tea and pastry?" Lindy said as we passed a nice café.

Envisioning the lean TV people I'd be seeing shortly, I passed. "I've been overdoing it lately—my waistline shows it."

"Not so I'd notice. You look great."

"I look tired and wrinkled and old and ugly."

Lindy laughed—a warm, loving laugh. "That's the silliest remark I've heard from you."

I shrugged. "I was never a pretty woman, not like you or Hillary; not even when I was young."

"Then love has made you blossom because you've got a type of beauty now, something much better than conventional prettiness. It's more than that, though," Lindy said, waving her manicured hand around for emphasis. "It's the *mystery* of you, Mickey. What woman wouldn't like a little mystery to her, huh?"

"It's my clothes."

"Whatever," Lindy said. "Stop punishing yourself. You look great—a little tired maybe. A week in the Amazon should cure that . . . I guess." We both laughed, though this trip was no laughing matter.

Later, when Lindy dropped me off, she kissed my cheek.

"Here's to a fabulous trip," she said. "Take care of yourself, and Wilson, too." It almost sounded like a warning. Had Lindy sensed the threat of Ruth Raleigh, too?

THE TRIP was two days away. Buoyed by Lindy's words and determined to cut off Ruth Raleigh at the pass, I overrode my insecurities and reached out to Wilson—massaging his back, cuddling up against him in bed, paying calls on him at the Raptor Center when I could. Maybe he'd been waiting for a sign from me, but at last, he responded. For twenty-four hours, he was my Wilson again.

Our last night before leaving, after a romantic candle-lit dinner, he excused himself and drove over to his office to take care of some final details. I didn't feel shunned. I imagined he would awake me later and make love to me the rest of the night. I felt like we needed to store up, that a hammock in the rain forest would not exactly lend itself to amorous adventures, none that I could figure out, anyway. As it happened, the next morning I woke to the phone: Wilson. He'd worked late, fallen asleep at his desk, wouldn't be back for another hour.

I made coffee, finished my packing, and waited for Wilson to share breakfast with him. Two hours and fifteen work-related e-mails later, plus one more to Steve, I got another call from Wilson.

"Wilson, the plane leaves today," I told him.

"Just another hour, sweetheart. You know that new owl we got yesterday? She almost died last night. I'd like to be sure she's fine before I leave."

"Can I finish up your packing?"

I could hear him humming, a habit he had when he was tense or worried, as he hung up without responding.

Pressing the phone to my cheek, I wondered how in the world I'd allowed this state of affairs to come to pass. Then Helen walked in, vacuum in hand. Recently she'd had a new perm and a terrible dye job, her hair now more orange than yellow. "You all right?" she asked.

"Fine," I said, but Helen knew better and stood waiting for me to say more.

"I'm a little tired, is all," I said.

"When you get yourself settled in, life will be a lot simpler," she returned pointedly.

"Sometimes problems aren't that easily solved, Helen."

"If you don't solve them, some other woman just might." With that, Helen switched on the Hoover.

chapter 13

THE PLANE WAS IN A STEEP DESCENT, THE LANDING kind, but the cabin lights were off and no one made a seat-belt announcement. I panicked. Were we crashing? What if I died? I clutched my laptop tighter. For me, the only thing worse than death would be survival. My dual lives could never be explained. I checked my watch: It was three A.M. Then the plane leveled out and we touched down lightly—Manaus, Brazil. I was in the Amazon.

As we drove through the darkness, I felt more than saw the city's flat shapes and subtle slopes, the poverty and beauty intermingling in the shadows. More than one and a half million people, many of them new immigrants, now made Manaus their home, Wilson, ever diligent on his homework, told me.

"But there aren't enough jobs, and the city keeps sprawling into the forest because the peasants have no other land to farm," our Brazilian driver, compliments of Ruth Raleigh, interrupted. "It's the only way they can feed themselves."

"The land turns fallow," Wilson whispered, "and the poor end up burning more of the forest."

We drove alongside the Rio Negro, dotted with the lights of small boats bobbing on the embankment, a counterpoint to the starlit sky. Before long we turned into a large circular drive lined with palm trees and brilliant red flowers illuminated by spotlights from a handsome brick hotel—our first destination. Even the air outside was lush.

Leave it to Ruth Raleigh to find a resort in the rain forest, I thought, with a mixture of relief and disappointment. Frightened as I was of camping in the wild, I had geared myself for adventure all the way. These few nights in Manaus were a lucky break for me. I could e-mail Steve and my staff from here.

LATE THE NEXT MORNING Wilson and I strolled around the resort's own version of the rain forest, this one behind glass panes. "I thought we were here to see monkeys and birds in the wilderness, not cooped up behind glass," I commented.

"I wish you'd make an effort to get along with Ruth," said Wilson. "Use your charm to convince her the sanctuary is perfect for their purposes."

I turned to him, a hand on one hip. "Wilson, that woman is not interested in my charms. She didn't plan on your inviting me, did she?"

Wilson shrugged and stuck his hands in the pockets of his chinos. "I don't like spending a lot of time with a bunch of strangers. Besides, we're practically married."

"That's not the point!"

"The point is I want to see the Amazon with you."

The point is, Michelle and Daisy scolded, *you have no business here, and you let that marriage remark go unchallenged.*

I took Wilson's hand as we resumed our walk to the terrace for brunch.

·   ·   ·

SUNSET FOUND US reclining on easy chairs in a shady nook on the same terrace, this time sipping Caipirinhas, my scolding voices lulled by the warm breeze. "What's in these?" I asked Wilson, holding up my glass.

"Lime juice, sugar, and a kind of raw rum," he said lazily. "Reminds me of a dark tequila and mighty good times on the streets of Laredo."

"Reminds my stomach of things better left undrunk."

We watched Ruth Raleigh slink toward us from the lobby entrance. "She's really pretty nice, isn't she?" Wilson asked, his voice pleading with me to agree.

"Oh, yeah," I said, taking another sip of Caipirinha, "pretty nice."

Young women in Technicolor versions of ceremonial native costumes began to set up for the evening's entertainment. In their brightly feathered headpieces, short-short purple skirts, and gold bodices shaped evidently to resemble armor, a few ran through some dance steps. All looked bored, but the prospect of the event excited Wilson. Innocent, wonderful Wilson, I thought, and hoped he didn't notice when one young nubile in a headdress reached into her backpack for a cell phone.

"Introducing your lady love to the wonders of the Amazon, I see," Ruth Raleigh said, and without invitation pulled up a chair. Ruth said "lady love" in the same condescending tone she would have used for "little wife."

"But won't you join us?" I asked. Wilson caught the sarcasm in my voice. To make up, I smiled with what I considered a simulacrum of sincerity as the witch draped herself over her chair, showing her legs to great advantage. "Have you made many trips to the Amazon?" I asked.

Ruth turned a smile on Wilson as if he had asked the question. "Of course. I'm the adventurous type."

"I envy you," Wilson said. "I've dreamed of this since I was a kid."

While Ruth spouted to Wilson about her love of the rain forest and her deep commitment to its preservation, I drained my Caipirinha and ordered another. As Ruth explained how this TV series was going to be a hip update of Tarzan and Jane in the jungle, I finished my second drink. When I asked for another, Wilson looked at me with some alarm and suggested we order an appetizer.

"I'll save myself for dinner," Ruth said, and rubbed her stomach as if it weren't already obvious that she didn't have one. Then again, neither had I a month or two ago. Why hadn't I appreciated that fact about myself sooner?

I looked Ruth up and down, then said, "I don't believe in saving myself for anything. I have ravenous appetites, I believe in indulgence. Otherwise, a kind of parsimony of the soul sets in." I smiled sweetly; Ruth excused herself. I liked that—*parsimony of the soul*. I made a mental note to include it in a column.

THE NEXT MORNING the television people, Wilson, and I stepped onto a double-decker boat just as planes, flying in formation, began swooping toward the water, peeling off, dipping wings, turning somersaults. "Our own air show, a fitting beginning," Wilson commented, and I agreed, although I would have done away with the storm clouds also brewing out over the horizon. If the boat rocked, I would be sick. Boats and I did not take to each other.

But the river and I did. Almost as soon as Manaus's modest skyline was out of sight, the Rio Negro, a vast river that drains much of the northern Amazon Basin, merged with the Solimoes and for miles the two flowed side by side—the Rio Negro the color of strong tea, the Solimoes a light brown, "white water" river. The Rio Negro is called the River of Hunger by the local Indians, our guide explained, because its poor nutrients made crops hard to grow and animals scarce.

Was I a river of hunger? Lately Mickey wanted more—sex, at least. Michelle wanted . . . to be seen. Daisy could be hungry, too, but she wouldn't know it. She'd think she was the steady flow of white water, the Solimoes. Since the announcement of this trip, I'd felt less and less in balance. When the rivers finally merged colors, the Amazon formed, gorgeous and expansive in its grandeur, and I, too, expanded and filled up spaces in my heart that had gone wanting.

I lay my hand on Wilson's arm. "I wish we could stay on this forever." The sun's warmth, the musical birdcalls, the engine's soft, rhythmic chug had all cast a spell.

He looked down and smiled his loopiest of smiles. "Well, woman of ravenous appetite, if you want, we'll do just that."

A wave of our early-morning pleasure washed back over me. Earlier I had made good on my "appetite" boast. I smiled contentedly. That I should be so lucky for even one day of my life, even one hour!

For the next leg of our journey, we forsook our "African Queen" for two small rowboats, and I was able to maneuver Wilson and me into the one sans Ruth Raleigh. Our guide, a dark-skinned, well-versed woman, paddled her insignificant group of mortals through a menacing dense patch of trees half submerged in the water. Large white hornets' nests like spun lanterns hung in the top branches, but their beauty could not surpass their scariness. As the boat bumped one tree and then another, I imagined the hornets giving chase, a python dropping on my head, deadly spiders biting my hand—well-deserved retribution of all kinds.

I wrapped my raincoat around myself. Then the trees parted and the tributary widened, and instantly the landscape altered, allowing in sky and light again. I spotted birds—some in vivid greens or blues, some in shades of red, others black with yellow chests—darting among the treetops. Wilson and the guide named most species, but I didn't care about their names, only their calls, their colors, their swoops, and, most especially, the beauty of their flight.

Monkeys, too, whole families, scampered noisily across trees, and thick sloths trudged up the trunks while multicolored butterflies flitted closer to the water. Again, Wilson called out names, but names belonged in another world of time and place. For this while, I escaped both. I became the monkey, the butterfly, the parrot, even the sloth in its labored lumbering.

In another maze of trees, even more dense and foreboding than the first, giant water lilies, maybe two feet wide, made a perfumed skin on the river's surface. The guide lifted one lily with her oar and held it up. "See these veins?" she said, somewhat proudly. "An Englishman took them home to find out how plants so fragile could support the weight of a baby. He used their pattern to design the Crystal Palace in London. Modern domes are based on them."

At the mention of London, I thought of Steve and our last trip there. We'd made a point to visit the fabulous "Palm House" in Kew Gardens and wandered together through its rooms of flowers and shrubs, noting the more remarkable plants. The building, though, more than its contents, had captured our fancy, for we favored works of human intelligence over nature's bounty. A spasm of nostalgia hit me for that couple who walked a little too swiftly, a little too sure, through that glass house of wonders. What had happened to them? And who was I, this awed woman in a dinghy in this world of sensuality?

THE NEXT MORNING we left Manaus and drove for three hours on mud-slick roads bordered by dense thickets, then hiked another half hour through the woods with our backpacks. At last we came to the camp, which was run by the American Rain Forest Foundation. The director of the foundation, Seth Williams, along with a chef in a tall white hat, greeted us and showed us around the clearing and its domiciles: a kitchen, a dining area, and two tin-roofed sheds lined with hammocks. Farther away Seth and a couple of his workers had rigged two showers and two flush toilets. They had even dammed a little stream for outside bathing, complete with environmentally correct soaps and shampoo. "And the cook's uniform is no ruse," Seth joked. "I promise you gourmet meals during your stay."

If I hadn't known better, I would have bet that Ruth Raleigh had seen to that, too, but it was the sleeping arrangements that made me truly suspicious: My hammock was on the end, Wilson's was next to mine, and Ruth's was next to Wilson's. How this had happened, I did not know. There went my hopes for late-night visits in Wilson's hammock, if such a feat were even possible. Getting in one alone seemed complicated enough.

Unpacking, of all things, proved equally daunting. I wished I had put my stuff in Ziploc bags or canvas with zippers like everyone else, including Wilson. And why hadn't he told me? Did he just assume Daisy Strait knew about *every* kind of packing? Ruth had placed all her stuff—makeup, toiletries, swimsuit, shoes, lingerie—in color-coordinated plastic bags. Later, when she hung up a pair of tiny lace g-string panties to dry, I wanted to kill her.

Ruth was young. That was the worst of it. In all these years I had never given age much consideration. I used creams and subtle makeup and didn't dress like a twenty-year-old, but basically I thought of myself as ageless. Compared to Ruth, however, I felt like an old hag and could think of no reason why Wilson would choose a hag over a beautiful young bod, especially one that had something resembling brains in her head. I now understood all the hullabaloo about turning fifty: In three years I would no longer be ageless. The smarty-pants me should have figured that one out sooner.

Or had I, and was all this some sort of midlife crisis? Was that why the usually austere and well-groomed Michelle Banyon was walking wild-haired in a rain forest so serried and dark I couldn't find the birds? Along with the rest of the group, I investigated the ants and small insects and tiny flowers that grew under the canopy of eternal twilight. Wilson had gone crazy over those damned ants. He spent half the time on his knees, eyes level with the ground, Ruth hovering close by, clucking enthusiastically.

THAT NIGHT, I had three Caipirinhas and a goodly amount of wine. We heard a deep twang like a rubber band and Seth

Williams disappeared into the fauna, returning with a tree frog, its green so vivid it defied the idea of forest camouflage. I fell in love with that green, that flaunting of beauty. However, when the group began passing it around, I held back until Ruth took it upon herself to hand it to me.

"Don't be so uptight," she taunted in a voice oozing with friendliness. "Surely you aren't afraid of a little frog."

My fervent wish was to have the courage to stuff the gorgeous green beauty down Ruth Raleigh's throat, though no frog should have to suffer that fate.

Louisa, a graduate student doing research at the reserve, came to my rescue. Gently, the young woman, her black tendrils framing warm blue eyes, lifted the frog from Ruth's hands and gently, ever so gently, coaxed me into touching it, then holding it—to group applause. I laughed. Wilson, looking so much like the proud father of a gifted child, kissed my forehead. I was in the rain forest! The outside world—every outside world—slipped away. I didn't feel so old after all.

At bedtime, I went inside the toilet stall with only a modicum of fear that a snake might lie curled inside. The Caipirinhas and wine helped, but not enough to keep me from later imagining the same snake crawling up my mosquito netting. Before the night was over, the alcohol exacted its price: sleeplessness. For hours I lay there under the mosquito netting on the alert for any sign of snakes or tarantulas or, quite possibly, jaguars. I wished I could cuddle with Wilson, who was snoring pleasantly. The idea of a quiet cuddle had clearly not entered his decorous mind.

Instead, I had listened to Ruth's patter all evening: "Oh, Wilson, do you think we could re-create this little bit of heaven"—a clump of ordinary bushes!—"at your refuge?"

"Oh, Wilson, wouldn't that stream make a delightful sight re-created in Texas?" Just thinking about that voice, "Oh Wilson, Oh Wilson, Oh," made me want to throw up. The Caipirinhas, unfortunately, made me want to pee again.

Groping in my bag, anticipating all manner of creepy-crawlies inside it, I searched for my flashlight and cursed this new life of excessive drinking. To make matters worse, this time I could not force myself to go inside the stall. I agonized over my failings—and felt them, something I seldom did in the past. Usually I got bad colds instead. Or a pain in the neck. Nothing I had to connect to feelings.

But love had taken me into myself as well as out of myself. Right now the dominant experience was panic. Unlike Wilson, I was a coward, and not just a physical coward. Wilson had the courage of his convictions; I wasn't sure I had any convictions at all. If I did, I would choose Wilson and leave Steve. Or leave Wilson and work harder on my marriage with Steve. Because underneath my bravura, as Helen had intimated, I didn't have the nerve. I was a coward clear across the board.

WHEN LOUISA APPEARED on the narrow path leading to the toilet, I had just opted to relieve myself behind the shack. Like me, she was wearing comfortable cotton slacks and a large denim shirt for pajamas—I had packed something right. "Everything okay?" she asked. "I noticed your flashlight on and wondered . . . I mean, you've been standing here a long time. . . ."

"If you would guard the path, just in case somebody else gets up . . ." I let out a sigh. What the hell, Louisa already knew

I was spineless. "I cannot walk through that door in the middle of the night."

"I'd be afraid to *crouch*," she said. "Snakes have been seen only on the outside, though. Would it help if I checked inside first?"

I nodded my humiliated head.

As we walked back to our hammocks, I asked my new friend about her wakefulness. She loved to hear the night sounds, she answered. She loved to lie awake all night listening.

In my agitation, I had hardly heard them. "Do they tell you anything?" I asked, hoping for some secret to navigate this trip, this life.

Louisa laughed. "Not yet, but they keep away loneliness." She walked in silence a minute, before adding, "They connect me to the earth."

Back in my hammock, I listened hard, but connection didn't come.

chapter 14

WHEN I WAS A LITTLE GIRL, MY HAIR, THOUGH CUT short, was always tangled. My mother or sister would brush it and I would cry. Back then, I remember coming across pictures in an old book depicting bodies writhing in hell. Shortly afterward I saw a television show in which an earthquake caused pandemonium in a city. The pain of tangles, the writhing, and the turmoil converged for me in the word chaos, a state I spent many years and a great amount of time and energy trying to avoid. Yet here I was in the epitome of chaos—the jungle.

Despite my insomnia, I woke early enough to spy Ruth Raleigh applying lipstick, blush, and eye makeup—mascara in the Amazon! I might be a coward but I was not absurd. From now on I would be Nature Woman incarnate, I decided as I stretched my back and shoulder muscles, stiff from the night in the hammock.

My new determination to find my inner Amazon caused a remarkable lessening of fear and squeamishness. I, too, began to take notice of the wonders on the forest floor—its teeming life, the treasure trove of medicinal plants, the myriad hiding places. I relished the dulcet hum of afternoon rain on the forest's canopy and the sanctuary of the forest itself after a hike in the morning's sun. I listened for howler monkeys, tried to pick up the scent of their dung as Louisa had taught us. I learned to distinguish birds and their calls, at least some of them.

On one hike, I was as alarmed as Wilson when we learned that insects and bees did not like to cross open spaces, and even a narrow road cleared through trees could limit their movement.

"Do you think it's their fear of the unknown?" I whispered to Wilson, not wanting to interrupt Seth.

Wilson shook his head no, then grinned at me and mumbled, "Maybe."

Whatever the reason, insects stayed close to "home," cross-pollination lost out, and neither side of the road had all the usual vital herbs and plant materials needed to make medicines. One narrow road meant some insects didn't have the food sources to live, which then threatened the animals that survived on the insects. A domino reaction. And an urgent situation. It occurred to me that I had cut more than one swath through my own being. The roads in me separated Michelle from Daisy from Mickey, who seemed to be waving worriedly at one another across the divides.

THE RAIN, the heat, the pulse of nature had an effect on Wilson, too. We were exploring again with Seth, who was giving us a tour through a tall-grass prairie his foundation operated as an experiment in land use. Wilson leaned over to me and whispered, "Let's slip away tonight."

As much as I missed him, I had developed a healthy respect for this wilderness. Love in the forest, night or day, seemed much too dangerous a proposition. "Seth told us not to go off alone," I said.

"What?" Seth called back from his place up ahead.

"Nothing," I said loudly. "Wilson is contemplating an unguided expedition."

"We'll be with each other," Wilson continued softly. "Come on, Mickey. It's that or a ruckus in your hammock as soon as the snoring starts."

"She *is* loud, isn't she? That could be a challenge worth undertaking," I mused aloud. And a way of serving Ruth Raleigh final notice, I thought.

"What's all this coy stuff?" he asked, which I translated as, *Don't I excite you anymore?* Did love always make people as insecure as the two of us? I squeezed Wilson's hand.

"After lunch, then," I said. "I'll figure out something."

"Famous last words," he retorted, and walked ahead, leaving me to remember that I was hot and thirsty and had not come up with any way around his marriage proposal. Obviously he had not forgotten my onetime, sort-of promise—had, instead, taken hold of that small lifeline of hope that I had tossed. Now, what kind of cockamamie problem solving could I come up with for an afternoon screw?

AFTER LUNCH, while the others read or snoozed or swam, Wilson and I snuck into the canopy of the forest—down one path, then another path, then one more. In my anxiety to find the perfect spot, I led us, carefully keeping track of the rights and lefts for our return. As I started to make one more left turn, I felt a tug on the back of my shirt.

"Hey, lady, I know there must be a body under these clothes," Wilson said. "Let's find out." He swung me around and pulled my body close to his, then leaned down to kiss my eyes, my lips.

I clung to Wilson's buttocks as his hands found my breasts. "Lean against that tree," I whispered to him. Kneeling down, but with my eyes cast up, I did make one plea: "Watch for creepy-crawlies. Other than the obvious."

"Is this a game? Come while I'm on bug alert? Besides, I want this for both of us." He tried to pull me up.

I squirmed away. "You can make it up to me later."

"You said you were starved—your 'very own river of hunger.'" His lips had found my neck, below my earlobe.

"I am, but I don't . . . I mean, I really cannot be on bug alert myself. I cannot possibly make love outside!"

"You could at home," he reminded me.

"That tree didn't hold snakes and—"

"Don't be too sure," he interrupted.

"Wilson, honey, I just cannot."

"Not even for a quickie?"

"Really quick?"

"Really quick."

I sighed and gave in to his tongue in my ear. I felt the bark imprinting designs on my back and then soon forgot my discomfort as Wilson skillfully brought me to sheer pleasure. How could I resist him? Nature Woman returned in all her glory.

THE SAME COULD NOT be said of my performance on our way back to the camp. As we walked side by side, arms around each other's waist, our four feet squeezed into a path made for only two, Wilson said lightly, "Let's get married in the Amazon."

I smiled up at him. "It wouldn't count back home."

"Then let's get married back home." His husky voice made no pretense at lightness this time.

Mine did. "Marriage is a highly overrated commodity. Haven't you heard?"

He let go of my waist and stepped ahead of me on the path.

"Wilson, wait up!" I called as he began walking faster. He stopped but didn't turn around. I stepped in front of him, held his face between my hands. "Wilson Collins, I love you. I love you so much. Please," I pleaded, "just let me love you." I paused. "For now."

His jaw clenched, he moved away from me. We walked into camp, all signs of ardor vanished. He would grab no more meaningless lifelines, and he was right. I had been a jerk for dangling them.

RUTH RALEIGH HAD a sixth sense. All evening her breathy "Oh Wilsons" dotted the conversation, and Oh Wilson, the arboreal portion of the afternoon evidently forgotten, relished every breathy murmur from her mouth. He responded in a shy, charming—maddening—way. Though why would he not? I asked myself. I knew he wasn't doing it to make me jealous. I collapsed back into Caipirinhas, and Wilson maintained a formal mien toward me.

Morning brought no improvement in his mood, so I suggested another tryst in the woods. His response: a distant "Maybe later."

Taking advantage of Wilson's disaffection, now available for all to see, Ruth monopolized what little time she hadn't already claimed under the guise of turning Texas—Oh Wilson's corner of it—into a rain forest. I hated Ruth Raleigh.

Not narrow roads but whole continents separated me now from the rest of my life. As Michelle and Daisy, at least I had enough sense to maintain boundaries of propriety. But Mickey was out of control. Mickey drank Caipirinhas like water at lunch and stuffed herself with the *feijoada*, the fish, the bread, the crème brûlée at dinner.

Drinking through lunch, however, turned out to be a blessing—of sorts. At least it helped to cushion the next assault. Two days later, Wilson took me for a walk. Straight out he told me that I would be returning to Manaus with the crew while he, Ruth, Seth, and the head cameraman traveled on to another camp. I demanded to go with him.

"There isn't enough room in the van. I told you that."

"Ruth Hot Pants told *you* that."

"Count the seats yourself, Mickey. As it is, we're squeezed. They hadn't originally planned on even me going."

I hated how his voice softened in direct proportion to my loudness. "I'll bet they hadn't!"

"What's that supposed to mean?"

"Ruth Raleigh has you under her thumb."

"You're not making sense," Wilson replied, this time with an edge of his own. "I thought you'd be pleased. It's the best indication yet that they've decided on the center. You know how much it matters to me. And you, too, I thought."

"It does. It does matter. But you matter much more, you jerk."

"Then marry me, Mickey. Marry me now." His hands remained clenched by his sides.

I hesitated, fumbled, but couldn't say the words he so desperately wanted to hear. Wilson's face and shoulders drooped, and I wanted to cry.

"All right, Mickey," he said. "I accept your reasons, whatever they are, but we don't have anything left to discuss."

I had expected him to deflate. I'd expected that sometime in the future, all passion spent, parting would take its natural course. But not now.

"Not now," I said.

"Now," he answered with more gentleness but no less determination. "I want you gone from Manaus when I get back in two days and gone from Rollins when I get home next week."

"You would stay in Manaus without me?" My voice sounded small. We had planned to linger there for a few romantic days after everyone else left.

"I want to do some sight-seeing," he said flatly. "I told you that."

"You're staying with Ruth. That's why you're driving me away. Admit it!"

"Ruth Raleigh is a twit. I have never been interested in twits, in bed or otherwise." Wilson turned back toward the camp.

I could not move, did not care if I ever found my way back. Let the jaguars and snakes have me, it would serve him right.

Just as Wilson began to veer out of sight, he turned around. "For the record, I did not plan to drive you away. I lost my wife. I lost my son. I needed to know I wouldn't lose you. I hoped you felt the same. You don't, and I can't see any reason to prolong my misery."

His prideful back broke my heart. His words brought me shame.

MY LAST NIGHT in Manaus, I excused myself from the remaining crew, who had planned to party. "A headache," I begged off. "I forgot my hat and walked in the sun today."

Room service that night consisted of Caipirinhas à la carte. Maybe the staff would think the señorita was having a party. Maybe the señorita was. The next morning, too hungover to pack, I tried the hair-of-the-dog remedy, ordering up a Bloody Mary and a club sandwich, then ordering another of each. Sufficiently revived, I decided to tour the newly restored Opera House, the grandest jewel of Manaus's colonial era, when rubber barons, many of them European, ruled.

"Is one hundred years old," the taxi driver announced.

"I hope I endure half as long," I answered as I got out in front of a well-scrubbed late-nineteenth-century facade, complete with dome, balustrades, and fanciful friezes. Inside, an English-speaking guide ushered me from the marble-encased lobby into the churchly hush of the theater with its plush red seats contributed by the French. The young guide in her trim navy skirt and white blouse pointed to the painted dome. "That's on canvas. The Italians painted it in their own country and shipped it over," she said. "The stage curtain was sent by the English."

"A Continental cooperation?" I asked, thinking of Michelle and Steve and Daisy and Wilson and Mickey.

"I suppose there was a certain amount of friendly rivalry," the woman answered, smiling. "Their wealth was staggering. The colonialists sent their laundry to England."

"Can you imagine the smell?" I asked. "Those women in their weeks-old petticoats and layers of silks and taffeta." We laughed. "Those poor singers and actors—trying to perform! And the peasants in the streets and the fields. They had to carry the whole damned civilized society on their backs." I waved my arms about the room. "All this in the name of a culture in peril of obliteration by . . . by . . . nature." I finished in a half-sob. The guide stared, but I was lost in forest vines and dangerous animals and sultry nights.

Later, on the balcony of my hotel room, I shared my sorrow with a couple of Caipirinhas and a glorious sunset rebounding off the river, all those reds, golds, blues, and an ache that began in my throat and traveled through my body. Nothing should be this beautiful, I thought. Nothing stays this way. I closed my eyes.

THE NEXT MORNING, I spent a long, long time in the shower pretending I was still Nature Woman of the rain forest—a life force, destructive, regenerative. I would be strong, move on. I dried off resolutely, then caught sight of myself in the mirror. Was that me? All those curves. I looked like I'd grown another dress size. And what was there to wear? My camp clothes were smelly, and last night I had spilled a drink on my one dress.

I sat on the bed and felt sorry for myself. Wilson had never loved me. He abandoned me as soon as he didn't need me anymore. I knew all along that he would leave me. I began to cry. Knew all along that his love was too good to be true. All the frogs and the monkeys in the forest couldn't change my destiny to be unloved by Wilson. He was the ant that wouldn't cross the road. No, I was the ant. My head throbbed. Oh, poor insects! The room began to spin again and I wept until I fell asleep and when I woke I cried again. The sweet alcohol sloshed in a fragile cage, my glass heart. I paced and cried and knew I had no one to blame but myself for my fool's game.

· · ·

WHEN WILSON ARRIVED, he found a half-eaten tray of food, a room littered with glasses and bottles, and me—still half drunk. "I couldn't leave," I sobbed through fingers splayed across my mottled face. "I tried. I couldn't. I can't exist without you."

Wilson only stood warily by the door.

"Wilson," I gulped. "Will you marry me?"

I was drunk, but I meant it. Wilson was silent for an entire two minutes. His face showed nothing. He stood stiffly, his hands in fists by his sides. At attention. A guard at Buckingham Palace. Was he looking for a way out? My terror did not abate, even when he folded me in his arms.

WILSON, SENTIMENTAL BUT no fool, understood that speed was of the essence. Once our plane touched down in Texas, he found us a flight to Vegas. There we checked into the Bellagio, where brides and grooms and assorted tourists posed to snap pictures of one another in front of flagrant reproductions and glittering facades. Threading our way through a sea of blackjack tables and roulette wheels and jangling slot machines, I wondered if the gamblers in their Bermuda shorts and wordy T-shirts understood the odds stacked against them, hoping against reason. Marriage.

Once situated upstairs, Wilson opened the yellow pages. "How about the Divine Madness Fantasy Wedding Chapel?" he asked. "Or the Drive-Up Wedding Window?"

"Divine Madness suits me," I answered, almost smiling.

"There's a priest on the hotel staff, too," said Wilson, looking at the directory of hotel services and amenities.

"The Liberace Museum, that's where I want to get married," I heard myself say.

"You do?"

"My mother loved Liberace," I said. "She considered him cultured."

Wilson kissed me sweetly. "Do you know that's the most you've ever told me about your mother?"

"We don't have to be married there," I amended, wondering what perverse devil in me had pulled forth that request.

"You bet we do." Wilson was all energy and excitement. He tore out with a promise of a speedy return. "And don't worry about your clothes," he called over his shoulder. "I'm buying you a dress."

THE BRIDE WORE ORANGE, as in Day-Glo. A stretchy, short dress, two sizes too small. The sales clerk, perhaps mistaking Wilson for a pimp, had also sold him strappy stiletto plastic sandals to complement the dress. To top it off, I clutched a busy bouquet of orange lilies, red carnations, and yellow roses. Still, I did fit right in with the rhinestone and red velvet and blue satin capes. Oddly enough, I felt I had finally found my true home. My gaudy inner child was all for costume.

The justice of the peace, dressed in a sky-blue satin suit that also suited the decor, busied himself behind his podium, which was actually a plastic box encasing the largest rhinestone in the world. I eyed Wilson warily. Although he wore his usual navy jacket and gray slacks and his hair still curled a little behind his ears, my intended bore no resemblance to the tradition-bound, careful-with-his-money Wilson I had come to know and love.

I leaned into him and whispered, "Are you Wilson Collins?"

He laughed, not taking my question seriously, although I had meant him to. I pondered why Wilson thought of me as an orange person. The color accentuated the sallowness of my skin.

Our marriage interlocutor's mouth opened and closed. He must have been talking. I was sandwiched between the maid of honor—a volunteer at the museum—and Wilson. Civilization, such as it was, existed by force of sheer will and, without vigilant attending, would be overrun. I thought of the desert sifting through the cracks of Vegas, the jungle vines swallowing our camp.

Wilson nudged my arm. The maid of honor crossed herself, causing me to wonder if that meant I was involved in some kind of religious ceremony. If so, was I in even more trouble? Wilson nudged me again.

"Mickey, kitten?" He was smiling.

"I'm sick. We have to go now," I whispered.

"Just as soon as you say, 'I do,'" he whispered back, both a furrow and a grin on his face.

"I do."

The justice smiled, the woman smiled, I smiled.

"You may kiss the bride," the man in the sky-blue suit said.

"Are you up to it?" Wilson asked solicitously.

I nodded yes vigorously.

I loved Wilson's ardor, his innocence, his devotion, his spirit, his courage. And I'd found courage, too. Indeed, I had. With no more thought, I threw my arms around his neck.

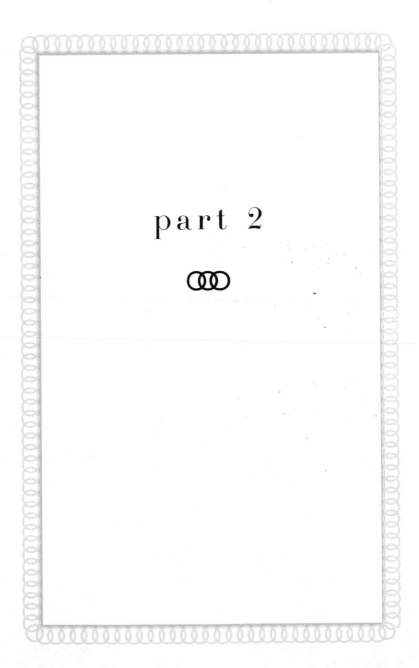

part 2

chapter 15

I LOVED WILSON. I LOVED STEVE. I'D LEAVE STEVE. I had to leave him. I would ask him for a divorce as soon as possible. As soon as I could muster up the courage. Well, at least as soon as he returned to the States. In the meantime, at Wilson's house in Rollins, Texas, I willed a stillness in time. And in this way, I continued to live my days in happiness and my nights in lust.

When I didn't do local consults or fly to a lecture, I spent whole trancelike mornings in what became habit: washing and fluffing my hair, touching objects Wilson had touched, putting on makeup and a clingy dress for lunch. When Wilson returned at noon, we ate and touched and anticipated evenings. Nearly always I took a nap, waking only in time to fix one of his favorite suppers the days I let Helen off early or to feast on one of her meals on the days she stayed. All the pressures and years of wanting dissolved into a radiant peacefulness that wrapped itself around me. Even a five-day trip to New York to check in with my office turned out fine, my leaving our easiest yet. "I only needed to know you were coming home," Wilson explained.

On my return he surprised me with a room on the third floor of the house that he had transformed into a special office—for me. "Nobody ever comes up here—the whole floor is yours if you want it," he said. The room, which Wilson had painted a pale yellow, suited me exactly. Not a Daisy yellow, but close enough.

Like so much else about my Texas life, the room inspired columns. I wrote one on the felicity of the color palette: "If there's no room of your own, why not try a color? A tint, a glaze, can brighten any wall. . . ." Virginia Woolf probably rolled over in her grave, but then again, maybe a pale yellow room would have been an effective antidote to the dank British countryside.

I made lists of titles: "Shelf Life: Has It Hung Around Too Long?"; "Fortunate Confusion: The Path to Creative Solutions"; "Hedonism: Worth the Try?" My wiser self nixed that last one. I could easily have spent days on end writing, reworking lectures, checking in with the Texas medical supply company to unravel its gnarly and antiquated personal communications system. I found I was less strident and more forgiving on the job. With the medical supply firm, for instance, I suggested that they not discard any old ideas, just put them to the side for the time being. That was certainly working for me.

Of course, once our friends discovered Wilson and I had gotten married, Rollins was at our doorstep. At first, I was beside myself, but Wilson relished the attention. He was proud of me and wanted the world, his world, to know it. I gave in and enjoyed being a bride, having never had the opportunity the first time around. The parties were fun. The gifts, however, made me flush—about the only thing that did.

Before long I resumed my occasional late-afternoon tea-cozies, as I thought of my conversations with my women friends. I loved my time with them. Having never "hung out" in my life, I found their camaraderie a steadying force. I looked to our conversations as a way to ground myself because, in truth, I was in the midst of performing a high-wire act, each foot balancing precariously on a thin steel cable.

Soon the carefully constructed equilibrium I'd concocted began to fray at the edges. When Steve sent me one of his sweet e-mails—*Mrs. Banyon. How goes work? Cast a good spell my way. Your devoted disciple, Steve*—I felt I might topple over and prayed a net would catch me.

The salutation alone set my temple pulsing. I was indeed Mrs. Banyon—and Mrs. Collins. How much prison time do they give first offenders? I wondered. Betrayal, the subject at hand, got more and more confusing. How could I continue as Daisy? As often as I kept assuring myself that, as Daisy, I could discreetly become the wife of a Texas naturalist, another part of me knew full well that Steve was bound to find out. My head throbbed as I tried to work out the overlaps. Lindy and Sonia already knew about Daisy. What about Amy Ward in my Texas office? How would I keep her from meeting Wilson? Could I keep Wilson as secret as I hoped? Really?

My very oxygen as Daisy depended on exposure, not a lot to be sure, but some, and in my private lives, any at all was dangerous. I needed to get my wits about me. To cut Daisy down to size was to deny some essential thing, some vital link to the world of possibility, and to trigger the ruination of the rest of me.

It's not as if I ever aspired to being a bigamist, but who hasn't fantasized about how else they might live? Or dreamed of other lives they could have had? If only. I had fallen down the rabbit hole of *if only. If only*, my personal refrain. *If only*, as I hoped for the right door to lead me into the light.

· · ·

SO IT WAS with real interest that I listened to Lindy Akers and Sonia Sartin discuss Anaïs Nin one afternoon. We'd finally found a window in all our schedules to meet for lunch and had convened afterward for coffee in Sonia's library, when Lindy noticed a first edition of Nin's published diaries on one shelf. Sonia confessed to being a fan when she was young, "until I discovered she lied." Sonia twanged *lied* into a four-syllable word and shook her head, laughing at her own naïveté.

"Didn't she write erotica?" I asked, vaguely remembering a book of hers being passed around in high school.

"Honey, she *lived* erotica," Lindy answered, flipping through the book. "I've read a biography about her. I keep looking for role models," she quipped.

"Well, if incest and bigamy suit you . . ." Sonia's voice trailed off into a smile.

"Why would I ever want two husbands? One was bad enough," Lindy said, snapping the book shut quietly.

"I wish you'd give someone else a try," Sonia scolded her.

Lindy sighed and put the book back on the shelf. "Nin's husbands and lovers aren't the point here. I liked the way she dared to carve a life for herself."

"Life carved her, too," Sonia said.

"But it was a conceived life. Wrong choices, maybe, and for the wrong reasons . . ."

"Or reasons she didn't understand," Sonia interjected, "meaning they weren't choices after all."

"Bigamy?" I heard a waver in my voice. "Did you say she was a bigamist?"

"Yeah, she had a husband of long standing," Lindy explained, "and then sometime after her affair with Henry Miller, she married a young gun on the West Coast."

"Without divorcing the first. Went on for years and years," Sonia added, her graceful long arms folded loosely across her stomach as she sat in a leather Eames chair, her feet tucked up.

"Could I borrow that biography?" I asked Lindy.

"Even the luckiest woman alive wants to partake in the fantasy," Lindy said in her driest drawl.

"No! " My voice hiccupped strangely and I made myself calm it. "My curiosity is piqued, that's all."

"Nin can be fascinating," Sonia conceded. "She had quite a cult following in her later years."

"Was she happy?" I asked, although I was pretty sure I knew the answer. There was no way in hell Nin could have been too happy for long with all that running back and forth, all the tending to, and worry. I put this out of my mind.

"From time to time, I suppose." Lindy shrugged. "Personally, I try to stay too busy to take a happiness pulse. It's a troublemaker. You start thinking you should be happier and before long you end up—"

"Daring too much?" Sonia finished for her, teasing.

ON THE WAY HOME I panicked. Even if I weren't a bigamist, I would end up paying big time for all this happiness I swooned around in. As much as I dreaded telling Steve I wanted a divorce, I had to do it soon. I wished he'd clinch the Hong Kong deal already and come back home. I wasn't fit for a life of crime, duplicity, or paranoia. I was convinced that my moment of reckoning lurked around every corner.

If I broached a divorce in the right way, Steve might not necessarily even consider it bad news. In some ways, we'd become strangers, I would argue. Without the expectations and complications of our marriage, we could be real friends again, over time. After all, we had to admit to a paucity of emotion in our marriage. *A paucity of emotion*—could that be a title for a column? *No, and not for Steve, either,* Daisy's voice answered.

For everybody's sake, the sooner I ended this mess, the sooner all of us would be happier. Otherwise, I might end up with a jail sentence.

MY RESOLVE TOOK care of itself. An e-mail from Steve came in overnight: *In Paris for two days and leave tomorrow for New York before returning to Hong Kong. Will you, by any chance, be in the city? Or, better yet, could we meet somewhere restful? If not, I'll meet you wherever you are. I await your answer. Truly yours, S.*

In all our years together, he had never once mentioned joining me on one of my business trips. He was either desperate or he had good news. Whichever, my heart sank. I hadn't meant *now.* Not this minute. Not so suddenly. Steve was my husband and, arguably, my oldest friend. Make up your mind, I chided myself—stranger or oldest friend.

I picked up my bedside notebook and saw a note I had scribbled in it earlier for a column: *Carve out the life you want. Don't cede your power to others.* With a flick of the wrist, I hurled the spiral notebook across the room.

chapter 16

STEVE AND I SUNNED AT AN OUTDOOR CAFÉ ON Madison Avenue. It was pleasant, so much cooler than Texas. I drank coffee; he sipped Calvados. This was our third café of the day and his second Calvados, reserved in the past as an after-dinner drink. In between cafés we'd strolled through Central Park and into the Whitney Museum, where Pollock's busy splatters and de Kooning's jagged women confronted us. I hurried us by a Rothko, thinking its somber, meditative mood was too close to Steve's own emotional palette at the moment. Did we respond to the Abstract Expressionists because they spoke a language of the heart that we dared not speak between ourselves? Or had our marriage itself become an abstract expression? Our life together was built around a loss, an open wound sealed with scar tissue. I kept waiting for the right moment to reveal itself when I might broach the subject of divorce with Steve, but when I looked over at him, I could tell something was already terribly wrong. He had been brooding since his arrival the night before, and I was worried.

Did he know something? Was he ill? Had he lost his job? His gauntness and weariness made him look so much older than usual. I put aside my own distress over the idea of ending our marriage. "You all right?" I had asked three times, but whatever was happening, I wasn't to be privy to it. The night before, he'd turned on his side away from me and was snoring within minutes. I didn't know if he was really that tired or just depressed. Now he was making even less effort to hide his black mood. I was frightened.

"Steve, please tell me what's going on. Is it the contract?" Forcing this discussion would upset him even more, but he needed to talk whether he wanted to or not. Part of him did want to, I could tell. "Please, talk to me," I begged.

"This damn job—I'm exhausted. I've got no time for anything," he answered, as if I were an idiot not to understand.

I breathed a huge sigh of relief and laughed out loud. By his expression, I might as well have slapped his face.

"I'm sorry," I said, "but you've been looking so sad. I know you're going through a rough patch with your job, but it isn't life-threatening or anything."

"Not anything, just everything! I'm spending eighteen hours a day on this case, Michelle, and there's a good chance I've failed." For emphasis he slammed down his glass and sloshed Calvados onto his shirt cuff and coat sleeve. A cleaning frenzy followed.

"That drink won't stain your clothes or your hand," I reassured him, but to maintain my calm and foster his, I ordered another round for us both.

"This suit cost a fortune, you know," Steve said after downing what was left of his drink.

"The shirt, too," I added. Steve had suits and shirts custom-made in London. With Daisy's practical nature, I thought the suits a waste of money and the fittings a waste of energy, but as Michelle I certainly liked having a dapper husband.

"A striking couple," everyone said of the two of us, though at the moment, with my extra pounds, I wasn't sure I was holding my own in that equation. The fact that Steve hadn't noticed indicated his extreme mental and emotional disarray. Other husbands—Wilson, for instance—might go months without noticing the condition of their wife's clothes, but not Steve. His fine sense of the visual assessed me just as it did a piece of art or the good lines of a car or a table setting. Having heard other women complain of inattention, I honestly didn't know which was worse, too little or too much.

"You're doing too much," I told him, risking further annoyance.

"Since when was 'too much' a criteria for either of us?" Steve replied, rising to the bait.

"Since it turned you into a wreck."

"I am—" He caught himself ready to slam the glass down again, then modulated the drink and his voice. "I am not a wreck."

"Well, you're not a failure, either. Even if you should louse up the deal—and I can't believe you will—that won't make you a failure. It makes a loused-up deal."

"Never mind," he said, tossing back his third drink and standing. "We need to change clothes before the opera."

"You gulped that down," I pointed out as we headed toward home.

"What are you talking about?"

"That drink. You never gulp." I heard my Prada flats click against the pavement as I doubled-stepped to keep up with him.

"Oh, for God's sake, Michelle!"

"And since you don't curse or lose your temper with me, something must be really wrong. Why continually push yourself? Why not let things be for a little while?" Out of shape, I breathed hard to keep up with his furious pace.

Slowing down, he gave me a sidelong glance and a little

smile. "Who am I talking to? Not the Michelle I know." Alarms rang. Of course, he teased, but I made a mental note to be more careful.

THE OPERA WAS Gounod's *Faust* (another who had sold his soul) and our dinner afterward went well enough. Steve actually kissed me on the taxi ride home. Our earlier heated conversation upset us both, for in all these years of marriage, we'd probably exchanged cross words fewer than two dozen times.

Steve pulled me close. "Thank you for coming. I hope I didn't mess you up too much by demanding this visit," he apologized.

"You didn't demand anything," I said, overcome with affection for him, this steadfast, troubled husband. I patted his chest with the flat of my hand. "I'm glad you asked," I added. At that moment I meant it. He was my first love, my steady love. How had I ever thought a divorce would be best for everyone? I wondered.

Maybe the fight had been good for us after all. Once in bed, I propped myself up against the pillows. Steve lay with his head in my lap and began to speak—so low I had to bend close to hear. "I can't think of a good way to tell you this, Michelle, so I won't even try." He paused only a half-beat, then burst out, "I've screwed up the deal. It could cost me everything."

"Of course it won't," I responded automatically. "If you don't get the promotion this time around, you will the next."

"You don't understand. I overreached," he insisted. "It's too involved to explain, but I wanted this to work so badly, I got impatient and then reckless. I couldn't stop myself."

I could certainly relate to what he said, but he had to be exaggerating. Responsibility hung too heavily on Steve for him to do such a thing. Still, not so long ago, the same might have been said of me.

It took the rest of the night for him to explain why: how the telecommunications deal seemed to be falling apart, how his own miscalculations contributed to the mess, how even his partnership in the firm was in jeopardy.

"When we saw each other last, you steeled me and gave me some perspective on the situation," he told me. He folded his hands on his stomach and stared at the ceiling. "When I returned to Hong Kong, I thought I could patch the deal back together. I also hoped to work out a fallback if I couldn't make the original deal work. I kept thinking that with a little more effort and money I could salvage something out of it. Or at least restore what had been agreed to. Michelle, I wanted this more than anything," he finished, looking up at me quickly.

Something about his explanations so far made me feel we were walking around a big hole pretending it didn't exist.

"What exactly did you do that was so horrible? Lie? Cheat? Whatever happened, I understand. Believe me."

Steve moved away from me and sat up, crossing his arms across his chest. "I broke the law," he said, his voice rough. "I violated the Foreign Corrupt Practices Act—out-and-out bribery, if you must know," he said, finally giving up the game.

I regarded him steadily, waiting for more.

"Look, in that part of the world, it's part of how deals happen," he said. "But I don't mean the more-or-less official bribes. This time I went beyond the usual 'commissions' and convinced Brisco to commit his company's money to it. I was so damn sure this would work and we'd get it back a hundred times over! Except everything's collapsing and there's no way to hide what I've done.

"If I just hadn't been so certain! When I'm dealing with those corrupt-practices statutes, I know I'm walking into a minefield and that a misstep is always possible." He reached for my hand to hold but still wouldn't look me in the eye. "Fool that I am, though, I believed my tracks couldn't be traced. In this case, reasoning and determination turned out to be futile in one case and disastrous in the other."

I felt the weight of Steve's hand in my own. I didn't know what to do for this man, so harsh a judge of himself. I never had. In the past, he sometimes hobbled his brilliance with an extreme sense of prudence. And who was I to judge if now, in one grand gesture, he'd decided to risk it all?

"We'll find a way," I finally responded lamely, and leaned over to kiss his forehead.

"I'm a failure and stand to lose everything. There could be an investigation. . . ." His voice trailed off. "Anyway, whatever happens, I've got to reimburse Brisco's company close to a million dollars, preferably before they figure it out themselves." His shoulders slumped.

"Your yearly bonus alone comes to well over a half a million," I reminded him. "And they're grown-ups. Surely they'll understand you did this for them." I turned his face toward me. "You shouldn't dismiss what's happened, but you can't drive yourself crazy with guilt. I'm not trying to minimize this, but I can't imagine they won't understand once you've explained yourself."

"These people relied on my judgment! I feel a moral obligation, don't you understand that? It's over, Michelle. The best scenario is that I'll be out on the street." He rubbed his eyes with the heels of his hands. I kneeled next to him and kissed his fingers.

"We'll survive," I tried to reassure him. "We'll use your money to pay off whatever debts you feel responsible for and support ourselves with the earnings of D.S. Enterprises until you can set up a firm of your own. We won't starve. "

Whether it was the idea of reducing his standard of living or living off me that horrified him the most, I didn't know, but whichever, he let forth a long, low moan and turned away. More than anything, I wanted to comfort him. I wondered how much money I could make if I revved up my lecture schedule even more. Would I make enough to give him some, if it really came to that? Whatever it took, my first priority right now was to restore Steve to his usual triumphant self. I couldn't bear to see him like this.

AT WORK, I FOUND loads of "stuff" to keep me occupied— nothing urgent, but it still required my attention. I didn't mind; the activity felt good. Nobody organized better than Daisy. Apparently, these days nobody was writing a column as good as Daisy's, either. So Gloria said, anyway. She sat on the edge of my desk, her toned brown leg swinging back and forth. She walked to work nearly every day from Harlem, her only exercise, but it must have been about seven miles and it certainly paid off.

Beth sat on her haunches and busied herself with straightening the lower drawer of my filing cabinet, which did not need straightening. She liked to stay busy, too. I propped my elbows on my desk.

"You keep hitting nerves," said Gloria. "Your ideas have become so down to earth. I loved this one—'When Deep Breaths Don't Help.'" She flipped through the magazine where she'd flagged the page. "My mother really related to that. And this one, too," she said, picking up another volume. "'Shoulda Woulda Coulda: The Procrastinator's Lament.'"

"I know this sounds heretical," Beth said, "but sometimes I find it amazing that anyone anywhere cares about another piece of advice on organizing and simplifying."

I made a fist stab to my heart. "Hey, you're hitting us where we live!"

"Amen," Gloria echoed.

"You'd think people would have figured it out by now," Beth said. She certainly knew all the rules that fit *her* sense of order: no makeup, a simple diet, few possessions, a clear desk, and a clear mind. She believed in emotional as well as material frugality. She also believed in tradition: polishing and using silver, setting a table with butter plates, panty hose in summer, freshly ironed linen handkerchiefs. The rest she either dismissed or refused to consider.

"It's like a diet," said Gloria. "Surely the next one is going to do the trick. Why do you buy a new lipstick? To perk you up. And if you're perkier, you are different from the way you were ten minutes ago, and if that's the case, you are on your way to becoming somebody or something else. That's why Daisy will go on forever," Gloria said, pleased about her job security.

I hoped so. I hoped Daisy Strait Enterprises could become hot enough to bring in a lot more money. Bigamy, however, would not provide me with a proper platform, I reminded myself. I thought of what I'd learned about Anaïs Nin from that biography I'd borrowed from Lindy, how she had ended up supporting her first husband with her writing when his fortunes fell. I admired her for that and would do the same for Steve, although I surely didn't need to live out any more lives.

With Steve in such bad shape, I cursed Mickey for not finding a way to stay with Wilson other than by marrying him. But second thoughts wouldn't help this situation one bit. After all, I had an obligation to reassure Wilson and meet his needs just as I had now to reassure Steve and meet his. While ministering to Steve, though, Wilson and Texas seemed very far away.

OVER THE NEXT few days, Steve's surface gloom lifted a bit, but that was small consolation. For my part, I spun through revolving doors of guilt, alarm, exasperation. To add to my uneasiness, I kept trying to reach Dottie with no luck. Finally I got one of her roommates, who evaded my questions as to where she might be and when she might return. Steve suggested she might have a new boyfriend, but I didn't like the tone of the evasions and hated leaving town without seeing or speaking to her. All I could hope was that her roommate wouldn't erase the many messages I left on their machine.

On my last afternoon with Steve, a heavy rain began to fall. "Maybe the airport will shut down and we can play hooky one more day," he said wistfully, even as we both packed to leave. If he had said that six months ago, I wondered, would I have been joyful? Or would it have been too late sixteen years ago? Would I have already grown restless to get to work? Because I had needed to deny negative feelings about our marriage so early on, I had no way of knowing if I had ever wanted more. Outside, a curtain of rain washed the tops of the dusty cars that moved with care down the street. I wished with all my heart I could go back to the naive oblivion I'd spent my life in up until now. Then my fury rose: Why had he waited so long to need me?

chapter 17

AS I RODE ONCE MORE DOWN THE DUSTY ROAD TO
Rollins, an eerie calm descended over me. Nin had pulled off
her double life, I told myself. For the moment, I could justify
not divorcing Steve. Yet when I thought of Wilson and me as
a unit—compartmentalized, sealed and secure—I had this
idea that now that we were married, we would live happily
ever after. I know that sounds ridiculous, but we were my
fairy tale, and I wanted to believe it. With Wilson, I felt more
content than ever.

On my arrival, Wilson and I fell into a pattern. He was
quiet and busy with trying to create a rain forest in the middle of a late-summer Texas drought. And I, to be the perfect
helpmate and atone for my absence and my postponed
divorce plans, helped him as much as I could on top of keeping up with my own work.

Now that I saw a need for a real breakthrough with my
business, Daisy Strait Enterprises became the linchpin to all
my endeavors. And I finally heard from Dottie via e-mail, so
that was one less worry. She said she was sorry to have missed
me and that she'd never gotten my phone messages, which I
found perplexing. But she was busy, she said, happy. And
she would keep in better touch, she promised. I chose to believe her.

With my blinders on, I hardly noticed anything amiss

between me and Wilson. What I didn't confront couldn't hurt me, a rule I had obviously adopted about my life in general. Besides, I had enough work to keep an army occupied. It took a lot of energy to keep up all this freedom.

Then, about ten days into all this, I got brought up short, and by my very own body.

I, Queen of the May in bed since our relationship began, couldn't think of anything new to do there. Part of Wilson's and my fun had been our sex life, or perhaps I should say, my sexual awakening. He was my excitement, my craving. It was as if we were the first people in the world to think of all those delightful positions. Did marriage have to take the bloom off so quickly? Perhaps we'd grown complacent. Perhaps neither of us had quite understood the importance of my lust. I did now. Without my fascination with the machinations of both our bodies, nothing much occurred. Without my boundless enthusiasm, Wilson's drive diminished, too. To compound our problem, neither of us spoke about it. Instead we continued to "do it," but with none of our old zest.

Wilson did not appear to mind so much. I even thought I detected a little relief. He had sometimes teased me about my sexual exuberance. I hadn't thought he really meant it. Now it seemed marriage had charged him up, all right, but for his work. He adapted. I did not. A neophyte to rapture, I parlayed the small inevitable diminishments that come with everyday life into catastrophic rejection. Incapable of ignoring his remoteness, I began to quarrel.

"You don't take me into consideration at all," I accused if he stayed an hour too long over an impromptu beer with a friend. "Of course I do," he protested, but I never believed him and he knew it.

"You never compliment my desserts anymore," I complained if he did not express his gratitude. Though Helen cooked most of our meals, I'd become the pie expert. "I eat them," he answered, looking puzzled and hurt. "The least you can do is apologize for leaving!" I'd shout after him if he had a bird emergency. It seemed to me the county was plagued by sick and abandoned raptors.

Sometimes we made up; sometimes we would spend the rest of the evening reading or working in silence.

When I complained that he was gone too much, he would point out, as one might to an unreasonable child, that I was often gone, too, and besides, after our trip to the Amazon, I knew that he had an extremely busy time ahead. "We're married now," he said one night, as if that explained everything.

So, while my constant griping led to even more withdrawal by Wilson, my sense of desertion increased my neediness. I continued to pick fights, to cling, to create scenes, never mind its negative effect. As miserable as I was, I can't say that some secret enjoyment wasn't involved, too. After all, I was playing notes in myself I had never known existed. Creating scenes called forth all kinds of inner drama. Some part of me relished trying out the new voices and stood back and applauded every time I became the wronged, tormented diva.

On some level I understood that I was making up for years of benign neglect by Steve. I'd sat on those emotions so well for so long, I didn't even know I had them. It was only thanks to Wilson's maturity and need of me that I didn't ruin the thing between us, despite all odds.

There were still good days when I felt neither needy nor panicked by what I'd done. I was even content with our more conventional sex life. On those days my spirit danced. I had Wilson, whom I loved, a sense of the land, a community, and new friendships. When I divorced Steve, then I would have no need to punish my libido with my guilt and perhaps no need to punish Wilson with my insecurities. Most days, though, I sorely tested Wilson's unconditional love with my erratic behavior, needing proof that somebody could love me even when I stopped being the good girl, the understanding wife.

THEN SOMEONE SHOT one of Wilson's beloved alligators, the one named Ally. She'd gotten herself off the center's grounds and into a downstream tributary of the creek. Wilson came home for lunch that day, something he seldom did anymore. Delighted with his unexpected return, I ran down from my attic room only to embrace a red-faced, furious Wilson. "Those sons of bitches! They killed Ally, who never hurt anybody. She was our only breeder. I know who did it. I *know*."

"Who?" I said.

"Joe Lyndon and his cronies. But the sheriff won't do a damn thing about it. 'Got no proof,' he says."

Wilson glowered and ate his ham-and-cheese sandwich. I did try to sympathize: "I know how proud you were of Ally." But sympathy infuriated him even more.

When his mood had not improved by evening, I tried another tack. "Can't you find another alligator?" I asked in my sweetest voice.

"That's not the point. These ignorant fools are afraid of them! Those creatures are part of the life cycle, they're part of life's mystery!"

"Mystery is overrated," I said as I climbed the stairs back up to the safe haven of my attic office. Only Daisy was level-headed these days.

Before I could shut the door, he called up, "Mickey? I'm sorry, honey. Come have a beer with me?" A pause. "Please?"

THE NEXT MORNING I awoke feeling lighter than I had in days. Spooned against my back, one arm flung across my hip, Wilson slept, and I lay still enjoying the moment. When I felt him harden against me, I turned toward him. As we kissed lazily, tongues lightly brushing, he opened one eye, then both eyes, wide. The next instant he was out of bed.

"My God! It's daylight!" he said half-accusingly.

"That's the general idea of mornings." I watched him fumble into his clothes. "Is there a fire you're attending or what?" I asked, more bemused than annoyed.

"What happened to the alarm? I've got men coming to dig another pond, and after that an eight-thirty conference call with Ruth. At nine-thirty I begin interviewing botanists—six botanists back to back—to find the right one to hire for this project. It couldn't be a worse day."

"And I thought I'd married into small-town life," I said, stretching lazily.

"This *is* small-town life, sweetheart. I led you astray." He leaned down to kiss me.

I clasped my hands around the back of his neck and pulled him toward me. Definitely aroused, I would settle for a quickie, but he gently unlocked my hands and whispered, "Later."

With that I threw back the covers and pulled on my jeans,

halfway hoping he'd tell me to crawl back in bed. He didn't. I thundered down the stairs to start the coffeemaker. Strange, but only then, with the pungent smell of coffee so thick around me, did I finally admit to myself that I had planned on the honeymoon never ending. As the heady aroma filled the room, I blinked back tears.

"THE LEAP OF FAITH: When Flying Feels Like Falling." "To Be or Not to Be: Ambiguity and Its Discontent." "Torn Between Two Loyalties: How to Deal with Competing Claims," I wrote, up in my sanctuary. Steve once told me the philosopher Isaiah Berlin considered this last topic to be one of the great tragedies of the human condition: How do we deal with contradictory claims of equal merit, claims on our souls? I rested my chin in my hand and stared at the computer screen, trying to focus. The human conditions that interested me most just now were one called "loyalty" and another called "ambiguity." And perhaps one called "fear."

"LOOK, HONEY, I know it's not always easy having a man around as much as Wilson is," Helen said one morning, to my surprise. For one thing, Wilson was hardly ever around as far as I was concerned. "I know what that's like. Sort of slows you down. I mean, now that Ben's retired, I'd go crazy if I didn't have this job to come to. The problem is every day is like Saturday. Use to be on Saturdays we'd piddle around together, get our chores done, maybe early evening do a little fishing out south of town. Nothing wrong with Saturdays except now there's no Monday."

Message delivered, Helen emptied the laundry hamper into her basket and left the room.

That evening over dinner, I suggested to Wilson that we take a short road trip to Dallas. "There's a David Smith exhibit that's supposed to be wonderful."

"David Smith?" said Wilson.

"The sculptor," I said.

"No time," Wilson answered, mashed potato in his mouth.

"So why can't we talk about it even if you won't go? Why can't we have conversations about art and life, the way we did in the beginning?"

"Did we talk about art and life?"

"Well . . . yes. Don't you remember? *Birds in Flight* . . . Brancusi?"

"I was trying to woo you, that's all." Wilson smiled at me, then bit into his sirloin beef.

"And I'm not worth wooing now?"

"I'm married to you now, Mickey."

"Damn marriage, then! And damn you!"

With great precision, Wilson put down his knife and fork, wiped his mouth, and got up and walked away.

I waited until he was in the shower to slip into our bedroom for my nightgown. I planned to sleep in the guest room. About the time I had settled in with a book, remembering how much I liked sleeping alone, Wilson, naked, crawled in beside me. "What if we go to that exhibit Tuesday afternoon, check into the Mansion, and have the most expensive dinner in town?"

"I would like that," I answered. Wilson looked so pleased with himself that I put my arms around him. He didn't let go of money easily. For him, this trip proposal was tantamount to offering me the Hope Diamond. Over the next several hours, our libidos behaved admirably. I hoped these exquisite moments wouldn't always be dependent on such dramatic foreplay. My nerves couldn't afford much more Sturm und Drang, even for great sex.

THE NEXT MORNING as I fixed his breakfast—Canadian bacon (so much leaner than regular bacon or sausage) and scrambled eggs (made with one whole egg and two beaten egg whites)—I decided Wilson and I had reached a turning point, and happy days were here again.

chapter 18

JUST WHO IS DAISY STRAIT AND WHY IS SHE SO Mum About Herself? When I walked in my office, the bold-faced headline screamed out at me from Page Six of the *New York Post.* Beth, who scanned the papers every morning, had left the spread open on my desk for me. Wow, Page Six—for an instant I was thrilled that I'd made the famous celebrity and society gossip page, where hoards of New Yorkers turned every morning for their scuttlebutt.

"The phones haven't stopped ringing!" Beth said excitedly when she rushed in.

"There's a rumor you don't even exist!" said Gloria, not far behind. My staff basked in the reflected glow of my new celebrity status.

"How did this happen?" I asked, sitting down and staring at the newsprint.

"We think maybe Pam leaked the story," said Gloria. "I suppose she wanted to stir up trouble, but this could be your big break."

Big break*up*, I thought to myself. I had to concentrate. On Daisy. On Mickey. On Michelle. Since arriving at La Guardia, Michelle had come back full force. I had to face the truth: I needed all aspects of my life. Those thirds made a whole for me. Daisy or Michelle or Mickey alone wasn't enough. Whoever I wasn't at the time, that's who I longed to be. Now London

Bridge could tumble down for all of me in one fell swoop, to mix some metaphors, which was the least of the mixing.

"Look, Daisy Strait Enterprises has nothing to hide," I proclaimed bravely. "Whatever happened to that interview I did for *Serendipity* a while back?" I asked. The journalist had talked to me for three hours and pestered my staff with questions for days afterward but nothing had come of it.

"I got the impression they tabled it," said Beth. "But I bet they'll run the story now."

I breathed deeply. "I'll talk to anyone. I have a message, sweet and simple. This company is about helping people have a better life. It takes all of us to get that job done. We are not based on the cult of personality," I declared. My troops looked on admiringly. I was quite pleased with myself.

"I'm not sure there's harm in discovering Daisy's true identity," Beth said tentatively. "I know you like your privacy. But it's not as if you're a common criminal or anything."

I swallowed twice before answering. "It's not about me, it's about the philosophy."

"It's the message, not the medium?" Gloria paraphrased.

"Exactly," I said. "I'd like to keep it that way."

"You're saying you *don't* want to jump on this?" said Gloria. "You don't want to try to get some mileage out of it?"

"I'd rather keep it simple," I said, smiling at the familiar Daisy phrase. "Go back to Texas and work from there. I don't want to participate in the cult of celebrity," I reiterated.

"It could be good for business, though," Gloria said pointedly, as if perhaps I'd forgotten.

"Daisy Strait is about acknowledging the struggle of everyone to become less encumbered. It's an ongoing process. What better way to extol my ideas than by living them?"

"Well," said Gloria, doubtfully, "maybe your reticence will add to your mystique. At least maybe we can get more bookings out of it."

I admit I felt good about finessing the situation, but I also knew it was a temporary solution. In a culture that thrived on sniffing out malingerers, even a no-nonsense efficiency consultant could become fodder if she had secrets she was hiding. How long could I go on dodging the spotlight when so much depended on stepping into it? For now I just hoped I'd been given a reprieve.

BACK IN TEXAS, though, the surprises didn't stop. Over dinner Wilson announced casually that he had mortgaged the farm to finance more upgrades and landscaping at the bird sanctuary. "We're too close to being chosen to let money get in our way," he said, apparently unfazed by what he'd done. If our trip to Dallas was the Hope Diamond, then this was the whole diamond mine. What had come over him?

I had the sinking feeling that I would spend the rest of my life supporting two husbands both emotionally *and* financially. His gamble could turn into a classic case of losing everything. We both knew that this television series was not a sure thing at all.

As I began clearing the table, Wilson rose to help me, a kind of apology on his part, but I insisted he finish up the mandarin chocolate soufflé. I needed a minute alone to sort my thoughts. For all practical purposes—as far as he knew, anyway—we were a team. We were married. I had worked like hell to help him with his campaign to fix up the bird sanctuary.

And I'd done more work on the house, too. You could

actually see the elegant eighteenth-century secretary now. I had hung an Andy Warhol print I bought in Dallas next to it and the effect had a certain wit. The same was true of his Victorian parlor, now host to a couple of Art Deco lamps and ashtrays that I had found in the clutter. I'd had fun playing with all the tastes abounding in these rooms, but it had taken a lot of effort. He should have told me he was planning to mortgage the farm. Wilson had let me down. He had held out on me, the same way Steve had. But just what, little lady, I asked myself, do you think you are doing to them?

OVER THE NEXT few weeks, the twin engines of guilt and necessity once again propelled me forward. I was determined to make everything right. I cooked okra and greens and roasts and sweet potato pies for supper on Helen's days off. Despite the influx of money from the refinanced farm, Wilson still needed more, and I redoubled my efforts to help him raise what we could to convince Green Works that the Collins Bird Sanctuary was the ideal Amazon setting. "Shouldn't they have decided by now?" I asked Wilson, as if I never had this problem. "What's taking so long?"

"They haven't received a final green light from the network," said Wilson. "We have to be patient."

Since it was especially politic for us to be a part of the community at this juncture, I accepted all dinner invitations and began to see another side of small-town closeness. Though everyone I knew in Rollins worked hard, nobody was as driven as Wilson, not so it showed, anyway. In this town, I came to understand, one must never appear too ambitious or too greedy—or in my case, too desperate.

Because of my contact with so many women, I also began to get some notion of just how difficult the lives of working women really were. All the streamlining strategies in the world couldn't relieve the inherent tension any more than telling people to cut back on friends and to control access could change those dynamics. Real friends, the kind I was discovering here in Rollins, provided nourishment and comfort and couldn't exist without cultivation.

If only I had more time. Of course, there was never enough of it. I labored long hours for Daisy Strait Enterprises and was pleased with my accomplishments. I picked up more consulting jobs for companies in the region and worked as usual on my column. If simple solutions weren't the whole answer, at least they supplied much-needed Band-Aids, those most unfairly maligned objects. Of course, I knew that had I followed the basic tenets of a simple life in the first place (one husband at a time, a focused life, a strictness of priorities), my morass would not exist.

I told myself that my problem was not the lack of strict priorities or focus but the presence of abundance. I wanted to shed nothing and keep everything, including Steve, if only that were possible. At this point in my ruminations, I would arch my back and move my head around, try to release some tension in my shoulders and tackle another column. *Guilt is the nemesis of simplification,* I must have written a dozen different ways.

I e-mailed Steve daily and checked in with Dottie from time to time. There were no "if only"s now, just "when"s and "then"s. When I figured out how to make more money. Then I could rescue Steve. Then I could divorce him. Then Wilson and I could live happily ever after. I'd have time to savor my new friendships, deepen old friendships, be a better aunt.

confessions of a bigamist

. . .

GRAYEST DAY in grayest town in grayest year of my life,
Dottie wrote me. *So gray, it's black. What's the point? Have
you figured it out, Aunt Michelle? By the way, I'm back home.
Daddy came for me. D.* I must have reread her words ten
times, feeling their heavy finality. Once again I couldn't help
but feel that I had failed her. Despite my best intentions, I had
not paid close enough attention.

I tried to remember how Dottie had looked the last time I'd
seen her, but couldn't think of anything out of the ordinary.
She'd seemed frail, sure, but then she always did. I'd gotten
used to it. All right, I ignored it. I'd decided that was how
dancers looked—lean and gaunt—and that she was a lot
tougher than I'd given her credit for earlier. I realized now
that I simply *wanted* her to be tougher. She always put up a
good front in person.

Although Dottie hadn't come right out and asked me to
come to Indiana, I took the plunge and made a reservation on
an early-morning flight. I felt responsible and negligent—I
wanted to make things right. When I called Andrea to tell her,
she sounded more than a little surprised at my announcement. Dottie sounded puzzled, too, but pleased. I'd never been
to Andrea's home, but it was as if an alien force had taken
over me, pushing me out Wilson's door.

"YOU SHITTIN' ME?" he said when I told him I had to leave
the next morning. The front porch swing moved back and
forth rapidly.

"It won't take long," I assured him.

"How do you know? If it's such an emergency, there's no reason it won't go on for a good long time. I need you here, Mickey. We're getting so close to making this thing happen— and you're my lucky charm." He tried to smile but the worry lines in his forehead weren't going anywhere.

"It's just that I've been having some staff trouble. I'll get it worked out soon," I said. Maybe I should have given him a few days' notice, not been so impulsive. He responded better with more notice of my leave-takings.

"What's going on here, Mickey?"

"What I told you—the same as I've told you before."

"You never tell me anything," he responded.

"I've told you lots," I said while trying hard to think of examples. "Look, we've gone through this. Before we got married, you were proud of what I do."

"I am, but you make it hard."

"Wilson!"

He threw up his arms. "What am I supposed to do? Tell me what!"

Before I could humor him, Michelle and Daisy spoke in unison: *"Grow up!"*

"You are hardly Ms. Reliability," he managed as a parting shot before going up to bed.

Of course, he had a point. The most reliable thing about me was that I often disappeared. In my fantasy script, when we were together, we were to play as gods. But Wilson was not only a mortal man, he was insecure, lonely, and traditional in the extreme. He craved Ms. Reliability while I craved a divine romance, in the highest sense of the word. One that could withstand the capriciousness of all my selves.

chapter 19

"AUNTIE M! OVER HERE." AND THERE WAS DOTTIE, to my relief, looking a few pounds healthier and more upbeat than her e-mail implied. I'd forgotten just how quickly moods and problems changed at her age. I hugged her tightly. If my child had lived, she'd be nearly as old as my niece. Dottie was as close as I would get, and I felt a love so piercing it hurt.

"Do you think your mother minds much? My sudden visit?"

"Who cares? It's a relief—the visit and the suddenness. I can't believe you're really here. I wanted . . . I didn't want to impose." Dottie sighed and blinked away some tears, though one escaped and slid down her cheek. She picked up my suitcase and we walked toward the car. Glancing sideways at me, she confided, "I'm fine now but I guess I'm no picnic at home." She laughed as if to make light of this. "Anyway, my mother's decided you're good for me—well, not exactly good for me, but she worries too much. They think big-city life was bad for me, so she's scared I'll leave home again. She's also scared I'll stay." Another hiccup laugh.

"I was worried about you, too," I said, choosing to ignore both the "not exactly good" comment and the fact that she wasn't quite tracking.

"Oh, I'm sorry about that. I guess I exaggerated some. It's just that this place is so dull! My mother is smothering me with attention. Hardly lets me cross the street without her. She didn't even want me to pick you up, but I told her I wasn't an infant."

I had wondered where Andrea was. The last-minute lipstick, blush, and eyeliner on the plane—they'd been for Andrea's benefit mostly. It wasn't so much that I was nervous about being on her turf, but I wanted to look my best, maybe to rub it in that I was successful and put together. If I was honest about it, I probably wanted to prove once and for all that I'd won that unfinished competition from our childhood and that she should have been nicer to me growing up. I scolded myself for falling so quickly into the script of our old battles. "Where is she, anyway?"

"Home cleaning your already-clean bedroom and cooking some meal that she said you liked growing up."

"What is it?"

"Beef Stroganoff? Is that a dish?"

"Sure is." And one I'd not had in years and did not remember liking much—let alone having—when I was young. Still, the thought of Andrea remembering, or thinking so, touched me. "I thought my short notice would save her from making a fuss."

WALKING INTO ANDREA'S suburban house was much like walking into one of the many we grew up in, although the early-1950s furnishings seemed incongruous with the faux-Colonial tract house. There was an ultramodern new kitchen and ornate bathrooms, but the blue-green plaid study was decorated with pictures of cocker spaniels, and my sister and her husband used the twin beds and bureau that had been our mother's. Andrea's home made Wilson's feel positively eclectic instead of merely junky.

Andrea didn't appear to be at home, and Dottie finished the tour by showing me my room. "It's a little girlie," she said before disappearing down the hall with a "Back in a sec."

The room most definitely had touches of a young girl—a young Michelle Harmon, to be precise. Andrea had hung one of my Impressionist prints on the wall and plopped an old teddy bear of mine on the bed. My old tennis racket was atop a bookcase. Since my mother had turned my room in our last house in Ohio into a sewing room the year I'd left for college, Andrea must have saved these things before the renovation. I wondered why. I'd always assumed all my early mementos had been tossed out long ago.

I sat on the bed and pondered what kind of message Andrea was sending with this odd shrine to my past. I half suspected it was another form of her piety, or a not-so-passive rebuke that I never came to visit. Then again, Andrea had only visited me three times: once in Michigan when I lost the baby, once for drinks in New York when she and Larry and Dottie had come for a convention, and her last recent visit when Dottie was sick. She'd never said anything about how I decorated my place. I couldn't imagine what she thought of it. Really, we only saw each other occasionally at our mother's in Ohio while she was still alive.

Whatever Andrea's reasons for holding on to my possessions, I felt even more unreal than usual surrounded by an old discarded identity. As my questions mounted, Dottie walked in, a plate of cookies in hand.

"Mom left us a note saying she's at a church meeting she forgot about. Daddy's out of town on business. You're to have a cookie and something to drink. You look like you could use a real one, though I doubt that's what she had in mind."

"I think I'll pass, but don't tell your mom, okay? Maybe you could eat for both of us."

"I hate cookies."

"I guess one won't hurt me." I reached out my hand. I couldn't bear for us both to reject Andrea's thoughtful gesture. It struck me suddenly that Andrea was exactly the kind of woman I created Daisy for, even if I did suspect my sister's actions were motivated by her expectation of reciprocal rewards. If someone gave Andrea or my mother a hard-luck story, they returned the effort with an effusion of care and sentiment, their rectitude beyond reproach. This capacity for pity took them to the greatest heights of virtue, but there always lurked a sense that they took satisfaction in stock-piling debts of obligations. Those who enjoyed playing the victim were rudely and sadly surprised by my kin's ultimate exploitation of them. It was an ironic twist that Daisy's austere approach both repudiated my sister's choices but could also have made her life better.

"Auntie M, are you all right?" Dottie looked at me curiously.

I laughed to cover my confusion. "Much too much going on," I said, rubbing my forehead. "Is that a new necklace?" I asked, trying to let go the past. The sapphire glittered against the soft hollow of Dot's neck.

"Yeah," Dottie said, fingering the pendant. "They're trying to bribe me into good health. Will you be staying awhile?"

"A few days—if you'd like."

"You know I would." Dot sat down beside me conspiratori-ally. "Sure you don't need something? A glass of milk, maybe? My mother would love it—milk and cookies. She's always wanted a daughter who liked milk and cookies." That tone again.

"Maybe I'll lie down first. Come back in thirty minutes and you'll find a new person."

Dottie gave me a quick tight hug. "I like you this way fine." She walked out before the emotion in her last sentence got the better of her.

And which person was I? The strain of trying to remember had begun to wear more than I cared to admit. Sinking back onto the pillow, right arm crooked over my eyes, I thought I smelled the faint scents of shoe polish and newly cut grass, sweet roses, freshly ironed sheets, old library books, the musty suitcases we packed and unpacked, the smells of my girlhood. I thought of my mother, always straining and flustered, running her fingers distractedly through her hair.

IT SEEMED NO TIME had passed when I heard a knock at the door: "Michelle?" It was Andrea. We hugged awkwardly. "Would you like a cup of tea or coffee? I've made both," she said.

"The tea, please." Wanting to be of help, I followed her down the hall, only to remember what I should have said first: "My room, what a surprise!" It did not escape me that I had tried to block out everything that she had tried to restore. In the kitchen, I picked up a cracked teapot I remembered from my childhood. It seemed to have a place of honor now on the counter next to the old cookie jar.

"You kept everything?" I asked.

"You said you didn't want it," Andrea answered defensively.

"I didn't . . . don't. I guess I never understood the significance."

"Somebody has to preserve a family's traditions."

"All right," I said, putting the teapot down.

"Don't be condescending, Michelle. You are always so damn condescending." Andrea put her hand over her mouth. She was shaking so much she had to sit down. "Sorry. My nerves are shot," she said, her voice breaking. "I'm at my wit's end."

"Dottie said you were worried about her," I said, hoping to encourage her to open up.

"Did she tell you we brought her home because she'd landed back in the hospital?"

I shook my head no.

"She says I overreacted—that it was just a flu bug. Larry buys her line. The doctor on duty in New York said she obviously wasn't taking care of herself and showed symptoms of depression. He recommended that she see a therapist. Frankly, I'm not sure that bout of pneumonia wasn't brought on by depression, too."

"Maybe she went back to dancing too soon," I said, sitting down next to my sister. "She looks better now anyway, and her spirits seem better than I expected. Maybe it's the other way around—sometimes people get depressed when they are physically sick. It's hard to believe anything is seriously wrong."

"Then why did you come?" Andrea snapped before crumpling further into the chair. After a few quiet sobs and a lengthy nose-blowing, she added, "I'm sorry. I'm glad you're here."

I put my arm around her. "Hey, forget it, okay? You're exhausted. Go lie down."

"I can't treat you like that."

"I won't melt or disappear. Tonight I'd like to take you and Dottie to dinner."

Andrea shook her head. "I already started the meal. You're my houseguest."

"All right, but you rest now. I have plenty of work with me to keep me occupied."

BACK IN MY time capsule, I placed my laptop on the vanity, found a phone jack, and checked the e-mail at my Daisy Strait website, hoping that might reorient me. These notes usually came from fans, and I felt legitimized when I read their missives, as if a camera lens turned slightly and my edges came into focus. This was the world I created, the one I'd brought to fruition. But the mixed messages I'd gotten here, at Andrea's, weighed on me. Dottie's behavior since my arrival seemed to belie her e-mail, but then I remembered the wayward tear at the airport, the quick intensity of her hug. And Andrea's revelation and outburst were shockingly uncharacteristic, too.

AT DINNER I dutifully spooned another helping of beef Stroganoff onto my plate and told Andrea again how delicious it was. I realized I meant it and swore that I would stop suspecting her every action. Like our mother, Andrea had short wavy blond hair, laced subtly with gray, which was brushed straight back from her face. Unlike our mother, though, she had a softness in her jawline, which looked especially defenseless to me now.

"If I'd had more time, I'd have fixed more of your favorite

foods," said Andrea. "I'm trying to convince Dottie that eating is okay."

Dottie cringed and the rest of the meal limped along. Though my niece had a chipper air about her, it was all air— she hardly said a word. At one point, to make conversation, Andrea told us about an accident that had happened on the town lake that day. She had heard about it on the radio on the way home from church.

"Two people drowned," she reported. "They haven't identified the bodies."

"Why not?" I asked, my fork stilled, midway to my mouth. "Why haven't they identified the bodies?"

"You don't have to register if you go out in your own boat. That's why you have to tell us, Dot, when you go out there," said Andrea, pointedly. "Or when you go hiking. People disappear from hiking trails all the time."

"They do?" I asked.

"I haven't been hiking since the seventh grade," said Dot.

"I hike whenever I get a chance," I responded. Yes, and why not? Maybe disappearing was the solution to all my problems.

THE NEXT MORNING, as we sat on my bed talking, the chinks began to reveal themselves in Dottie's perky demeanor. She confessed to a terrible sense of failure over her inability to make it as a dancer in New York. "I just wasn't good enough," she said sadly. "The competition was too fierce and my talent too small." When I protested, she assured me that she wasn't being modest or too hard on herself. "Believe me, I know that I danced well in Indiana. The trouble is everyone in New York danced well back home. There's another standard there and I don't happen to fit it."

Without her passion, she seemed like a shell. It was heartbreaking to see that her spunk and determination had vanished.

"I THINK I AGREE with that doctor about Dottie. Maybe she should see a therapist," I said to Andrea as we put away the breakfast dishes after Dottie had left to run an errand for her mother.

"I do, too, but she won't hear of it. She hangs out with that old boyfriend of hers but doesn't see any other friends. I can't get her to talk about going back to school or anything else she might do. She made good grades her first two years in college."

"She is capable of so much. And she's such a charmer."

"She has certainly charmed you," Andrea said, polishing the stainless-steel faucet as if it were a precious piece of silver.

I took the hit but let it pass. "So what can we do?"

Andrea stopped wiping the kitchen countertop and sat heavily. She looked older than her years, certainly older than any woman her age in New York. "I don't know. A therapist might help.... Then sometimes I think, Well, maybe she knows what's best, maybe she does only need to take some time out. Then I get scared. She is such a fragile little thing."

Andrea looked at the pattern on the floor. "I thought about asking you if she could stay with you for a few weeks. Remind her of her options. Growing up, she held your life out as a promise. But if she went back to New York before she was

ready . . . You couldn't protect her every minute, you know?"
Andrea's eyes pleaded with me to disagree, *not* to know.

"I do know," I had to say. I moved closer, leaned over the
table to place my hand on top of my sister's. As if my touch
unhinged a private door, Andrea bent toward our hands and
cried softly. I stood as close as I could, my other hand on top
my sister's soft hair. I felt ashamed of all the cynical and
immature thoughts I'd cherished about her.

Then Andrea's steely nature straightened her back once
again. She pulled a tissue from a pocket, blew her nose, got up
and splashed water on her face. "I'd like some reconciliation
with her before she leaves again. As it is, she can't bear Larry
or me." She patted her face dry, her eyes puffy and vulnerable.
"We did make a lot of mistakes, didn't pay the right kind of
attention. She's right to an extent: We saw her only as we
wanted to see her." She shook her head. "I don't think I could
stand to have her leave the way you did. I have always felt
guilty."

Before I left Indiana, I managed to persuade Dottie to get
outside help. Andrea and I didn't have the courage or energy
to pursue our own talk further, but something had certainly
thawed between us.

chapter 20

WHEN THE ELEVATOR DOOR OPENED TO THE EN-
trance hall of my New York apartment, the whiteness
enveloped me like a cherished blanket, the austere serenity
calmed me, soothed me. Inside, the harmony of proportion
and the reflecting shades of late-afternoon sunlight and
shadow stunned me with pleasure. How could I ever do without this rarefied world—or Steve? The last time I had seen
him here he'd been desolate. We had so much in common, I
thought ruefully, and our home mocked us both. Did I honestly think I could be happy in the scrappy Texas countryside
with only Wilson? Somehow the clean lines of the home I'd
made with Steve sharpened my mind and made me consider
the life of the mind, how much I valued the intellectual connection Steve and I shared, which I found so stimulating, not
to mention the indulgent solitude Steve's travels afforded me.

What the hell had I done? I stood in the center of the living room, disoriented, then collapsed on the sofa. I forced
myself to focus, composing myself enough to leave a voice
mail for Wilson, who I knew was at a dinner at Sonia Sartin's:
"Just thinking of you. Take care and know I miss you."

Steve got an e-mail: *I feel so good about the possibilities,
Steve. Sweet dreams. Michelle.*

I wrote Dottie, too: *Hey there—Just arrived in New York
and wish you were here to have dinner with me. Maybe soon*

you'll feel like coming. I'm keeping my fingers crossed. Your Auntie M. I was trying my best to encourage her. She still had a shaky belief at best in her future.

As much as I wanted to cocoon myself in my apartment, I also knew my only hope was to keep moving forward, one foot in front of the other, and show up willing and eager at the office the next day.

INSIDE DAISY STRAIT ENTERPRISES, the air was crackling with electricity. I knew immediately that something was up. Beth and Gloria began talking at once, their speech pitched high with excitement. Tippy Medved, one of the hottest literary agents in town, wanted to represent me, they said. She'd seen my columns, loved my message, my voice, and believed I had a book in me. "Your modesty worked in your favor," Beth said. "She was so impressed." They followed me into my office.

"You can take Daisy Strait's philosophy to a whole new level!" said Gloria.

"Slow down," I said, sitting at my desk. "Now . . . what are you saying?"

"She thinks you could make a book combining old columns with new material," said Beth.

"It's a great idea, don't you think?" said Gloria, almost delirious. "Some days every single demand is legitimate and sorting them out is impossible and about all you can do is take 'em one at a time and hope for the best. You tell us to forgive ourselves for not being perfect and not having enough stamina or the fortitude of a saint.

"I've followed the Daisy Strait doctrine for years," she went on. "I've pared down and pared down and still feel myself going crazy with all my obligations and don't feel I give enough to any of them. I can't ignore my kids. My mother and auntie depend on my legs to do their shopping because of their arthritis. My brother is so messed up that I'm the only one who talks to him. A favorite uncle sits all day alone in his apartment in Albany just waiting for my phone call. One of my best friends is going through a horrible divorce; another, a horrible marriage. And those are only the big deals.

"They don't include the ratty stuff like calling the plumber three times to fix the toilet or getting my mother's phone turned back on. She forgot to pay the bill, then fought with the phone company. There's a man I sometimes see who can't understand why I'm always bummed out. I tell you, my work feels like a relief from everything else. A dozen projects here don't get me down."

"I had no idea," was all I could say. I was amazed by the sudden stream and collision of words. Beth seemed to be, too.

"Oh, I'm not trying to unload on you," said Gloria. "I'm telling you this because you touch on something fundamental to so many women. Your book will make people realize that what we need is more than a system—and I'm not knocking those one bit—but what we need even more is just acknowledgment of our predicaments."

I started shuffling papers on my desk. The confiding, coupled with her praise, embarrassed me. "Thank you, Gloria. That means a lot to me."

"Would you like to set up an appointment with her?" Beth asked me.

"With—?"

"The agent?"

I took a deep breath. "Yes, of course," I said.

I sat for a few minutes after they left, resisting the impulse to pick up the phone. I wanted to tell somebody the good news but then wondered if telling could jinx everything. What if I really could make money on a book? What if I really could help Steve and pay off the mortgage on Wilson's farm? What if I fulfilled my own Daisy dream? Unable to sit a moment longer, I put on my suit jacket, stashed my papers in my desk drawer, and informed Beth that I was leaving for an early lunch before my afternoon lecture in Tarrytown.

"I hope it's a celebratory one," Beth answered. Perhaps she felt we should all lunch together, but I needed the privacy. She smiled bountifully. "Gloria is convinced your book will be a bestseller."

I felt a wave of pure giddiness but tamped it back down. "Maybe we'd better not start counting the dollars quite yet."

"Oh, let's do! A little recklessness might be good for us."

Everyone seemed to be changing right in front of my eyes. I gave Beth a thumbs-up sign. I did not know then how fragile my architecture was, how this news like a minor tremor could start a landslide.

I checked my watch. Two hours before the commuter train to Tarrytown. I wished I could use a car and a driver, but they didn't fit Daisy's image. I wished I could celebrate over lunch. I wished for . . . well, millions, I thought, turning up my coat collar against the nip in the afternoon air.

Maybe I could tell Steve. Even his pride could accommodate my potential success. He could set up a practice of his own or repay his debt without anyone being the wiser. I could tell Wilson. . . . But I had to stop fast-forwarding. Baby steps, I reminded myself. First you have to write the thing.

It's going to be fine, the Daisy in me said. *Enjoy the moment.*

You have to write it, Michelle, ever the level head, pointed out again.

What does it matter? Mickey asked. *Y'all tumbling, plunging into hell. Rescue Steve and Wilson? You can hardly look after yourself.*

It's about time you figured it out, oh romantic one, Michelle sniped. *There's no way you could ever marry Wilson and live happily ever after—not at the expense of Steve and me. I would never allow it and you know it. Steve can't be discarded like yesterday's papers. He is not* clutter.

Both of you hush. Daisy is in charge now and Daisy feels free. I have enough sense to take work demands anytime over sticky emotional obligations. I have, for the first time, possibilities of real success. It's your blessing, too, so get with it.

The problems won't disappear, Michelle warned.

For one hour and forty minutes I sat in Grand Central Terminal and stared at the clock, watching the minute hand go round and concentrating hard on collecting my selves, worried that without great effort, I might fragment irrevocably.

THAT EVENING, as I came into the apartment, the phone rang shrilly. It stopped, then started again. I rushed across the room. It was Roberta Simpson, asking me to attend a charity benefit with Buzzy. "I'm sick about it, but my face is a mess from laser surgery. I did it so I would look good for tonight, but I didn't heal in time. I've been to two different makeup artists today, and they can't do a thing with me. That's why I'm calling so late—and telling you the truth. Buzzy has to go and refuses to walk in alone. I've got to humor him. The charity is one of my clients."

"What about Randi? Have you tried her?" Randi was a mutual friend, just divorced and miserable.

"She's really let herself go—on purpose! she says. You know how picky Buzzy is. He has to have a stylish thing on his arm or he'll wilt."

"Then find him a model."

Roberta knew plenty. She loved the fashion crowd. "Think not. He wants stylish. I want stylish and safe, and that's you, Michelle, dear. So safe, I've entrusted you with the truth rather than the high-fever flu story that Buzzy is to dispense. I'll make it up to you. Please."

I immediately regretted accepting, then panicked when I checked my closet. Dress after dress had to be put aside for not accommodating my extra dozen pounds. Did I own nothing that wasn't sleek? I had bought a few new pieces to wear as Daisy, but those clothes weren't appropriate for any formal occasion. Maybe I could do a Scarlett O'Hara and transform myself with a curtain.

OVER A FANNY-HUGGING, bosom-popping, long white crepe dress, I clutched a white silk sheet, draped balloon fashion. My other hand gripped a glass of mediocre champagne. A couple of people had already asked who designed my ensemble, and modestly, indifferently, I shrugged my shoulders as if I couldn't bother to remember. With people more or less complimenting me, I stopped worrying about my homemade number. The king-sized sheet, however, although skillfully bunched, fortified by safety pins and all the white thread in my house, required constant monitoring with my left hand.

"I find these things dull, don't you?" Buzzy shouted a little louder than necessary over the cocktail hour noise.

"Dull," I echoed, and pulled my sheet tighter about me. I hadn't dreamed I would be stuck sitting with him in a corner, but Buzzy didn't want to mingle before dinner, and very few party souls came over to speak to us.

"Now, that woman over there," he said, nodding his head toward a petite woman, "the one in the red gizmo. She is not dull, if she's who I think she is, and she has to be."

"And who is that?" Trust Buzzy to have good gossip, I thought, and tugged up the bodice of my dress.

"No names," he whispered, "but I can tell you that back in my crime-fighting days as an assistant U.S. Attorney, we used her once as a decoy courier."

"What's that?" For some reason I thought of wooden duck decoys, but I knew that wasn't what he meant.

"Someone who carries drugs as an undercover agent," said Buzzy. "Most exhilarating time I've ever had. Sometimes I think I'd gladly trade all this"—he motioned around the room as if it belonged to him personally—"for the kind of highs I got back then. Making money is a kick, but danger, intrigue, that is something else."

"I never knew this about you, Buzzy."

"It was before we met. Just out of law school. Roberta and I had come up here from Idaho. . . ."

"I always thought you were—" This time I interrupted myself as I was about to say "a lazy party guy," but changed it to, "That you had a . . . a good Samaritan side."

He stood up to dance with me. "Shall we?"

I rose and tightened my grasp on the sheet.

"I don't know if I was a do-gooder or just a kid who liked the chase," he said wistfully.

At the end of the evening, on our way to the car, Buzzy put his arm around me and whispered, "Now that you know a lot more about me than I know about you, mystery woman, you've got to tell me one thing."

I smiled in reply, a bit queasy.

"Am I mistaken, or is that a sheet?"

IN LESS THAN A WEEK, I'd met with Tippy Medved and we'd put together a proposal for my book. I could tell why Daisy appealed to her: Tippy Medved was the personification of minimalism—a crisp, fitted black suit, sensible shoes, a smooth hairdo. "I'm really excited about this, Daisy," she said. "All you need to do now is decide which columns you'd like to include and add some new material. We can figure out together how to structure the book. I'll help you at any point you want. I'm here for you. Now, when can I expect more?"

"Soon," I answered as gamely as I could.

"Make that sooner if you can. This book has a lot of potential. There's nobody who won't identify with the situations and your understanding of how truly hard it is to change a damn thing going on in your life. It hits home."

"Did anyone ever feel this way about a book by Anaïs Nin?"

"What?"

"Anaïs Nin."

"That's what I thought you said." A long pause followed. "Well, I guess . . . no, no, I doubt it." Another pause. "She wrote a very different kind of book. A little more . . . difficult."

"Not her erotica."

A much, much longer pause, then, "No, certainly not her erotica. But Daisy?"

"Yes?"

"What has this to do with your book? Am I missing a connection or something?"

Maybe the best solution would be to divorce both husbands. After the initial grieving, Steve would do well. He already lived alone most of the time. If that didn't suit him, he would find somebody who could be satisfied with a lesser number of lives. He would be fine. Wilson, too. One of the reasons for my "irrational" anger with him was that part of me suspected I'd been, though in the best of ways, just another of his enthusiasms.

Maybe no one marriage could contain the all of me. Why not let Daisy have her go without encumbrances? Find out what a simplified life is truly all about.

chapter 21

BACK IN ROLLINS, LIFE FELT AS CRAMMED AS EVER, and cobbling together my book occupied a good deal of my evenings after dinner. I had risked the jinx and told Wilson about my meeting with Tippy, and he was genuinely happy for me, I could tell, because his eyes shone with the same mix of hope and confidence as when one of his birds was nearly ready to fly. Once again I rationalized that my work had to come first. There was no way I could handle two divorces with my book looming above my head. After a sybaritic night with Wilson, I'd pad back to my desk for another couple of hours, where I would exhort myself and others to consider ourselves every now and again: *Allow for grace notes—a cup of tea, a stretch, a smile, a fleeting moment of congratulations for work achieved, if not completed.* Sometimes I actually followed my own advice.

Before turning off my computer, I ended many nights with an encouraging e-mail to Steve. *Believe it or not, an agent approached me about doing a book. I just know things are going to turn around for us—I can feel it.*

Fantastic! You can do it in no time, I'm sure, he e-mailed back. *Do you need me to negotiate your contract?*

No word from my agent, I wrote another time. *She's waiting for me. Book isn't done but I'm working hard.*

What about a TV tie-in? wrote Steve. *Finished yet?* I knew these questions reflected his desperation. I sympathized.

"BETH?" I SHOUTED over the phone. "Are you there?" My cell had gone dead for a minute—so frustrating.

"We were hoping you'd call today," she answered. "There's great news! Have you spoken to Tippy?"

"No, I turned my cell off so I could work. What's up?"

"You should probably call her," said Beth, "but we can't wait. Just a sec. I'm putting you on the speakerphone." She actually giggled.

"How does three hundred and fifty thousand dollars sound?" That was Gloria.

"What?!"

"Tippy sold your book to Simon and Schuster—just on the basis of the proposal!" said Gloria. "They're planning to announce a first printing of a quarter of a million copies."

"Oh my God! That's a lot! Are you sure?!" I said.

"They want you to do a huge tour," said Gloria, happily. "This is it, Daisy! You'll have the kind of visibility you've always wanted. You have put us on the great map in the sky!"

"Whoa, horsey," I said, picking up one of Wilson's terms. "We haven't sold those books quite yet."

"No, but we'll get the publicity, no matter, and in a million years we could never generate that kind of exposure on our own."

I flinched at the word *exposure;* my heart raced. After a flurry of calls—to Tippy, to the editor, to my office again—my head was hammering. I was exhilarated and terrified; I felt like what it must be like to leap out of the gate on a bucking bull. Outside, the Texas heat and humidity were building to a late-day storm—I could hear the coming rumble. I checked my watch—I was supposed to meet Wilson at a cocktail party at Annette's a half hour ago. I saw a flash of lightning. If I sped, I could just beat the rain.

I WALKED INTO the party more in Daisy than Mickey mode, though Daisy would not have worn a pale-blue cotton shift guaranteed to wilt in this Indian summer heat and humidity. Brian handed me a mint julep. "Go find your husband. He thinks the storm might have blown you away." He pointed me toward a front window where Wilson stood watching the black clouds.

I walked over to kiss him. *You can have your house back, you can make two rain forests,* I wanted to tell him. *I will be rich. I will buy you anything and serve it to you on a silver platter.* "You looking for me?"

"There's a tornado watch; I was worried about you."

"There's always a tornado watch. You told me so yourself. Here, have a sip of my mint julep."

He pushed my cup away. "I hate mint juleps. Just a damn affectation."

"They are very Southern."

"Annette is not a Southerner. She's a Texan. Her husband is a Texan. Their parents are Texans."

"So have a beer. Calm down. What's got into you? Did something happen at the center?"

"You were supposed to be here nearly an hour ago."

"And?"

"I was worried."

I felt my neck lock into a vise and swung around to join Lindy and Annette in the living room. Imagine! A sixty-minute lapse and Wilson turns into my gatekeeper! Soon, however, he came over to me and, to my surprise, grinned and put his arm around me. He was the damnedest man. He pulled me in a little closer.

"Stop that, you two," Wendell Jackson teased.

As huge hail pelted at the plate-glass windows and doors, another woman whom I hardly knew joined the group. "Rumor has it that you're working on a book," she said to me. "I told Hillary and Lindy that you wouldn't last long around all us unimportant people."

I excused myself. The town was a magnifying glass, and I did not want to start apologizing for who I was. In all fairness, though, my friends here treated me like another old shoe. And Wilson and I loved each other, and money was just around the corner. We could travel, I said to myself as my brain spun into that now-familiar sensation of decision and revision.

When Annette exchanged my empty mint-julep glass for a fresh one, I promised myself to start watching calories tomorrow. I had to get back into my best shape for the limelight. But not this evening. I was bursting with my news and wished I could tell someone, but I wasn't ready yet. I wanted it to be mine just a while longer.

"Mickey, dear," called Hillary. "I have something to show you!"

Wilson walked over just as she reached into her purse and pulled out a page torn from a magazine.

"I was just about to show this picture to Mickey. This woman looks just like her." She handed the photo first to Wilson, then to me. "Do you have a rich cousin?"

The caption read, "Roberta and Harris Samuel Simpson at the Save the Sea Benefit." I saw the white sheet clutched tightly in my right hand, my left on the arm of Buzzy Simpson. My face had the look of a dazed accident victim, my lips parted slightly in such a way as to suggest a smile, or a sneer, depending on the viewer's interpretation.

Wilson construed it as a sneer. "That woman looks like a bored, snooty bitch, not a bit like Mickey."

"To me she looks more like someone having a really miserable time but trying hard to fake it," Lindy said.

Hillary stuck the picture close to my nose. "But don't you see, Mickey, how much she looks like you? The way you would look in a three-thou dress with your hair blown straight?"

I examined the picture again, this time surprised to see that Buzzy looked almost as uncomfortable as I did. "In fact, we are cousins," I said. Wilson's face registered surprise. Quickly I added, "Distant. Never see her."

Utterly deflated of my secret triumph, I folded the picture and gave it back to Hillary. It was impossible. Daisy and Michelle and Mickey could not coexist for long side by side, not even in my wishful thinking. A successful Daisy would be too much in demand; a reticent Michelle could not hide behind her. Inevitably those two would have to reconcile with each other because, no matter how private I tried to remain after I became a truly public figure, Michelle Banyon's face would appear every so often as the woman behind Daisy Strait. Inevitably, I would have less time for my personal lives; worse, as had suddenly been demonstrated, I could get found out. I'd been lucky that I'd been identified as Buzzy's wife. My heart skipped a beat.

When Wilson suggested we sneak out, I readily agreed. The idea of Wilson discovering my treachery terrified me. In another life I was going to be famous. I wished this one didn't have to matter so much.

THE NEXT MORNING, I woke up grinning as I remembered all over again. Three hundred fifty thousand dollars! I rolled over to Wilson and whispered in his ear, "I sold the book. For lots of money."

"Hmm . . . nice," he murmured.

"No, Wilson, I really did."

"Did what?" he said groggily.

"My book was sold to Simon and Schuster!" I could hardly contain my glee.

He pulled me in closer and squeezed me tight. "Oh, honey, I'm so proud of you." I could feel him harden and my thighs opened. "You're the best," he whispered, and we celebrated in the slowest, most delicious manner.

ONCE AGAIN, our days took on the comfort of routine. I got breakfast, tidied up, passed a few minutes with Helen, then spent the next hours upstairs with my computer. On my reducing kick now, I came down to the kitchen for a lunch of cottage cheese and a piece of fruit.

By late afternoon, I attended to the last of my office e-mails from New York and Dallas before resuming life downstairs. While Helen prepared dinner most nights, on her evenings off I took over, though now grudgingly. Sometimes Wilson brought home pizza or fried chicken, even though I kept insisting I was on a diet. After dinner, I returned to work upstairs while Wilson watched TV or went over papers or went to nurse a sick raptor.

I was impatient to finish my book. The book promised deliverance—for Steve, for Wilson, and for Dottie. Yes, Dottie, too. I had decided I wanted to make enough money for her to use however she wished in the future. She could go to a school of whatever kind anywhere in the world if she wanted.

With all these deliverances, surely I could then figure out something for myself, but right now my only thought was finishing. I was in a time warp, suspending all decisions and anxiety while I worked on the book. I caught the flu, but I worked anyway. Rest became impossible. Each night I grew quieter, almost ticking off the minutes until I could politely leave Wilson. I began skipping lunch altogether. I turned down all invitations from my friends, using the flu as an excuse far longer than its actual duration. My skin verged on gray and I was losing a shocking amount of weight. Even Wilson noticed.

When he suggested I see a doctor or take it easy, I snapped at him: I had work to do. He had known that when he married me—*married* sounding interchangeable with *jailed.* Not once did he get angry; on the contrary, he understood. I was grateful but defensive, which I felt bad about but couldn't help. He must have sensed as much, for he essentially became invisible.

AND THEN CAME the meltdown. My beautiful computer, my one reliable link to sanity, the one object in the world I could count on, stopped at ten minutes after ten o'clock on the third Wednesday morning in October. I spent the first hour assuming that I could fix it; I spent the next on the phone with the computer company technician, who thought maybe the hard drive had gotten damaged.

"But my files!" I shouted. "I've lost my files!"

"Didn't you make backups?"

"No, I *trusted* this, you idiot!"

I hung up. The next hour I spent in disbelief, trying frantically to resurrect all my work. In an attempt to calm myself, I went to the kitchen in search of comfort food. I looked without success for a consoling morsel, practically crawled into the refrigerator. I settled on a half jar of green olives, but the lid wouldn't turn. Someone walked up behind me and I swerved, raised the jar to throw it—only to see Wilson.

"You scared me!"

"Oh, Mickey, honey, I'm sorry. I thought you heard me. You all right?" he asked.

"A little hungry," I answered, now so weak I had to sit down before I could get the bread.

"Want a sandwich?"

I nodded yes. Already he was fetching a knife, the bread, the peanut butter, a glass of milk. I remembered to thank him, but in some far-off, flat voice I hardly recognized as my own. My arm didn't want to move. I am paralyzed, I thought. My body and my mind are paralyzed.

Wilson handed me a glass of milk and said, "Hot today."

I nodded and sipped the milk. While he made my sandwich, he continued talking about the heat as if nothing at all was unusual in our circumstance. I looked up, mute.

He put his hand to my forehead. "You look sick, like you need a rest maybe."

I shook my head no. "My computer's had a breakdown. My steady, sturdy"—my hands trembled—*"reliable"*—I clutched the table—"machine. A perfect machine. Never gave me any trouble. Made my life so . . . easy. Simple. I have a simple life with that computer," I explained, my eyes begging him to understand.

Apparently he did. "Machines and birds are easier to deal with than most else in this world," he answered, his kindness undoing me.

I put my head on the table and began to weep. "My computer is dead." My tears were way out of proportion to the event, but I couldn't stop myself. I sobbed uncontrollably. Wilson sat beside me and pulled me close, stroking my hair. As soon as the convulsions stopped, he gave me a napkin to blow my nose.

"Now, what did the computer do?" he asked gently.

I looked up at him, furious with his tenderness. "Had a breakdown, I told you."

"Yes, but exactly how did it act during its breakdown?"

I described how the clock in the corner of the screen froze and then jumped ahead, how the screen flashed. "It looked like a hiccup," I said. "The technician I talked to called it a burp. Then the screen shrank to a dot in the middle and went black. A black hole."

"So what we really need are lost files? The computer is replaceable. Could I see it?"

I managed an "Okay." We climbed the stairs to my haven— at least it had been until this disaster—but I hesitated at the door. Wilson seldom came in here. This room had been his gift to me and he had respected the boundary.

He began examining my laptop as if it were some rare

species of bird. "Could be the hard drive, but it sounds like bad memory to me," he said. "We'll fix you up in no time."

"I didn't know you knew so much about computers," I said, spent.

"Whaddaya think, lady? I'm just a one-note Willy?"

We both laughed. In that instant I put all my faith in him, more than I had ever before placed in anyone.

WILSON, HIS PAJAMA TOP unbuttoned, sat up in bed, back straight against the mahogany backboard, his legs stretched in front with his ankles crossed. I also wore one of his pajama tops unbuttoned. Wavering shadows played across us—the full moon.

He cradled my head tight against his chest. "I love you, Mickey."

Radiance flooded through me, and my heart opened to catch all the brightness. We fell asleep to the seductive glimmer of the moon and its shadows.

chapter 22

IT WAS SO NEW, SO DEEP, THIS LOVE I HAD WITH Wilson. I was no longer so dazzled as to think the magic would be there always, but it could resurface if I didn't strangle it. Better than that, I wanted to nurture it, to treat our love tenderly, to blow softly on the flames. It was time to clean up the mess I'd made. It was time. I knew Steve was headed back to the city for a quick trip, so I hurried there, too. I would tell him . . . I would tell him . . . I would tell him the distance had caught up with us. Or: I wasn't the Michelle he'd married anymore. I would tell him people change, I'd changed. It was time.

UNFORTUNATELY, the conversation didn't begin as planned. Steve, alarmed, barely put his suitcases down before he asked me what was wrong. "I'm fine," I assured him, thinking my nervousness must be worse than I imagined. "You freshen up while I get us a drink."

Instead, he pushed me toward the sofa and insisted on getting the drinks himself. I heard him in the kitchen washing his hands, opening the refrigerator door, stirring the vodka tonics. Maybe I would tell him on my second one, or the third. Placing a tray with our drinks and macadamia nuts on the marble-top coffee table, he loosened his tie, then said I looked like death warmed over. "And your clothes are falling off you. Are you sick? Have you been to a doctor?"

I felt I'd failed some test. "I've been working hard. The book and everything . . ." My voice trailed off. Here I was, trying to please him again, making excuses. "But I'm not sick," I said, too quickly, too sure.

He relaxed back into a soft cushion of the sofa. "Well, how is it coming, the book? Can they make you a star?" he asked, more than half joking, which I resented.

"More than that, we are going to be rich."

"On three hundred fifty thousand?"

"I'm serious, Steve."

But he wouldn't take me seriously. He made the proper clucking noises and excused himself to go to the bathroom. "Should I change?" he called from the bedroom. "Or is my rich wife taking me out to dinner?"

"Out to dinner?" I hadn't given food any thought, only the drinks and how I might tell him we were through, but he came out in his business suit, not understanding that my response had been a question.

"Don't you realize I stand to make a lot more money before this is over?" I said, defending myself. "One of the morning shows wants to try a week's worth of mini-segments with the idea of making me a permanent fixture. And my speaker's fees will jump enormously—to ten thousand dollars maybe. I can speak three times a week for fifty weeks of the year," I told him. "You do the math."

He stared at me strangely. "You can't possibly keep up a pace like that." With that, he went again to the kitchen. He came back this time with no fanfare and no tonic, only the chilled vodka bottle. Holding out my glass, my hands trembled, whether because of anger at his not taking me seriously or another attack of nerves, I had no idea. Steve noticed and covered my hands with his.

"I think I'll get something delivered," he said.

"Steve! I am telling you something important. You . . . you just damn well pay me some respect!" I took two big gulps of vodka in hopes of holding back tears. My whole body began to shudder.

Steve sat close. "To say I respect you is the least of it, Michelle." He fell into his formal, lawyer's voice: "I have always had the pride of self-sufficiency, and that makes me slow to admit how much I depend on you. I always have. I just haven't found ways to express . . ." His voice cracked. And then he did the most shocking thing—he put his head on my chest and cried, the sound so strange and garbled, as if he had no prior knowledge of how, and, so far as I knew, he had none. "I'm scared," he mumbled into my hair. Then he grew quiet for a long while. I patted his back awkwardly. Somehow, the only way I knew to handle this was to stare at a smudge on our wall. I wondered how our impeccable wall had gotten such a smudge. For a long time he continued to clutch me, his life raft. That's what he called me when he finally sat up and poured us each another drink.

"Hey, Steve," I said gently. "I think it would do us good to eat something. Let's order in some Thai food."

"Anything you like," he replied, but I feared that what I liked had no place in my life, no place at all.

I WENT THROUGH the motions. Steve stayed in town for a week, catching up on Stateside work. At night we saw friends, took in the theater, plotted how he might rev up negotiations with the Chinese. In the past, when he was stressed about his work, he had gotten annoyed with me if I showed too much interest, and sometimes if I showed any interest at all. Now he talked about his negotiations freely.

"Losing doesn't mean you're a failure. It only means that you lost," I reminded him yet again one evening as we walked to a favorite uptown haunt of ours. Maybe I was talking to myself. Was I a failure for being a coward, for risking losing Wilson, the man who continued to show me how much more was possible in a relationship? Perhaps sensing my distress, Daisy stepped in, ever helpful: "Why don't we brainstorm some new strategies for you?"

"Don't talk about something you don't know anything about!" Steve snapped.

I grabbed his arm—to shake it? To stop him long enough to ask how he could know so little about me? To tell him I was leaving? I was too upset to honestly know. When he turned his agitated face to me, I tucked my hands around that same arm and kept him close. We huddled together. He could have been Wilson.

TIME FLOATED IN and out of focus. I lost myself in present moments but could not compartmentalize sufficiently to carry off the trick for any length of time. As men and memories and moonlight and history spiraled around me in a mad rush, I felt my only hope was to be the eye of the hurricane— to be as still as I could inside the spin.

The odd thing was, even as I tried to keep from toppling, I kept coming up a winner. I met with my editor, Miranda Lundgren, who felt sure we had a bestseller on our hands. She talked of a coast-to-coast tour and bookings on national talk shows. The newest material that I'd sent her, though, for inclusion in the book, "needed tweaking," she said. In places, I'd gotten away from the idea of simplifying, had gone too much into life's complexities. "Like this one," she said, reading out loud. "'When Every Day Feels Like Monday' or 'Yard Sales, Pshaw! You Never Know When You'll Need It Again.' Your readers might get confused."

Right then I should have put my foot down, but I'd lost track of which way was up and which way down.

According to Tippy, every women's magazine in the country was vying for my column as well as an excerpt from my book. And that morning TV show was moving forward with plans to audition me for a regular slot. What my staff and I had only speculated about was actually happening. The fickle spotlight of recognition might actually single me out. I was, everyone kept saying, golden.

But I felt paralyzed. I used my reliable distraction of work as a survival tactic, but I couldn't work twenty-four-hour days. Steve waited for me at home, and every hour with him reenforced the inevitability of him and me. This wasn't rationally considered. It just was. We were a given. We shared an obligation of love, hidden under the rubbish of a lifetime together. We reached out to each other as best we could.

When he finally returned to Hong Kong, I was thrown back on my tenuous self. Every day became a triumph of will over disintegration.

Be calm, I told myself. The eye of the storm. Stay in motion. Even my self-encouragements conflicted with each other.

On impulse, I made a quick weekend trip to Rollins. On the drive from the airport, I felt as if I had recovered a treasure—sensual, forbidden, desired—and had to keep touching Wilson, stroking his cheek, his hand on the wheel, his thigh. I told him I was desperate for him but I think I was just desperate.

"Hey, careful there, sweetheart. The traffic's a little too swift for playing around."

"I thought you'd like to be aroused."

"Believe me, I am," he said. "Now, scoot over and buckle up before we get ticketed or have a wreck."

That incident pretty well summed up our first hours together. I kept hovering and he acted as if I should "buckle up." What Wilson wanted was another kind of intimacy. Saturday we took a long walk around the sanctuary. We strolled hand in hand along the edge of the creek, keeping our eye out for the new alligator Wilson had purchased. "She's a beauty, Mickey," he said. And I laughed at the idea, but loved his endless enthusiasm. Wilson pointed out the recently planted grasses and shrubs bordering the water, and with the denser foliage I could see his imagination taking shape. I thought about my own creation and how Miranda Lundgren said my manuscript "needed work."

"They want me to change Daisy," I told Wilson. "They want to steal Daisy from me, and she is my one true story."

He tucked me under his arm. "Mickey, honey, they can't if you don't let them."

"I have to let them. My staff, my agent, my editor—they'd all be too disappointed. And they would lose money. We would lose money."

"Forget the money. We don't need it and the others will survive, I'm sure."

I wished that were true. I thought about Steve's heart-breaking tears and Andrea's bewilderment and Dottie's shaky ego, and then I gave in to the rhythm of my footsteps with Wilson's, how well he and I fit, our hips bumping together softly. That night he made love to me so sweetly, and in the early morning he surprised me with breakfast in bed. By the time I left before noon, he didn't appear upset as much as weary and resigned. What did I expect? The way I came and went must have seemed like whims to Wilson. I began to wonder whether my comings and goings weren't a symptom of my own fear of the fullest life with this wonderful man. As I got behind the wheel again and waved, I had to consider: Was I really trying to drive *him* away?

BY SUNDAY AFTERNOON I was in my New York City apartment, dragging myself into the kitchen for a grapefruit, as if the tart taste might shed insight into how I might get out of my insane predicament. Maybe I could get rid of the old lives and find myself a new one, join the Witness Protection Program and move to a desolate spot or a Middle American cookie-cutter town or a place on the edge by the ocean somewhere, adopt a new name, a new identity, and let these tangled ones go. Or maybe I would just lock myself up in my elegant rooms with their spacious solitude, become a hermit, and never get into trouble again. I would be perfect, the perfect . . . But loud sobs and moans, my own, interrupted thought. Pacing back and forth, lying on my bed, spread-eagled, curled in a ball, facedown, drinking water, holding my breath—nothing stopped the sobs, my only solace the lights in other windows. If only I could reach through one, find one to take me in, a window to save me, my Wilson, my window.... I punched the buttons on the phone. "Wilson?" I whispered, my voice shaking. But he didn't sound like Wilson. He sounded like somebody angry with me.

"You'll feel better if you talk about it," I insisted. Did I say that to all my husbands?

He must have smacked his bedside table with his hand. "I will not *feel better* if I talk about it. You are not listening to me. It sounds like something's really wrong with you and you aren't doing anything about it. If you won't come back here, then I'm coming to New York to see about you. You can't go on like this."

"No!" I shouted, then I took a breath, calmed down. "You hate New York."

"Not as much as I love you. I'm worried. You're not acting like yourself anymore."

"When I'm there, I'm a good wife." How could he attack all aspects of my wifeliness?

I could hear him sigh. I could picture him composing his face, composing his temper. "You... you are a... fantastic wife, but you won't tell me what's wrong. Are you worn out? Are you sick? Are you sick of me?"

"No," I said. "Never."

"When you're here, you either can't settle down at all or you hide out upstairs. I don't recognize you. You don't act like my Mickey anymore. "

"I'm not," I said, choking on a sob. "Or not completely. Listen, I'm sorting out my life, you know? Like I sort out closets?"

"Closets?! No, Mickey, I honestly don't know. You sound so... fuzzy. Please, tell me what's wrong."

"Nothing that can be fixed. Nothing," I said miserably.

"All right." His voice had an odd tone to it, not one I'd heard before.

"I can't talk to you now. I'm very busy," I said, and hung up.

THE LONGER I considered my situation, the less decisive I became. Buying fruit juice and bread from the grocer took hours. What kind of juice? Which bread? On the street I would forget where I was going. At the corner I'd stop, bewildered. Turn left? Go straight? Should I make the changes to my book? Raleigh Lundgren had made many suggested edits, her red pen everywhere in slashes and delete curls. It wasn't fair. They'd bought the book for its nuances, now they wanted to strip it down for a mainstream audience. And how could I be on television?

In my white room, I became obsessed by the catastrophe that seemed imminent. It was too bad, I thought, that Steve couldn't have been my lover and Wilson my husband. Steve wouldn't have wanted or needed to marry and would have been content to remain a lover. One husband and one lover would have been so civilized. The full horror and scope of what I'd done hit with a violence.

Sleep was fitful and rare. My voices nattered on and on, bickering and constant. I dreamt I was standing at a podium with vines creeping up the sides, binding me to the lectern, a foreign babble spewing from my mouth—and then ringing, the phone ringing, my phone.

"Did I wake you?"

A male voice. I struggled to open my eyes. "Wake me?" I tucked my cell phone next to my ear.

"I did. Go back to sleep. I miss you."

"Me, too," I said, for I was missing me.

I looked at the crumpled papers and clothes that littered my bedroom floor. They offended my sense of order. Did Daisy, the tough-love maven for cluttered souls everywhere, have to disappear in order to keep her husbands happy? Her center couldn't withstand the pressure.

WHICH PARTIALLY EXPLAINED why I found myself standing in front of a group of well-groomed women in a Philadelphia suburb and puzzled as to what sort of group they were exactly. I should have paid attention during the preliminaries. I should have brought the prep sheet that Gloria always readied for my talks—where, when, who. I had no business wallowing in my own debris. I had important things to say and do.

"I know all of you have important things to say and do, so I won't take any more of your time than is necessary to help you do them more efficiently." I glanced down at my notes, my fingers rifling page after page, frowning because I had no notes, only the doodles I had made on the train.

"But I know this talk by heart," I said, looking up and beaming at my audience. "You know it, too. You know that if you were a robot instead of a human being, you, too, could live and work and play efficiently. You would not compromise your daily schedules with daydreams, or with talking too long on the phone with a distressed friend, or with eating up time and energy worrying about your parents or your children or the morning quarrel you had with your husband."

My audience was with me, a great many nodding their heads, but I had no idea where to go from here. I was rephrasing what Gloria said she liked best about my columns, but there was no train of thought attached. I needed Gloria to remind me. "Maybe what we all need is a buddy system. I'll go to your house and tell you what to get rid of and you come to mine and tell me. We are too close to it ourselves to make sound decisions. And I don't mean just papers, furniture, and knickknacks, I mean people, events, the worries we carry about with us." I stopped a minute to think. The group was hanging on my every word but I'd forgotten about them, I'd become too interested in what I was saying.

"The buddy probably shouldn't be your best friend—she knows too much about what's important to you, identifies too much with the rut you've put yourself in. Better to get a near stranger. This may sound like an outrageous solution to you, but I see it as good, plain common sense. What you have to do is *act* on it. For God's sake, ACT ON IT!"

I pounded the podium and glared at my listeners, who were attentive, applauding, a little puzzled, their clapping somewhat hesitant, as if they wished to be good children but weren't certain how.

"My children," I addressed my listeners, some older than me, "let me tell you, it is no easy matter getting through this life, making choice after choice every day, ev-er-y da-ay. I mean, should you floss after breakfast as well as before bed? You can ask your hygienist, but only *you*"—an extended arm, a wagging finger—"can decide.

"Now, what to wear today? You've got a gym class. You've got a meeting. You've got a lunch. You've got to pick up children or grandchildren and spend a couple of hours with them spilling things on you or spitting up or whatever else little kids do." The audience tittered (*nervously* would have been added by someone less absorbed in her own words).

"You could buy an everyday uniform, something serviceable that may not be haute couture but is sure as hell wrinkle-proof, and may not be perfect for any one thing but adequate for all." The women nodded again.

"I might tell you to invest in a few year-round cotton knits fortified with whatever that stuff is that helps them hold their shape and then buy thermal underwear to keep you warm underneath and do what you want about sweaters and coats and all that crap, just so you don't make them too bulky to carry on a plane in a roll-on—" I had to stop to catch my breath, but I was hot, I was on a roll, should have been in Vegas gambling—no, forget Vegas, go back to "buddies."

"You could be helpful to your buddy, too. She's told you which kitchen pans to throw away. You could tell her which husband to toss." My voice caught, but I suppressed my sob. "I mean, nobody in her right mind needs two of them. But then, who, I ask you, is in her right mind?" There was laughter but lots of looks passed around as well. I certainly had their attention now. I fixed them with my dark and glittering eye. That's how I saw myself right then, as possessing such an eye, for "The Rhyme of the Ancient Mariner," a poem learned in grade school, had popped into my head. I had no long gray beard but I had a lot of truths for these people. *The bridegroom's doors are open wide.*

"You may think I am too severe in what I am asking of you. You may be right. Decluttering is a severe process, a ruthless one. *Ruthless,*" I repeated, tears falling rapidly. "If there just weren't so many damn choices. They are enough to drive God crazy. And they have," I said, weeping, "they have." I wiped my eyes with my fingers and turned to look in my bag for a tissue to blow my nose before returning to the lectern.

To say I did not register the significance of the group's hum is perhaps an understatement.

"Though who am I to speak of clutter? In fact, *who* am *I?* Somebody tell me, please." I took a deep breath. "That was a digression," I explained, my voice calm, unconcerned, "an aside, so to speak." Yes, I am in charge, I assured myself.

"But I am pleading with you," I continued, arms stretched out to my disciples over the rostrum as far as I could reach, standing on my tiptoes, "begging you for your sake. The extra time isn't for more of the same shit. The extra time is for yourselves. You need time to reflect, to walk by yourself, to be with those few special friends who really care about you—" More tears. I took a few minutes to collect myself, then in a dramatic voice I announced, "Make time for some really fabulous sex." I jumped backward from the podium. "You must. When you have spent your whole damn day in the service of expectations and obligation, you may not feel like any sex— unless it is the volleyball variety, you know, just another sport to relieve some tension. But I am not talking about that 'slam bam, thank you, ma'am' kind, though it sure beats not wanting sex at all, an all too common predicament of the over-worked couple of today."

Had I paid attention, I would have noticed the audience had now turned a collective dark and glittering eye on me. I leaned into the group, some of whom had walked out after the "volleyball sex" remark. I whispered, "If you don't have a significant other or hate him or her, you might try museums. Nice people hang out there." A few more women left. Heretics, I thought scornfully, then remembered something I had read somewhere years before. "By the way, did you know that the French in the nineteenth century thought sexual abstinence

caused rabies?" The audience laughed; I winked. "That justified a lot of hanky-panky. But to hell with hanky-panky! That,
my friends, is clutter!" I had taken to pounding the podium
again and pointing that indefatigable finger, a Dr. Strangelove
kind of tic.

"I am talking about real passion. I am talking the earth-
turning kind. Which, my good, good friends, takes time. It.
Can. Be. Yours. Time is of the all." A moment's pause, an audience's silence, then I picked up my theme in a lighter voice.

"So, out, damn clutter. Out! I say, for I have come to bury
Caesar—clutter, that is—not to praise it. And I have. By damn,
I have!"

I gathered my doodles and my bag, walked magisterially
off the stage amid a smattering of clapping hands and strange
looks. But who cared? Nobody gets many opportunities to be
Daisy Strait, the Ancient Mariner, Lady Macbeth, and Antony,
all within an hour.

The woman who had chauffeured me from the Philadelphia station ran to catch up. In the car, the St. Laurent–clad,
buffed-body matron said, "That was the most unusual performance I have seen in my entire life."

"Thank you," I replied with modesty. The rest of the brief
ride passed in silence. There was no denying it, Mickey,
Michelle, Daisy, and any other stray part of myself were having a collective breakdown. I had to make a stand.

I CALLED WILSON to tell him I was coming to Rollins to discuss our problems. "We might as well admit it," I said. "I don't
think marriage works for us—you any more than me."

He waited so long before answering, I wondered if the line

had gone dead. "Maybe not," he answered, his voice even flatter than mine. "I love you, but . . ."

"You love a lot of things," I finished for him.

"As do you."

"I didn't know I'd been such a burden to you."

"Mickey, I'm trying to be honest about us. I get restless for my old life, the same as you, and feel guilty because I pushed you so hard to marry me. I've tried hard to make it work. But you keep slipping through my fingers. It's frustrating."

"You've ruined everything!" I shouted, forgetting why I'd called him in the first place.

"I'm trying to tell you that what's happened between us isn't all your fault, by a long shot. About the time I needed a little distance, you would leave. And then I'd want you more than ever. I can't stand it when you're gone."

"Until I return."

"I love your returns."

"I hate you!"

Another one of his damn pauses before he answered: "Tell me where to send your things."

"I'll send for them myself." I don't remember hanging up the phone. I don't remember much of anything after that. A merciful numbness settled over me except for one, brief sickening moment of realization that, had he asked, I would have stayed. We had shared the mystery of inevitable forces.

chapter 23

I WENT ABOUT MY LIFE AS IF I WERE NORMAL again. Imagine, that's what I used to think I was: normal. How you act is what you are, I reminded myself, and from long, long practice I acted.

One morning, in the company of Beth and Gloria, I made my first trip to the set of the *Sunrise Show*, the one considering featuring a segment with Daisy once or twice a week. They called it a "dry run," but I knew it was really an audition. We walked onto a luxe kitchen set, slightly reconfigured, they said, from when they'd used it with a former weekly guest—a chef, it appeared.

"But I don't cook. I mean, that's not what I am—a cook," I told the man who introduced himself as the segment producer and who showed me the bright green kitchen with three different preparation tables.

"No? Well, maybe you could occasionally toss off elegant but simple dishes."

"I barely know the ABCs. You would have to bill me as a children's cook for adults," I cracked, but no one responded.

The segment producer gestured to one of the preparation tables. "We could turn this half of the set into a demonstration room," he said, "where you could counsel someone off the street about how best to fold their towels or label spices." He laughed and added, "Everything simple," of course, before I could protest. "And right over here," he said, pointing me toward a couch and an easy chair, "you could show how to reupholster and decorate your basic family room or, in the case of New Yorkers, your basic everything room. You'd be surprised with the versatility of this small setup."

"This is not what Daisy does," I answered. "None of it. I'd be better off with a closet."

"Closets? They're decorating closets these days?"

"Organizing them. I don't know about *they,* but that's what I do." I saw Gloria and Beth exchange a look. Gloria pulled me aside.

"Listen," she said, "we can make this work. Beth can edit their scripts—"

"*Their* scripts? They don't even know what I do. They don't—" But Beth joined us and begged me to hear the man out.

I waved my arms at the set. "How can this help anyone? And what does any of it have to do with Daisy?"

The question, however, was what Daisy could do for television. To that end, I was next taken to a dressing room, where makeup was applied and I was told Daisy would have to give up her black-framed glasses, then led back out to practice reading from a TelePrompTer.

"Good morning and welcome. I'm Daisy Strait, and I'm here today to give you some tricks of my trade. That is, how to organize and simplify while beautifying your life. It's easy if you know how." I stopped. "It's not easy at all," I told the producer.

"Right. From the top again," he replied. "This time, pick up the pace."

For the next forty-five minutes, I either picked up or

slowed down the pace, reading with "a smile in my voice," as they suggested, grinning and "bubbling," whatever that was, and sometimes employing a kind of strict schoolteacher countenance.

"Why can't I just do it naturally?" I finally asked. "The way that works before my usual audiences?" By this time two more network people had joined the producer.

"We're trying to decide which Daisy works best," one of the production team said.

"*Which* Daisy?" I practically shrieked. Gloria shot me one of her glares, which under normal circumstances would have shut me up, but these were not normal circumstances. "There is only one Daisy," I said, "and I decide who she is. *I* decide. And she will not be *tweaked!*"

At which point, Gloria sprung into action and hustled me off the set, apologizing for our abrupt departure because we were running late for our next appointment. I didn't know of any appointments. I wondered if she'd heard of my Philadelphia fiasco.

ON LATER REFLECTION, I'm sure she had, for I noticed that my speaking engagements dropped precipitously. Just as well, for I was dragging myself through the days, expecting some sort of release. As yet it hadn't come. I hadn't been capable of looking at my manuscript again either or inputting Raleigh's changes. No matter who cajoled or threatened, I remained paralyzed on that score. Even so, I congratulated myself on having finally made a decision to give Wilson up, even if it left me in total despair.

Not long afterward, I woke from a restless night with a raging fever, my nightgown plastered to my skin with sweat. There was a bug going round the office, so I wasn't too concerned. "I ought to come look after you," Gloria offered on the phone. "I started the yucky thing."

"I plan to order in and not turn a lick," I told her, my voice sounding just like Helen's, drawl and all. I did not turn a lick but I didn't order in, either. Feeling much worse than Gloria had led me to expect, I didn't have energy to read or watch television. Aspirin barely kept my fever down. For three days I lay in bed while assuring my staff that I was all right. In my e-mails to Steve I made no mention of it at all. I wished I could tell Wilson—I wanted him to know and to be sorry. Instead, I took more aspirin. I'd run out of milk and juice. I tore the mold from the last few pieces of bread.

In my fevered state, I thought maybe I'd receive a sign, some meaningful hallucination that would illuminate how contradictory impulses could be reconciled, or lived with. I was burning up. I thought I might vanish. Truly, everyone would be better off. I had to say my good-byes.

Toward that purpose, I managed to pull on a pair of black slacks and a sweater; I picked up my laptop, an automatic impulse, remembered my purse, and shut the door behind me. On the floor below, a young woman stepped into the elevator, and the fresh scent of her shampoo lingered after she departed briskly ahead of me. She made me think of Dottie. I was a Dottie once. How long had it been since I'd washed my hair? I should have, but all the "should have"s and "should have not"s in my life brought on a wave of nausea more ferocious and thoughts more punishing than the virus that afflicted me.

Outside it was winter but I hardly noticed the cold—my

head was hammering, I was fueled by my fever, a lightness consuming me. No more encumbrances, only freedom. I was giddy with it. I floated. I had escaped. The only pursuers were noisy ghosts, fragments with my many voices, as I hailed a cab, the first step back to a familiar capsule in the sky.

I DID NOT collapse when I arrived in Indianapolis or as I waited shivering, my head pounding, on the front step of Andrea's for someone to come home. I did not close my eyes either, too afraid I'd be unable to open them again. Breathing took an effort—my lungs hurt as if the altitude were high.

When Dottie drove up, she looked astonished. I saw her mouth move as she gasped "Auntie M," although she did not look particularly excited to see me. Debilitated as I was, I noticed that. I also noticed a boy sitting in the car and that the two of them whispered in a furor before opening the car doors and Mike Something-or-other got properly introduced.

"Let's get you inside," Dot said, and took my arm to help me up. "Aren't you cold? Where's your coat? Where is your suitcase, Auntie M?"

"Oh, lost. The airline can't find it."

"I thought you always use a carry-on—you know, more efficient?" She turned the key in the door.

"I carry on, all right, but not this time—the suitcase." I smiled at my own joke. "I guess I'm not carrying on at all," I added in what must have sounded like a slightly hysterical voice. I started laughing. "Maybe that's it. I'm really not carrying on."

I saw the expressions on the faces of the two young people in front of me—Dot in a wool coat and a yellow sweater I had sent and the boy, all neat and shined and ready for an afternoon with his girl but not the girl's crazy aunt.

"It's a private joke of mine," I explained, although by now I could barely hold up my head.

Dottie led me to a chair. "Auntie M, are you all right? I think we need to get you to a doctor."

I shook my head. "No doctor, honey. I'm just tired . . . a little bug." I tried to stand but had no strength. "If you could make a strong cup of coffee with lots of sugar. That will do it. Works wonders." Dottie fled into the kitchen after ordering Mike to stay with me.

"And two aspirin," I called out to her. "I need two aspirin."

Mike took the initiative and came back instantly with the pills and a glass of water. I gulped down three, by which time Dottie returned with the coffee. "It's instant," she said, "a double scoop."

"Imagine, your mother with instant coffee." I attempted to focus on the conversation instead of floating into some ethereal sphere—blue, it was—that hovered around my head. "I can't tell the difference," I announced at the same time I caught a fleeting exchange of panicked looks between Dottie and Mike.

"Mom and Dad have gone to the lake for the weekend," Dottie said.

So I had interrupted their weekend tryst. Have at it, I wanted to tell them. I am no one to judge. Yet sex was folly, of that I had absolutely no doubt.

"That's fine," I heard myself saying. "I've only dropped by for the afternoon. I'm on my way . . ." I motioned vaguely toward the west. "But I will freshen up and have a little chat. That's all I've time for."

I accepted Dottie's hand to rise. For a split second the blue haze encircling my head turned black, covered my eyes, before turning back to blue again.

In the bathroom, I took my time getting up from the toilet and gripped the sink tightly. I splashed my face with water, applied lipstick, and dabbed some on my cheeks for good measure. In the mirror a ghost stared back at me. Too bad Dottie would remember me this way, but Dottie had already moved on. She didn't need me anymore. Boyfriends, mentors, there'd always be someone to take my place. Same with Steve. And Wilson. They only thought they couldn't do without me. In truth, they did gorgeously without me, so long as the choice was theirs and not mine, so long as their pride stayed intact. And neither would mourn Daisy, who had, in her own way, kept *everyone* going.

But how ridiculous to think I mattered so much. Maybe to be matter, conscious matter, is to want to matter, an ordinary human condition, except I had had to make me matter more. My ambition. My unholy needs.

"AUNTIE M? You okay in there?"

"Be right out," I replied, only then noticing that I was lying on the floor, my knees curled into my chest. I rolled to my other side. Someone hammered loudly, maybe Dottie on the door. With effort I rose and put my head between my knees to keep from blacking out.

This time a knock. "Auntie M?"

I opened the door. "Maybe I'll lie down a minute."

"You look white as a sheet. Do you want more coffee?"

I nodded. "And two more aspirin."

"I don't think she should have more aspirin," I heard Mike say in the kitchen as I made my way slowly down the hall to my childhood—I mean the guest—room.

"But if they help her. She's sick," said Dottie.

Was I a guest in my own childhood? Maybe I'd had a guest-hood. And this was a childroom.

"Yeah, but Coach told us to watch out with them, and every guy on the team is a hell of a lot bigger than your aunt." Mike's voice drifted down the hall. "You want me to come back later?" he said.

"I don't know. She can't go anywhere in this condition. Do you think I should call my mom?"

"If you do, we'll lose the weekend. Give her a couple of hours and call me first."

Dottie returned with aspirin and coffee. I smiled my thanks, then lay back on the pillows of the bed. She pulled a chair up beside me. When I tried to talk, my temples began hammering again. "That damn noise was going on in New York, too. And on the plane—it was really bad on the plane." I remembered almost nothing about my trip except the noise and the effort it took to board.

"What noise, Auntie M?"

I had sunk too deep into the blue haze to answer.

I AWOKE FEELING BETTER. The pounding had stopped, except when I moved. It occurred to me that no one except Dottie knew where I was. Already I had disappeared. Kind of. How lovely. So free. Magazine in hand, Dottie sat in the small chintz-flounced bedroom chair, the same chair I had hung my clothes on throughout my early life, with almost the same fabric. What had gone on in Andrea's mind? To re-create her own past was one thing—in some ways she had never left it—but to re-create mine was quite another.

"Look at you, Dottie, wasting your pretty afternoon here. Have I slept long?"

"Auntie M, I think we ought to call the doctor. You look really . . . sort of . . . really dead."

I propped myself up. "I'm better. You mustn't worry. I came to tell you that I love you and that you must be careful about love, honey. No, I don't mean love, I mean lust. Now, that is very dangerous. . . ." But I didn't want to whine about love or lust. After all, here I was—almost fifty and no beauty—and I had two wonderful men in my life, and most women would be happy to have either of them. The last thing I should do was moan. I tried to remember my train of thought. "This lust business can blindside you into love. You think you can distinguish, you think you have control. . . ." I tried to conjure up Daisy, who never lost her concentration—well, almost never. "Dottie, what I really need is another cup of coffee. And some ice cream. Do you have any ice cream?"

Dottie hopped up, practically running out of the room. She must think I'm batty, I supposed as the blue haze began to move in again. This time, though, whole parts of my body were shutting down in protest. Forcing myself to my elbows, I shouted as loud as I could to Dottie. "Skip the ice cream. Just bring coffee—three scoops and double the sugar." I lay back down with a casualness belying reason. "Dottie, quick!" Blood gushed out with the words.

. . .

THERE WAS A PULSING LIGHT, a strobe across Dottie's worried face. And Mike's. I called out to him, "Be good to my niece." I was rising in a wind. I felt weightless, lifted. Maybe I'd reached the flight room. I wanted to share my joke. I would like to cheer them up a bit—Dottie, scared beside me, holding my hand as an oxygen mask closed on my face, whirled me into the blue, blue haze.

I hoped Steve would think to give Dottie money for adventure. But how would he know to? And how would Wilson know anything? If I could live long enough to tell somebody to call, swear secrecy. Andrea would be best, *but it is so blue.* I jerked the mask away. "Call your mother. Tell her to hurry."

"Mike already has."

"Do you see that blue? Is it the sky?"

"You'll be all right now, Auntie M."

"MRS. BANYON?" a man asked.

I nodded and opened my eyes. He was barely a man; he looked Dottie's age.

"Your niece tells me you've had the flu? Were you on any medication?"

"No. I believe in mind over matter." *Banyon. I am Mrs. Banyon.*

"She tells me she found an empty aspirin bottle in your purse."

I nodded to confirm.

"Have you been taking them frequently?"

"Since I got the flu."

"How long has that been?"

"A few days? I've lost track."

"Are you eating?"

"Eating? I haven't been very hungry."

The intern nodded and tapped his pencil against his forehead. "That might explain your loss of blood." He went on to speak of aspirin and stomach lining and internal hemorrhaging and blood type and consent form. "You have to have blood immediately."

"I know that," I snapped. *If I hadn't known that, I wouldn't be here,* I felt like telling this kid, who called himself a doctor. "I also need a clean sheet of paper. Two clean sheets of paper."

"Your niece wants to come in."

"After I write my notes." On one, in a jagged scrawl, I declared my love to Steve and requested he take care of my staff at Daisy Strait Enterprises and help Dottie "find a larger life—if she wants it." The other I addressed to Andrea, asking her to inform Wilson that his wife had died. She would have to figure out how since I didn't have the energy. I instructed her to make the call from a phone booth, and to tell no one else about it. *This is my terrible secret, and I am trusting you, Andrea. I so appreciate your help. Thank you. There is no one else in the world to turn to.*

P.S. I would hate for Dottie to know. After I'm gone, she will idealize me, much worse than this idolizing now, which will pass; the other won't. Which will be hard on you and make you stop liking me. But for her sake, not ours, let her have me as special. (The other way is just a little too special.)

I hoped my messages were legible. My hands shook so much I wasn't sure. I folded the paper as carefully as I could and gave the notes to the intern. I wished he would stop pacing and looking at his watch.

"Heavy date?" I asked, wanting a story.

He gave me a wan smile. "The heaviest," he answered as a nurse put a blanket on me.

"Under no circumstances turn those notes over to anyone but the names on the outside. Do we have a deal?"

The intern nodded as the nurse prepared me for the blood. "Where is Dottie?" I asked.

The intern stuck his head out the door and Dottie rushed in. She looked petrified. I felt sorry for her; for the intern, too.

"I've sure managed to ruin a perfectly good afternoon, huh? Tell Mike I'll make it up to him."

Dottie smiled. I tried to also. For her sake, I wished I could stop shivering. What a hell of a thing to put her through. *What a hell of a thing to put us through,* all my voices spoke at once. *If you weren't so damned scared of life . . .*

"Dottie, could you talk louder? I can't hear you."

My niece sat by my bed and said whatever came into her head. She told me about her first ice-cream cone. She described its flavor. She remembered Granny rocking her, could feel her arms around her. I tried to remember how those arms had felt. All mothers hold you sometime. "Don't all mothers do that?" I asked nobody in particular, but there was much commotion about the blood arriving and I got no answer.

As the drip began, tension visibly ebbed from the room. Dottie's voice grew steadier, lower. The intern's jaw relaxed and he stopped his pacing. In a while they rolled me out of emergency and into my own hospital room. Sometime later Andrea appeared and glanced quickly toward Dottie before turning to me. "You've given us a good scare."

"None equal to the one I gave Dottie. Take her somewhere nice to dinner."

Dottie laughed. "It's after midnight, Auntie M."

"But we've only made it to your eighth birthday," I protested. I wasn't ready for the evening to end.

"Tomorrow," Andrea replied, and patted my hand.

"I could come back and sleep in the chair," Dottie whispered. I made myself refuse the offer. She kissed me good night.

After everyone else had left, the young intern returned with my notes. "You won't be needing these now."

"I'd just as soon you keep them through the night."

"Sure, though that's not necessary."

"I know," I answered. But I didn't know. Throughout the night I monitored my machines. Life, type B positive, dripped back into my veins.

chapter 24

TWO DAYS IN THE HOSPITAL AND I PROMISED TO spend a few more with Andrea—the doctors ordered and I readily accepted. After sending off e-mails to Steve and my staff to let them know I was okay, I surrendered to the ministrations of Andrea and Dottie, who indulged me by bringing magazines, newspapers, and library books, and fetching water whenever my glass was empty. Dottie installed her elaborate sound system in my bedroom, and Andrea pulled out tapes she had made from our father's LP collection. She and I listened raptly and a little nostalgically to the softer side of the master sergeant, a jazz aficionado who loved the vocal artistry of Nellie Lutcher and Billy Daniels and Don Byas, who all dated back to our grandfather's time.

I felt loved in the way that I imagined lucky children feel. My days were simple. Andrea brought me breakfast in bed, and I loved lying there with the sun streaming across my covers. I hadn't earned that light but I took it.

After pouring us both coffee, Andrea usually settled into the chintz chair and we talked awhile, often taking Dottie's emotional temperature. My niece was seeing a therapist now and her mood had lifted, but Andrea and I worried that Dottie still hadn't recovered any of her old drive. It was only a matter of time, we counseled each other. This morning, though, our conversation took another turn when I stepped tentatively into the forbidden territory of our childhoods. I told Andrea I resented her closeness to our mother, how I felt they formed a magic circle with no entry point for me.

"I did everything she told me, so she let me hang around," said Andrea, evenly, "but that's not closeness. Really, I was too much like her, and she didn't like herself at all."

"If she didn't like herself, then why did she have all those affected airs? And her piety! So holier than thou!" I lifted my arms in mock obeisance.

Andrea almost smiled. "You know she and Daddy both came from small Mississippi towns and weren't much more than eighteen when they got married. She considered her parents white trash and herself uneducated. Ran as far as she could from what she'd known." She got up to straighten the blinds.

"So she negotiated the rest of her life with some weird rule book based on her idea of Southern gentility?"

Andrea peered outside through the slats. "They both saw the military as a way out, but I think early on she just froze. She was so threatened by Daddy's accomplishments."

"I always thought she enjoyed the prestige he received as master sergeant. Didn't that count?"

Andrea took a sip of coffee and sat back again in the chair. "He grew away from her. Rightly or wrongly, she felt he was her only recourse. Who can blame her for being so angry?"

"I got the brunt of it." I was glad for the nest of pillows around me.

Andrea sighed. "I think she saw some of her younger scrappy self in you. That must have irritated her to no end. Reminded her of what she'd lost."

"I lost it, too," I confessed. "And I didn't even know it." I let out a shrill laugh, which Andrea ignored, caught up in her own thoughts.

"She wanted better for us than what she'd had, though I think her capacity for love got lost in the misery they dealt each other. Something in her got numbed too early to do much loving."

I thought of Steve and myself, how numb we were, too, so early on. I wondered if Andrea ever felt numb with Larry, or minded his frequent absences. Like Steve, he had work—in his case, in insurance—that often took him away from home for long stretches. The Harmon sisters and their absentee husbands, apples not far from the tree. But Wilson was a present husband, I reminded myself.

"We can't undo or redo," said Andrea practically.

If only she knew how I had tried to redo.

"I guess I used my anger to protect me from recognizing Mama's side of this," I said.

"I know," she answered dryly.

"I always thought you and Mama drove Daddy away."

"I probably did want to push him out to show you that you couldn't have everything. I didn't reckon on his dying, or the guilt I'd feel later. Your high-school leftovers in this room? It's all I could save for you." Andrea slapped her thighs and stood up—she'd had enough.

"That's the way Mama thought—pretend we're a happy family," I said hopelessly. "If we don't face this, we'll be back in their lives."

"You mean, like pretend we weren't sick and weren't thirty minutes away from death?"

That stopped me short. "Okay. My life's in chaos. . . ." My voice dwindled away.

"So fix it," Andrea answered, and left the room.

confessions of a bigamist

·   ·   ·

I LAY IN BED and thought about the cast of characters that swirled about me—not just Andrea and Dottie, but Gloria and Beth and the connections I craved. I missed Lindy and Annette and Hillary and Sonia. Even Helen. And Wilson? I had no words, only a terrible yearning, as if a dark cave had carved itself inside me and I could not bear to discover its contents. This kind of grieving allowed me to focus on what I did have. No surprise, really, for I had a lot of practice in refusing to acknowledge what I needed most. And what I had was pretty good. I still held within me all those parts of myself that Wilson had helped me discover. They weren't going anywhere.

THE FIRST MESS I cleared up was Daisy's before she turned into a caricature of herself. Neither the world nor my sense of obligation to it would corrupt Daisy, I decided. What the publishing house wanted was the same old package a dozen others had done but with a new ribbon around it, and that ribbon amounted to no more than lip service to the notion of complexity. I had intended something else entirely different. So I wrote Raleigh Lundgren a long letter explaining that I couldn't make the changes she needed and that I wanted to withdraw the book.

Next, I e-mailed my staff to let them know what I'd done. I also told them to stop all negotiations with the television studios, if, indeed, there were still negotiations. I reminded them that Daisy was about one-on-one and small groups and wacky phone calls from time to time. At any rate, the old Daisy Strait wouldn't be leaving. I liked her as she'd always been and that's what I needed. To place her on too large a canvas would cause us to lose everything she stood for.

The network people, I soon learned, were absolutely furious. I could imagine Gloria scowling as she read my e-mail on her computer screen, her arms crossed belligerently. She probably thought I'd lost my mind; Beth, too, though she wasn't as apt to say so out loud. She would be perplexed but sympathetic. At least that's what I hoped. Even now, I didn't want any of them upset with me if I could help it, but I couldn't. Amazingly, I didn't even feel guilty thinking of their disappointment, a whole new twist for me. Maybe my need to please had truly diminished after all. Besides, it was high time Daisy stopped trying to save the world.

I STAYED AT my sister's for over a month. The doctor had told me to increase my mobility slowly, so I walked with Andrea or Dottie every day in a nearby park, gradually increasing the distance. Andrea and I talked of Dottie's college plans. "I think she's going to be all right," I said. I watched my breath hover in the air. The night before, Dottie had told us she planned to go back to school and finish her undergraduate degree.

"With some luck and a lot of help."

"Maybe next semester she could find a school in the New York area," I ventured.

Andrea patted my hand and smiled. "Maybe a milder transition would be in order this time around."

I couldn't argue with that one, but I longed to have Dottie back in the city. When I started to tire, Andrea suggested we take a break on the nearest park bench. "How's your chaos going?" she asked carefully.

While I considered this offering, I dug out a tissue from the coat Andrea had lent me and blew my nose. As fine a sister as she was turning out to be, Andrea did have a few unresolved grudges of her own. And announcing that you were a bigamist would shock a lot less conventional people than my sister, who probably would be shocked enough if she thought I was having an affair.

After an uncomfortable pause, I attempted to explain. "You know, I always considered myself a pretty moral person—not necessarily a good person, but someone with integrity. Nearly a year ago, my life turned upside down. I found out that when it comes to my personal wants, it's easier than I thought to not play by the usual rules. I thought I could manage to have everything. And then I thought what I would give up wouldn't matter so much. But it did."

"You always did flit about," said Andrea. She blew a stream of air like a smoky trail from a plane.

"Did I? Well, I certainly haven't flitted much in my adult life, I can tell you that." I did not think of myself in those terms and that Andrea could annoyed me. "What I've done is not in the least bit frivolous."

"I don't mean it in a frivolous way either," she said. "In school you went from group to group, girl to girl, boy to boy, making yourself useful to all. It was your insurance policy. If one let you down, you had someone else, somewhere else to go. You've never trusted anybody to stick by you."

"But this time people trusted me. I had commitments to both and the obligations were equally compelling. I've let one down and betrayed them both. I almost ended up with nothing more than little pieces scattered all over the place." I held up my hands and made children's raindrops with my fingers. "No one really knows who I am."

Andrea smiled. "What about this makes you so different from the rest of us?"

"A lot," I answered in earnest.

"You know," Andrea said quietly, "after you moved to New York, I thought about leaving here, leaving Larry, and trying a new life for myself. You had managed somehow, and I felt more qualified than you. I got as far as visiting a friend for a week in Atlanta, even found a well-paying job, but I took my old self with me and discovered I wasn't up to the game."

"I didn't exactly think of myself as being in the middle of a game, more like in the middle of surviving," I said, defensive again, then stopped. "You almost left Larry?"

"Yeah, it was a long time ago. The point is, you could afford independence and I couldn't. I wanted that kind of freedom but not enough to live with the tension of it." Andrea ran her fingers through her hair, looking for words. "Real independence is scary," she said. "Look, I know I can't absolve you of what you've done, but I can tell you that a woman needs an inner world—her own secret path to help her get through, well, the mundane and . . . you know . . . the tragic." She gave me a lopsided smile. "Even if we don't act on it."

I threw up my hands. "Then why can't I be satisfied with the usual 'Let's pretend'? Why do I need to *live out* illusions?"

Andrea laughed. "Because you are either very brave, a complete fool, or a scoundrel. Maybe all three."

WHEN WE GOT BACK to the house, Steve was on Andrea's doorstep. He'd come as soon as he could—all the way from Asia. We had exactly twenty-four hours.

"I had to see for myself that you were all right," he said, cupping my cheek.

I hugged him tightly. "Thank you," I said. "Thank you, thank you." Looking at his mussed hair, that familiar little bald spot, and his dapper, if rumpled, suit, I felt the heft of all our years and I hugged him for a long time. "Come inside," I whispered in his ear. "You won't believe Andrea's house." I took his hand and led him through the door, down the hall to my time capsule. "This was me," I said, somewhat apologetically, but also a bit proudly, pointing to the old teddy bear, the tennis racket on the bookcase, the poster on the wall. I wanted him to acknowledge my past, but Steve had something more pressing to tell me.

Holding hands, we sat on my girlhood bed as he told me his good news: The ethics partner had grumbled but didn't banish him. He hadn't been fired. In fact, Brisco, who had put his company's money into the deal, had sympathized and led Steve to believe what he'd done wasn't all that uncommon. "'Companies find ways to gloss over these things'—those were his exact words," Steve said. "I think he'd just as soon I hadn't told him, but that's not my style."

"I know." I was glad to see Steve so relieved.

"I told him I'd pay every penny back out of my own pocket if it took the rest of my life." Steve laughed. "At the rate I'm going, it might. But hearing you'd been so sick reminded me of what's truly important," he said, kissing my hand, a rare romantic gesture.

"Steve, I need to tell you something." I would confess, too. I would cleanse my soul and we would start anew.

"Anything!" he said, and held my hand with both of his.

"I need for you to know that . . . well, that I'm not a good person. I haven't been a perfect wife." Once again, I chickened out.

"And I'm not a perfect husband," he replied. "I know it hasn't always been the greatest marriage and may have been sad sometimes for you. But we keep enduring, don't we?"

"Yes, we do," I agreed, and put my other hand on top of his, so that our hands were sandwiched together in team spirit.

We had a happy twenty-four hours and then he left. That was our pattern. That wouldn't change. Steve's style suited me, even if loneliness left its smear.

AS THE WEEKS WENT BY, I felt myself grow stronger. That said, it took a long time before I felt enough in possession of myself to call Wilson.

"It's Mickey," I said.

"I know."

Oh, that husky voice. I'd forgotten. "I'm sorry it's taken so long for me to get my things, but I've been . . . well, I just haven't done it. I'm sorry."

"I haven't gotten around to packing them up. I'm sorry myself," he said gruffly.

"Oh, no, it's my responsibility," I said, and abruptly added, "I'll come next Saturday to pick them up. Say a proper goodbye. I don't want us to be enemies." At that moment, I wished with all my being that I had figured out a way to have it all.

"Suit yourself," he said, and hung up.

"Damn him!" I yelled to no one. "And damn me, too!" But I would get to see him one last time. Why couldn't he be grateful as well?

chapter 25

THE MORNING PLANE RIDE TO TEXAS HAD A SET-tling effect despite my misgivings about the ordeal ahead. I'd been dreading the trip, but I owed it to Wilson to do this gracefully and resolve the conflicts between us. As I waited for coffee, I pulled down the tray and took a towelette from my purse to wipe the juice stain left on it from another flight. Flying above the rivers and mountains, I could feel that essential current humming inside me. Why had I ever thought I needed two men? Or any man at all? Without anyone, I knew now I was whole. Each man had brought out a different part of me and now those parts belonged to me.

"Going to be a scorcher in Texas," the flight attendant, young and friendly, said in a Texas accent as he poured my coffee.

"I don't mind the heat," I said, and smiled. I'd actually accepted that I was a cheat, a liar, a lusty broad, a lovesick fool, a moderate, a realist, a dreamer, a sophisticate, and a do-gooder—all rolled into one. For the most part, I'd made two men very happy. The price, I reminded myself, almost cost my life.

Don't kid yourself, Mickey whispered. *You're still afraid of life.*

It doesn't have to be chaos, I answered.

In your case, sometimes it does. Daisy's even altered her

*message because you figured out that willpower and rational
thought don't always cut it. You only thought you had yourself
down pat, another of your ruses that won't work anymore. Life
should be expansive.* Mickey again. *You shirked an obligation.*

I started to argue, but I knew that short duration doesn't
make a claim less valid. Besides, Wilson never felt like an obligation, I thought, fighting back emotion, all emotion. I wondered if the ache would ever go away and used another
towelette to wipe my hands, a Daisy gesture, my real Daisy,
not a packaged one dreamed up by publicists. I had accom-
plished that, too.

AT THE DALLAS/FORT WORTH AIRPORT, I went through
the familiar motions of taking the shuttle to the rental car station, seeing which car I would draw. Texas would always
mean the lure of the road to me, a dusty, seductive drive.

I turned off the car's air conditioner and rolled down my
window to catch the hot wind in my hair. High in the sky, a
bird, a speck against the bright blue, circled and soared, dipping, soaring until it vanished. Maybe it was one of Wilson's,
one he'd nursed back to health to fly again. That soaring freedom of the present. I'd had it, too. A benediction, unlawfully
gained, joyfully claimed.

"You go, bird!" I shouted out the window.

Annette had probably stopped digging up weeds in her
garden and would be having a ham-and-cheese sandwich
with Lindy or Hillary. I didn't want to think about them,
though. Instead, I willed myself to memorize everything—
the sprawl, the fast-food chains, the sudden opening of the
land and its black fields, the bony stands of trees. There really

were no hiding places here. Nor would there be a need for them anymore.

Coward, Mickey whispered. *Coward.* I willed her voice into obscurity.

AS I TURNED down Wilson's unpaved road, the gracious old farmhouse beckoned. The prism shifted and a rainbow jumble of images flashed before me: the black blur of Luck, the sand-gold particles of dust dancing across the kitchen table, the tumble of white papers and panoply of books, seemingly immune to my ordering, the blue of Wilson's jeans and work shirts as he climbed into his red truck, his blond-gray hair as he leaned over a small brown owl, the moon's silver shadow playing over Wilson's white skin.

Unreasonable expectation swept over me at the thought of seeing him one last time—I could look into his eyes, inhale his smell, maybe even touch his hand. I shouldn't think past that. I would only grab the moment, take pleasure in his presence. It was the only way I'd get through the next hour. I held on to my eager anticipation of him until my car came to a halt.

His truck was down by the barn, but he didn't come to the door. Luck didn't greet me, either. My stomach filled with ice as I turned off the motor and stepped outside. A cloud passed over the sun, causing a momentary graying. I heard a hammering noise. I stood still, waiting.

The hammering stopped, then started again. With angry steps I walked toward the sound, which seemed like it was coming from the barn. He owed me a real good-bye, certainly the courtesy of a handshake. And he had no business out in the midday sun.

He was on a ladder, pounding a nail like crazy with his wonderful back to me, his faded jeans slung low, a white T-shirt only half tucked inside them. He was the damnedest man. The cloud had passed and the sun glinted off the steel hammer and up and down the aluminum ladder—a Wilson surrounded by sparklers. A surge of joy welled in me, spilling out all over. My heart couldn't hold all the love flooding through. I had so much to share, it made me gasp.

"Wilson!" I called, and started running toward him, forgetting he wanted me to go, forgetting I was leaving. "Wilson!"

He turned his head and then he beamed. "Mickey, honey!" he shouted. "Come home!" He opened one arm out in a wide, sweeping gesture, then began to make his way down the ladder.

I had almost reached him when he turned toward me, six rungs from the bottom. In his excitement, he tried to jump the final distance but caught one foot and I watched horrified as Wilson fell forward and landed hard on the earth facedown.

I leapt the last few paces and put my head on the ground by his, pushed his hair away from his eyes. "I love you, Wilson. Please don't die." I cried as if he already had, but if he lived, I swore to myself I'd make my life work for as long as I could, not one obligation unfulfilled.

He raised his head enough for me to see his lopsided grin. "You haven't killed me yet," he said, his face smudged with dirt.

I wiped his forehead and cheeks with my fingertips until he took my hand and kissed the palm, the secret place in the center.

"There now, help me up," he said. And I did, as we began.

epilogue

ON NEW YORK'S FIRST REAL DAY OF SPRING, DOTTIE
and I stroll arm in arm through Central Park. We join a cluster of on-lookers watching a bicycle race and cheering on the
participants. Dottie is visiting me on her college break and it
is wonderful to see her young face flushed with pleasure, her
body lithe and strong. She has changed in those nearly imper-
ceptible ways of a young woman who is experiencing new
and pleasurable aspects of life. I flush with my own pleasure
in just being near her.

From where we stand, I stare up at the row of apartment
buildings ringing the park and glimpse the windows of my
living room. Last night I charged in there fresh from a talk
before three hundred women, the glow from my successful
presentation remaining with me as I changed out of a char-
coal gray wrinkle-free pantsuit. These days I talk a lot about
the importance of recognizing and accepting conflicting
demands. My audience loves it, but the truth is, I can't hear
those sentiments enough myself.

By the time Steve walked in the door from work, I had
changed into a new white wool suit and taupe sling-back
heels. I vamped a model's turn, just to feel the fabric move
against my body, just to show off my new outfit. On cue, he
nodded approval, but his mind was on the brief he had been

working on and would continue to work on during tomorrow's flight to India.

After a few days at home, Steve had become restless and was ready to immerse himself in yet another challenge. This time he was focusing on the growing Indian telecommunications empire. I guess I realized a long time ago that Steve is married to me *and* to his work. He, too, is a bigamist of sorts. I patted his bald spot fondly as he washed up in the bathroom. "What?" he asked, and smiled. We were going to have dinner with Roberta and Buzzy Simpson at the pretty restaurant near Lincoln Center that plays Haydn in the background. We would make love when we got home and he would leave me. Again. It worked for us. It was a thoroughly modern marriage—and I was a thoroughly modern woman. I had found a way to have it all and hurt no one in the process.

Dottie takes a swig from her water bottle and passes it to me. We applaud and whistle with the crowd as the sleek bikes—greens, silvers, blues, reds—dash by us. The colors blur, run together, much like my life. Dottie and I have a day in Manhattan with no agenda. Tomorrow we both fly out in our jeans and sneakers, Dottie to Indiana and me to Texas. Only after I say good-bye to her will I spritz and crunch my hair, the way Wilson likes it. Then there will be the roar from the engines' thrust as the plane lifts off and the thrill I'll feel to be on my way to the other life that each of us wonders if we could have had if only things had worked out differently. Well, things definitely worked out differently for me and I feel blessed.

What am I doing? Occasionally I ask myself that as I look down on the expanses of fields and towns and highways below me, a million lives being lived in different and interesting ways. There are so many ways to live a life. The way I live wouldn't appeal to everyone, but I am more content than an outlaw like me deserves to be.

Of course, there are those times when I look down to see what I'm wearing in order to be sure I know who I am, and I laugh.

About the Author

KATE LEHRER is the author of three previous novels: *Best Intentions, When They Took Away the Man in the Moon,* and *Out of Eden.* A Texas native, she lives in Washington, D.C., with her husband, Jim Lehrer.